JOAN HOHL
BOBBY HUTCHINSON
EVELYN ROGERS
BOBBI SMITH

Love waits somewhere in time, somewhere beyond the mystical boundaries
of the ages. Here are four breathtaking
and unforgettable journeys of the heart
—a dazzling collection of timeless love
stories by an accomplished quartet of
your favorite romance authors. Prepare
to be transported to places far beyond
dreams—as courageous lovers reach out
across the generations to fulfill their
passionate destinies . . . and to experience the power, the wonder, and the
rapture of miraculous love.

*Don't Miss These Romantic Anthologies
from Avon Books*

Avon Books
Presents

Love Beyond Time

JOAN HOHL
BOBBY HUTCHINSON • EVELYN ROGERS
BOBBI SMITH

A SUTTON PRESS BOOK

AVON BOOKS NEW YORK

AVON BOOKS PRESENTS: LOVE BEYOND TIME is an original publication of Avon Books. This work is a collection of fiction. Any similarity to actual persons or events is purely coincidental.

AVON BOOKS
A division of
The Hearst Corporation
1350 Avenue of the Americas
New York, New York 10019

Turquoise Yesterdays © 1994 by Sutton Press, Inc., and Joan Hohl; *Forever* © 1994 by Sutton Press, Inc., and Bobby Hutchinson; *Time-Stolen Love* © 1994 by Sutton Press, Inc., and Bobbi Smith; and *Always Paradise* © 1994 by Sutton Press, Inc., and Evelyn Rogers.
Published by arrangement with Sutton Press, Inc.
Library of Congress Catalog Card Number: 93-91009
ISBN: 0-380-77540-9

First Avon Books Printing: July 1994

AVON TRADEMARK REG. U.S. PAT. OFF. AND IN OTHER COUNTRIES. MARCA REGISTRADA, HECHO EN U.S.A.

Printed in the U.S.A.

RA 10 9 8 7 6 5 4 3 2 1

Sutton Press, Inc., dedicates this book to
Freddie and Martha

Contents

Turquoise Yesterdays

Joan Hohl

1

June 1993—Some distance from Virginia City, Nevada

The drive from Virginia City had not been too bad—that is, until Laura Brand left the black-topped highway and pulled onto a dirt side road. She was bumping and bouncing along in her rented Cherokee when she noticed the Indian, standing behind a makeshift table bearing a hand-printed sign that read simply: Jewelry For Sale.

Laura spared a quick, curious glance at the man as she rocked and rolled past his rickety table. Then in the next instant she stood on the brake pedal, skidding to a teeth-jarring stop.

Although Laura was not in the market for jewelry, there was something about the man that had caught her interest and tugged at her heart.

In appearance, he could only be described as shabby, worn, almost flea-bitten. And yet there was an innate dignity about him—the erect posture; the stoic expression indelibly stamped onto his ancient, lined face; the direct, unflinching stare of his black eyes. Something beyond the ordinary . . . timeless.

Hooked, and fully aware of it, Laura stepped from the Jeep, fatalistically prepared to part with a sizable portion of her ready cash.

"Hi," she called, waving and offering him a tentative smile as she approached the table.

"Good afternoon," he replied in careful, precise English, his voice deep and gravelly. "You have appreciation for hand-crafted silver and turquoise jewelry?"

"Appreciation, yes, but . . ." Grimacing, Laura let her voice fade on a sigh.

His wise eyes didn't appear to move, yet Laura felt his appraising gaze, as if he could see, or even know, everything about her. It was an eerie feeling, but strangely unthreatening.

"You do not adorn yourself," he finished for her in an understanding, unquestioning statement.

"Not often," Laura admitted, shrugging her shoulders slightly. "Except for rare special occasions, I usually can't be bothered."

"I see."

Oddly enough, Laura was at once convinced that he did see, a lot more than she could probably comprehend. And yet she still felt in no way threatened or intimidated.

Offering him an apologetic smile, she moved closer to the table to peruse the selection of pieces attractively arranged on a large square of dark blue velvet.

Laura's knowledge of jewelry making was decidedly limited, but she recognized the quality of workmanship in the finely wrought pieces.

"How exquisite." She delicately touched a stunning necklace in the style she knew was the traditional squash blossom.

"Yes," he concurred. "But for you, for the special occasion, I choose this." From a corner of the table his gnarled brown fingers plucked a small pouch made of the same midnight-blue velvet. He withdrew a wide, hammered-silver cuff bracelet set with a large oval turquoise stone.

Laura had caught her breath, and reached for her purse.

The wise old eyes watching her glittered like jet in the midday sunlight.

"This amulet holds magical powers," the Indian said, *after* the exchange of money for the bracelet had been made. "Listen well, daughter," he continued, thereby preventing Laura from interrupting or protesting, both of which she sorely wanted to do.

"While confined inside the pouch, the powers will remain passive and contained," he intoned. "To release and surround yourself with the powers, remove the amulet and clasp it about your wrist."

"Oh, honestly . . ." Laura began, only to be silenced by a slicing movement of his flattened hand.

"Hear this, pale one." His voice had grown in strength and depth. "I foresee dark clouds of trouble gathering around you. Wear the amulet. Now. It will protect you, keep you safe, guide you."

Unequal to the challenge of meeting his black stare, let alone openly defying him, Laura obediently clipped the cuff to her wrist.

Then, ten minutes after driving away from him,

she removed it and slipped it back inside the pouch.

"Magical powers." Laura made an unladylike snorting noise. "Right."

Muttering to herself the old truism that a fool and her gold were soon parted, Laura switched off the engine with an impatient flick of her hand, then reached for the door release and flung open the door.

The dry, enervating heat of early afternoon rushed into the Jeep, overwhelming the cool interior air.

"Wow!" Laura gasped, peering through the heat haze at the ramshackle buildings lining the rutted road. For an instant she was tempted to slam the door shut and restart the Jeep and the air conditioner. But she had set out to investigate this ghost town she had discovered while reading a historical guide to Nevada and poring over a map last night in her hotel room in Virginia City, and investigate she would.

The deserted place had a forlorn, haunted look, scary and forbidding, not at all romantic or inviting. Asking herself scathingly if she had been expecting a tall, handsome man of the Old West to meet her and welcome her into the past, Laura collected her grit and gumption and thrust a cotton-twill-encased leg out the door.

Nevertheless, despite her bravado, she reached across the seat, slipped the silver and turquoise cuff from its pouch, and clasped it around her wrist. Then, grabbing her backpack from the backseat, she stuffed the velvet pouch into a side pocket, slung the pack over her shoulder, and got out of the Jeep.

It was like stepping into the mouth of hell.

Laura's lips quirked in an amused smile at her silent observation, and she shook her head. She shucked out of her short denim jacket, tied it around her waist, and strode forward in her sturdy, protective hiking boots.

It didn't take long for Laura to lose interest in the old mining town, which had never really amounted to much. According to the guidebook, all that the handful of miners who had descended on the place ever found was a skimpy vein of gold that had petered out in less than a year, somewhere around 1860. The town consisted mainly of one street, lined by a collection of tumbledown shacks. The largest one bore a crude sign hanging askew from one hinge, informing Laura that it was the Pick and Shovel Saloon.

"Big deal," Laura muttered, dismissing the sign and the town by turning away and heading for the foothills beyond the motley structures.

Although the going was rough, the terrain rocky and uneven, she happily trudged along, her sharp-eyed gaze scouring the ground in search of her favorite subject, new and unusual plant specimens.

Laura was a botanist. From her earliest memories, she could recall being fascinated by anything and everything that grew.

Encouraged by her parents and her only sibling, an older brother whom she adored and who likewise doted on her, to use her mind and to achieve, Laura had sailed through school. After earning her postgraduate degree in botany at the small college in her hometown in southeastern Pennsylvania, Laura had felt proud and delighted to accept the institution's offer of a position as associate professor.

About the only thing other than plant life that had interested Laura to any lasting degree was the fabled Old West. She had grown up devouring books, movies, and TV series reruns dealing with the subject.

But although for most of her life she had felt the siren song calling her westward, this vacation trip was her first journey beyond the Mississippi.

Fairly quivering from the excitement of perhaps discovering some plant life that was new to her, Laura wandered farther and farther afield, away from the ugly town.

The brazen sun had begun its descent into the horizon when she noticed a small white blossom halfway up the side of the next hill. Perspiration slicked the back of her neck beneath the sable swath of hair she had tied with a scarf, and ran down between her breasts. Beads of moisture trickled down her forehead and into her eyes, causing them to sting and tear.

Blinking, Laura refocused her eyes, and could have sworn the white blossom waved to her, which was ridiculous, since not a breath of air stirred the dry heat.

Dismissing the fanciful thought, she wiped the sweat from her brow, then set forth determinedly to get a closer look at the flower.

Her breath growing harsh from exertion, she skittered down one humpback and began scrambling up the next hill. She was brought up short within yards of her quarry by a wide mass of bracken. Tiring, she started around the brush, then, shrugging, plunged into it. She had taken three long-legged strides when her left foot came down and she felt herself falling, her arms flailing as darkness engulfed her.

A startled yelp escaped her throat as she landed on her rump with a bone-jolting thud on the rock-hard ground.

Stunned, disoriented, she stared around her at what appeared to be a cavern . . . a very dark cavern. Gathering her rattled wits, she sighed with relief at the narrow beam of sunlight slanting through the opening above.

How long would that reassuring light be there? she wondered, beginning to shiver. The sun was on its downward trek. Soon night would come. She would be alone in the cavern. Or would she? Suddenly Laura remembered a TV documentary she had watched months before, filmed in worked-out, abandoned mines. The mine shafts had been alive with bats and rodents and . . . snakes!

Jerking to her feet, she rushed forward to stand directly in the path of the comforting blaze of hot sunlight. Telling herself to remain calm, she drew several deep breaths and raised her hands to wipe the now-cold sweat from her face. Sunlight glanced off the turquoise stone in her bracelet. Then, to her utter amazement, the light appeared to radiate and swirl in flashing blue rays from the stone. The shimmering energy crackled and sparked above her and descended to encircle her quaking form in a brilliant cocoon.

Stunned, Laura did what any self-respecting scientist would do under the circumstances. She threw back her head, opened her mouth wide, and screamed.

2

Hours had elapsed since she had tumbled into the cavern, hours in which Laura had been visited by any number of fears, but fortunately not by crawly creatures, especially the kind with poison sacs behind their pointed teeth.

Every one of those long hours had been fraught with speculative thoughts that had ended up scaring her senseless. She was thankful for whatever impulse had impelled her to tie her denim jacket around her waist rather than toss it onto the seat of the Jeep, for the cavern had grown cold with the sun's descent.

It was dark now, and the only thing that saved Laura from utter darkness was the small flashlight she had stuffed into her backpack as an afterthought before leaving the hotel that morning. Recognizing the wisdom of conserving the batteries, she had overridden a panic-induced desire to leave the light on, forcing herself to switch it on and off at intervals instead.

She had stopped screaming when she heard her voice growing hoarse. Besides, even through her fear, Laura reasoned that her chances of actually being heard by anyone were slim to none; the town a few hills back was a ghost town, the surrounding area deserted. What was the point in crying out for help when there was nobody there to hear her? And yet, despite knowing it was hopeless, she had called out every time she switched on the flashlight.

Turning the flashlight on now, she raised her voice once more. "Hello!"

Then she stilled, startled by the unexpected sound of a human voice, a male voice, calling in response. She stared up into the opening above her, which was only marginally less dark than the cavern's interior.

"Hello?" the voice came again, deep-timbred, suspicious-sounding, harsh with impatience.

"Dammit, is somebody down there?"

"Yes!" she croaked on a sob of relief. "Yes, I'm down here. Please, can you help me get out?"

There came a low, rough mutter—a curse?—and then a sharp-voiced reply. "Damned right, I'll haul your carcass out of there."

What was he mad about? she wondered in confusion, for the anger lacing his tone left no doubt that the man was as mad as a disturbed hornet.

Biting her lip in consternation, she peered at the opening. After what seemed like an hour, a weak, wavering glow illuminated the hole.

"I'm lowering a rope," her irate savior shouted. "Can you see it?"

She could, just barely. It curled and coiled like a long, skinny snake. Telling herself it was not a viper but her lifeline, she called back, "I see it."

"Good. Grab onto it and hold tight," he said. "I'll pull you up. Have you got it?"

Looping the straps of her backpack over one arm, she clutched at the rope. "Yes."

There was a quick tug on the rope; she tightened her hold. Then slowly the line and Laura were drawn upward. She felt a rush of fresh air an instant before her head cleared the opening. Strong hands grasped her upper arms, steely fingers dug into her soft flesh, and she was literally plucked from the mouth of the hole. She was swung in a half circle and deposited on the ground with bone-jarring force.

Since Laura had seriously begun to fear that the cavern would be her final resting place, she felt too grateful to her rescuer to take umbrage at his rough handling of her. She didn't even object when he continued to grasp her arms in his hard-fingered grip. Weak-kneed with relief, she welcomed his support.

"Thank . . . you," she sputtered between gasps of sweet, sage-scented night air. "I can't begin to—"

"How did you find it?" he cut her off in a harsh-voiced demand.

"Find it?" She frowned and peered through the darkness, trying to see his face. The wavering light she had seen from the cavern floor had been cast by an old-fashioned oil lamp with a handle, quite like the kind railroaders had used years ago. The lamp still sat near the rim of the hole, behind her less-than-congenial rescuer. All she could make out was his size—large, shadowy, intimidating. "Find what?"

"You know damned well what," he shot back in an angry snarl. Releasing her, he made a half-turn to indicate the hole. "The entrance."

Entrance? Laura shook her head in confusion. She didn't have a clue as to what this uncivil man was talking about, and at that moment she didn't much care. The effects of prolonged fear were taking their toll. Shivers cascaded the length of her body, and she was exhausted, her mind numb.

"That hole?" she asked blankly.

"Yes, dammit, that hole," he barked.

Laura was close to losing her patience, and to the edge of hysteria. "What about it?"

"What were you looking for down there?"

"Why would I be looking for anything in a hole in the ground?" Then, abruptly, the last vestige of her energy drained. She went crashing to her knees on the hard ground.

"What the hell!"

In a flash his strong hands were grabbing her once more, hauling her up, more gently this time. For such a big man, he moved swiftly, Laura thought with vague detachment, past the point of caring.

"Are you all right?" The harshness was gone from his voice, leaving it still raw, a little rough, but deep and surprisingly attractive.

"Yes. No," Laura immediately corrected herself. "I . . . I . . ." She took several gulping breaths, then gasped a startled "Oh!" when the earth spun as she was suddenly swept off her feet into his arms. "What are you doing?" she demanded, struggling against his tight embrace. "Put me down."

"Why, you like falling?" he asked, not unkindly, holding her close to his hard chest.

"I won't . . ." Laura began, then broke off, startled when she felt the muscles in his arms contract.

"Why are you wearing pants?" he asked in what sounded to Laura like disbelief and shock.

"Why not?" She frowned when his muscles contracted again.

"It's indecent, that's why."

She stiffened. "I beg your pardon?" she said, feeling both baffled and insulted.

"You should," he muttered, beginning to walk away into the darkness.

Laura was on the point of demanding an explanation for his remark, but abrupt motion drove the question from her mind and raised another one. "Where are you taking me?"

"Back to my place."

"Oh, no, you're not!" she exclaimed, beginning to struggle, this time in earnest. "I'm not going anywhere with . . ." Her voice faded as a large shape loomed ahead, barely discernible in the pitch darkness. "What's tha—" Once again her voice failed as she was swung away from his warm body, high into the air, then plopped unceremoniously onto what she realized was the back of a horse.

"A horse?" Laura was barely aware of speaking aloud, too busy grabbing for the saddle horn to notice.

"What does it look like? A humpless camel?"

She opened her mouth to deliver a scathing reply, but closed it again, because he was gone, striding back toward the hole.

Damn the man. A horse, of all things! Who did he think he was, the Lone Ranger?

For all her fascination with the Old West, by choice Laura had never been on the back of a horse, simply because she thought them too high off *terra firma*, too skittish, and too dangerous. She was pondering the proper, and least dangerous, method of getting down from the animal when her irascible rescuer returned.

"This pack yours?" he asked, holding her back-pack aloft for her inspection.

"Yes, thank you," she answered with genuine gratitude; she had completely forgotten it. She reached to take it, then shook her head. "Will you help me down first, please?"

"No." Slinging the pack over his shoulder, he shoved one foot into a dangling stirrup, grunted as he heaved his body off the ground, and swung the other leg over the horse. "Make room," he ordered, wedging his hips against hers.

Her protest died on her lips as his lower body nudged her posterior. A gasp of shock lodging in her throat, she wriggled forward, away from the hard, too-intimate pressure.

"I don't think . . ." she began stiffly, holding her body rigidly still.

"Good," he said, reaching around her to gather the reins looped to the saddle horn. "Keep it that way till we get to the house."

He made a clicking sound. The horse moved, and she clamped her lips together and grabbed for the horn.

3

Fortunately, it was not a long ride. Even so, Laura's bottom was feeling abused by the time he brought the animal to a halt in front of a shadowy building.

"Is this your house?" she asked, hating the uncertain, tremulous sound of her voice.

"Hmm," he murmured, in what she had to assume was assent. He stood in the stirrups, and Laura inhaled sharply when his body dragged against hers as he dismounted. "Now I'll help you down," he said.

Before she could respond, he raised his hands to her waist and lifted her from the saddle. Her feet made contact with the earth, and her legs buckled. She was forced to hang onto him to keep from falling. The next instant she was swept off her feet again and into his arms.

"You're the most falling-down female I ever came across," he said, striding to the front door. "You got some sort of affliction or something?"

"Of course not," she answered, glaring at him—to little effect, since he couldn't see her expression in the dark. "It's just that . . . well, I've never been on a horse before," she blurted out. "It's left me feeling—"

"Never been on a horse?" he said, his voice sharp with surprise.

"Well, no," she said defensively. "Riding isn't an everyday occurrence for most people back East, you know."

Her explanation stopped him in his tracks. "You're from back East?"

"Yes," she said. "You can put me down now."

"In a minute." Stepping to the door, and nearly crushing her against it, he shifted around until he could grasp the latch, lift it, and push the door open.

A door latch? Laura mused. How quaint.

"Where back East?" he asked, moving inside. He set her on her feet just inside the door.

"Pennsylvania," Laura told him absently, locking her knees to insure against falling again. "You can let me go, I'm all right now." She glanced around and saw . . . nothing. The darkness was complete. Afraid to move, she pleaded, "Could you please turn on a light? It's darker in here than in that darned hole in the ground."

"Stay put," he advised her, his boots scraping against the floor as he moved away from her.

A moment later Laura blinked as another scraping noise was followed by the flare of a match. Her eyes widened as he held the flame to a wick inside an oil table lamp.

No electricity? she thought, probing her memory to recall if she had noticed electric lines strung along the rutted dirt road leading to the ghost town. She hadn't.

Bemused by the idea of a person living in the back of beyond without the basic amenities, she watched as he lit two more lamps.

"Incredible," she murmured. "Simple but incredible."

"What?" Straightening, he turned to her, his face and body bathed in light. Seeing him banished all coherent thoughts but one from her mind.

Her rescuer was one breathtaking sight to behold, even taller than she had first thought, whipcord lean, and handsome in a rough-hewn way.

"Name's Jake Wilder," he said, eyeing her narrowly. "I own all the land around here. Do you have a name?"

His taunting voice snapped Laura out of her introspection.

"Well, of course I have a name," she said, bristling as she stepped boldly forward, her right hand extended. "I'm Laura Brand, and I want to thank you again for rescuing me from that cavern, Mr. . . . May I call you Jake?"

Though he hesitated, slanting a wary look at her hand, he finally reached out to engulf it within his own. "Uh, sure, if you like. May I call you Laura?"

"Certainly," she said briskly, withdrawing her suddenly warm and tingling hand. "I . . . ah, guess I can consider myself pretty lucky you happened along when you did," she rushed on, feeling odd, disoriented by the intimate sensations that had spread up her arm to her shoulder and down, permeating her entire being. "If you hadn't come along," she babbled on, "I might have had to spend the night down in that dank hole."

"The night?" His dark, naturally arched eyebrows inched up his forehead, and a distinctly sardonic smile accented his hard, masculine mouth. "You may have had to spend one helluva lot more that one night down there . . . Laura."

"What do you mean?" She frowned as she cast a quick look around her. Even with the three lamps lit, the interior of the room was shadowy. But the light was sufficient for her to note the sparse furnishings, the rustic appearance.

"It might have been days before I had reason to ride out to that section." His harsh voice captured her wandering attention. "I don't often go out to that . . . hole."

Her frown deepened at the emphasis he had placed on his last word, and she felt sick knowing she had been right to think she could have died. She stumbled to a ladder-backed wooden chair she had noticed during her brief perusal of the room.

"You gonna fall down again?" he asked, sounding both impatient and disgusted.

"No!" she snapped, tossing him a fulminating look. "I'm going to sit down. *If* you don't mind," she added, sinking onto the chair without waiting for permission.

He shrugged, bringing his shoulder and chest muscles into rippling play, and causing her breath to catch at his casual motion.

"Don't mind at all," he said dryly. "Save me from having to pick you up again."

"How very gallant of you." She began to feel downright put upon by his attitude.

"Never claimed to be gallant," he retorted. "You're the trespasser here . . . remember?"

"Well, I do again beg your pardon," she returned with feigned sweetness. "But I didn't try to fall into that damn hole, you know."

"Didn't you?" he shot back. "What were you doing poking around there?"

Suddenly the effects of her experience overwhelmed her, and her fatigued body sagged in the hard chair. It required a supreme effort to reply. "Trying to get to a flowering plant on the other side of it," she finally answered.

His eyebrows made a return trip up his forehead. "A plant? Don't make the mistake of taking me for a fool . . . Laura. Who sent you here?"

"Nobody sent me." She frowned, wondering what in hell she had gotten herself into.

"How did you get here?"

"A Cherokee."

"You came with an Indian?"

"Only the four-wheeled variety," she said, waging an inner fight to remain upright in the chair.

"Huh?"

His expression of baffled consternation was comical, except that Laura wasn't laughing.

Weariness placed her far beyond seeing the humor in his obvious confusion.

"My vehicle, four-wheel drive and all. You know?" she said tiredly. "It's a Jeep Cherokee. It's red. You probably missed seeing it in the darkness." She sighed, making a vague motion with her hand. "I parked it a few hills back, near that ghost town."

But her explanation seemed to increase his confusion, and suspicion blazed from his glittering dark eyes.

"Jeep? Red?" he repeated, shaking his head as if to clear his muddled thoughts.

His action distracted her, drawing her attention, and her unwilling admiration, to his dark hair. It was long and a bit shaggy, but deeply waved and lustrous, with russet strands gleaming in the flickering light. Her fingers itched to delve into those dark locks.

The impulse startled her, for she couldn't recall ever having experienced anything like it before. The sad truth was, she had long ago accepted that she was not a sensuous person. Unlike most of her female friends, she simply never noticed male attributes like terrific hair, fantastic eyes, great pectorals, or heaven forbid, slim, tight buns.

"Answer me, dammit!"

Distracted by her unprecedented reaction to the allure of his hair, not to mention his other equally impressive features, Laura gasped and nearly leaped from the chair at his impatient demand.

"You don't have to shout!" she yelled right back at him. "What was the question, anyway?"

Jake looked about ready to explode, but he managed to keep his voice even by speaking through his gritted teeth. "I asked you what ghost town?"

She grimaced; she couldn't recall another ghost town in the vicinity on the map. "How many are there?"

"Not a damn one that I know of," he said, his voice hard with absolute certainty.

"Oh, come on," she said, sure he was amusing himself at her expense, and past the point of tolerating his apparently skewed sense of humor. "You know full well that I'm referring to that old mining town a couple of hills west of here."

"Old mining town?" he repeated, scowling. "You mean Sage Flats?"

"Yes, that's it," she said, suddenly remembering the name of the town in the guidebook and on the map. "Sage Flats."

Once again his narrowed eyes glittered with suspicion. "Sage Flats ain't old, and it sure as hell ain't a ghost town. I wish it was."

That did it. Laura had heard enough. "Look, Mr. Wilder, I'm too tired to play your funny little game . . . whatever it is. I'm exhausted, I'm hungry, but more than anything else, I'm parched. I emptied my canteen hours ago."

Though Jake had frowned at her remark about him playing games, her subsequent complaints wiped the frown from his face and galvanized him into action.

"Why didn't you tell me you were thirsty?" he

growled, striding to a doorway set into the far wall. "You don't fool around with thirst out here."

"I don't fool around with thirst anywhere," she retorted, too weary to make an issue of it. But it didn't matter; Jake Wilder wasn't listening. In fact, he was no longer in the same room. He had disappeared through the far doorway.

Laura's eyelids were already drifting closed when seconds later he strode back carrying a tumbler of water and a thick slice of bread.

"Oh, thank you," she said, heaving a sigh. "That tastes so good." She raised the cup to her lips again, starting when his strong fingers curled around her wrist.

"Slowly," he cautioned. "Eat some bread."

She heaved another sigh of dwindling patience. "Look, I know all about dehydration and all that, but I wasn't even in the sun down there." Despite her protests, she took a bite of crusty bread. "Mmmm, this is good." She took another bite. "Tastes like homemade bread."

"It is bread." He stared at her, confused. "What did you expect it to taste like?"

"Certainly not like home-baked." She took another bite, her teeth crunching through the crust. "Oh, yummy, I haven't had bread this good in . . ." She broke off, her brows crinkling in consternation. "Come to think of it, I've never had bread this good before."

"They don't make good bread back East?"

"No way." She washed the bread down with a sip of water. "Mass-produced bread is pretty tasteless." Her eyes widened at a sudden thought. "Did you bake this?"

He shook his head. "No, I brought it back with me from Virginia City."

"You were in Virginia City?" she asked impolitely around the bread she was happily munching.

"Yeah." He nodded. "I told you you were lucky. If I hadn't been lookin' for my damn horse, I wouldn't have been near that . . . er, hole," he said, starting for the other room. "Finish the bread while I fix you something hot to eat."

"Horse? What horse?" she asked, still chewing.

"That damned bay that keeps breaking out of the lean-to," he stated from the other room.

Well, that certainly clears that up, Laura thought, shaking her head and beginning to feel a definite empathy for Alice, who had also stumbled into a hole in the ground. The difference was, Jake Wilder was no engaging, fuzzy white rabbit.

The bread was gone. Laura unabashedly licked her fingers before draining the last of the water from the glass. The food and drink had revived her somewhat, and the weak-kneed, light-headed feeling had dissipated.

The call of nature, and sounds of activity from the other room, drew her to her feet. She stood still for a moment, testing her equilibrium. When the room didn't spin and her body remained steady, she smiled confidently and followed in Jake's path.

She took one step into the room and stopped dead, her confidence ebbing as she glanced around her.

The room, obviously the kitchen—of sorts—was small, but that wasn't what had brought Laura to an abrupt halt. Her own kitchen in her townhouse in Philadelphia was even smaller, but compact, loaded with every convenience. This kitchen was anything but compact, and didn't possess a single convenience.

If the other room was rustic, this one was positively primitive. Feeling a renewed sense of disorientation, Laura gazed slowly around the room, beginning with her taciturn host.

Jake stood with his back to her at a wood-burning stove the likes of which Laura had seen only in museums. It was squat, pot-bellied, black, and ugly. Three lids, approximately six inches in diameter, were set into the flat stovetop. With a long-handled metal spoon, Jake stirred the contents of a large black iron frying pan that sat atop one of the lids. On another lid was a smaller pan, and the steam rising from it carried the aroma of cooking ham. A blue agate coffeepot on the third lid puffed the scent of coffee from its spout.

Laura's stomach growled in anticipation.

"It'll be ready in a few minutes," Jake said, not bothering to turn to look at her.

"Thank you." She made a face at his back in response to the embarrassment she felt at his hearing her body's noisy demand for food. Then, feeling foolish for the childish reaction, she glanced away from him.

The few other objects in the room looked as ancient as the stove. There was a metal sink with one spigot. One? Laura mused, frowning at the certainty that it was a cold-water tap. Primitive indeed.

From the sink her gaze drifted to the only pieces of furniture, a table and two chairs, both made of wood, and not too expertly at that. But it wasn't the crude table and uncomfortable-looking chairs that caught Laura's attention, or the tin plates and utensils set beside them. It was a well-worn broad leather belt, complete with a holster that sheathed a wood-handled, long-barreled pistol, lying on a folded newspaper at the end of the table nearest Jake.

In truth, it wasn't the gun itself that surprised Laura; she knew that Westerners armed themselves with both rifles and handguns, especially those living and working in desolate areas. It was the type of gun. She could identify it even in its holster, because it was unique. An illustrated book about handguns in Laura's library featured a picture of it—an experimental seven-shot open-top .44 and single action Army Peacemaker.

The strange thing was, the gun had been produced in the 1860s, and this particular weapon, though it had obviously been used, didn't look over a hundred years old.

Laura was staring at the gun, pondering whether Jake had any idea of how valuable the pistol must be, when another, more immediate problem made itself felt.

"Uh . . . Jake, would you direct me to the bathroom, please?"

"Bathroom?" He turned, frowning.

"Yes, please. Nature calls, you know," she said, smiling.

"Huh?"

She smothered a sigh. The man was so attractive; it was a pity he was proving rather dim.

"The facilities," she said, ditching subtlety for bluntness. "I've got to go . . . and soon."

"Oh." His frown turned into an impatient scowl.

"Why didn't you say so? It's out back." He cocked his head, indicating the back door.

Out back? Laura repeated to herself, making a beeline for the door. Why would anyone . . . Her thought splintered as she bolted through the door into the chill night air . . . and complete darkness. Damn, she fumed, she should have brought a—

"You might need this," Jake drawled from behind her, one arm extended over her shoulder, a lantern handle dangling from his long fingers.

"But where is it?"

"Straight ahead, you can't miss it."

Grabbing the lantern, she strode forward. After a few yards she came to another abrupt stop, appalled at the sight of a narrow boxlike structure illuminated by the flickering lantern light. An air hole in the shape of a quarter moon was carved into the door.

Staring at the outhouse in disbelief, Laura felt her stomach tighten at the stench. At any other time, nothing could have compelled her to enter this offensive excuse for a bathroom. But this was not any other time, and unless she made use of it . . .

Gritting her teeth, she lifted the rusted metal latch and swung open the door.

Fortunately, by the time she reentered the kitchen, the roiling sensation in her stomach had mercifully ceased.

"Good timing." Jake shot a half-smile at her. "Grub's ready. Grab a seat."

"I need to wash up first."

"There's the sink." He motioned with his head. "Soap's in the dish on the draining board."

She crossed to the sink, turned the spigot handle, and thrust her hands into the trickling water. As she had suspected, it was cold.

"I suppose there's no hot water," she said, reaching for the soap.

"You suppose correctly, but if you want to wait, I'll heat some for you."

"Never mind." She wondered why he hadn't thought to heat the water while she was outside. "I'll rough it with cold water this time."

"Rough it?" He snorted. "At least there's water running into the house. Most folks don't have that."

"Really?" Drying her hands on a coarse towel from the draining board, she turned to give him a startled look.

"Yeah, really," he mocked her. "Fact is, none of the shacks in town have it."

"None of the shacks in what town?" she asked, puzzled as she watched him turn from the stove, the large frying pan in one hand, the long-handled spoon in the other.

"Sage Flats, o' course," he replied, spooning scrambled eggs and fried potatoes onto the tin plates. "Ain't no other towns nearby."

Laura felt an uneasy skittering down her spine. Ignoring it, she forced a laugh; it sounded phony, even to her own ears.

"You're pulling my leg . . . right?"

He had crossed to dump the big pan into the sink, and was in the process of lifting the smaller pan from the stove lid. Her question made him pause, the pan suspended in mid-air as he stared at her in evident bafflement.

"Why would I josh you about that?" he asked, his tone questioning her common sense.

"Because both you and I know that Sage Flats is nothing more than a ghost town," she retorted, insulted by his tone and manner.

"Uh-huh." He shook his head. "Sit down and dig in," he said in a gentling tone, putting the ham on their plates. "You'll feel better after you've eaten."

She began to argue, but the combined smells of potatoes, ham, and eggs wiped all thoughts from her beleaguered mind. Without another murmur, she slipped onto the chair he indicated with a nod. Picking up a crudely made fork, she began to dig into the eggs, but hesitated when he shot a sharp, disapproving look at her.

"What?" she asked, shifting a puzzled glance from her plate to his stern expression.

"We didn't say grace."

Grace? She felt a surge of warmth for this seemingly hard, emotionless man. Jake Wilder, who, gun close at hand as he sat down at the table, insisted on saying grace over his meal. How utterly charming.

"Sorry," she murmured, lowering her head to hide her smile as she laid the fork on the table and folded her hands above her plate.

"Thank you, Lord, for the abundance of your bounty," he said. "Amen."

"Amen," she echoed demurely, then picked up her fork once more to attack her food.

Consuming his own meal, Jake watched Laura with open interest as she cleaned her plate down to the last smidgen of egg, ham, and potato. Finally, cradling her chipped crockery cup in her hands, she sat back to enjoy her coffee.

"Better?" he asked blandly.

"Much," she admitted, sighing in satisfaction. "Thank you. You're a pretty good cook."

"Or else you were that hungry," he drawled, moving his shoulders in one of those muscle-rippling, sense-stirring shrugs.

"Well, whichever, it tasted great."

"Are you ready to talk now?"

"Sure, if you want to." She frowned at the sudden tension in his expression. "What do you want to talk about?"

"You could begin with the truth."

"The truth?" Her frown deepened. "What are you implying? I told you the truth."

In a flicker, his expression changed from tense to skeptical. "Uh-huh." One dark brow shot into a high arch. "You came here from back East with a red Cherokee, and just happened to stumble into that hole while trying to get to a wildflower. Have I got that right?"

"Exactly."

"Bullshit." The lightning change in his expression was frightening.

Laura felt hard pressed to keep from jumping from the chair and running back into the hills. The man looked positively lethal. Forcing herself to remain seated and calm, she drew a deep breath.

"Whether or not you choose to believe me, I have told you nothing but the absolute truth," she said, somehow managing to keep her voice steady.

"And the reason you came out here from the East," he said in a tone of patent disbelief, "was to collect plants?"

"Yes," she said, then scrupulously qualified, "well, that and the fact that I've always felt an affinity for the Western mystique."

"The Western mystique?" His expression went blank with incomprehension.

Where has this guy been? Laura wondered, then immediately answered her own question. He's been out here, in the hills of Nevada, as wild as the plant life.

"You know," she said, waving one hand vaguely. "The essence, the ambience of the place."

Now he looked at her as if she were to be feared. "I don't know what the hell you're talkin' about, lady," he said. "You're gonna have to do better."

Laura's patience finally snapped. "I wanted to see the West, so I came out here!"

"With an Indian."

"No!" she shouted. "A Cherokee, a red Jeep Cherokee!"

"A Cherokee Indian *is* red."

"It's not an Indian. It's not human!" Her voice had grown so shrill from frustration that it startled her. Yet she continued, nearly screaming at him, "It's a machine, an automobile . . . with four-wheel drive."

His expression questioned her sanity.

She was beginning to have doubts on that score herself. "Look, Jake, what's the big deal, any-way?" she went on in a more reasonable tone. "So I fell into that hole . . . so what? I meant no harm."

"So you say," he bit off. "I just don't happen to believe you." His stare drilled into her, giving Laura the uncomfortable sensation that he was trying to see into her soul. "I believe you were sent here, either to poke around on your own, or to distract me while whoever hired you searched those hills for the mine entrance." His eyes slitted, and his expression was granitelike, shrewd. "I figured someone had grown suspicious when I picked up strange tracks at the base of that hill. Maybe I was followed once when I went to check on the mine, and didn't know it."

"Tracks? Suspicious?" She shook her head, totally lost. "Suspicious of what?"

"You know damn well what." Anger frayed his tone. "Suspicious of that hill," he blurted out—unintentionally, she was sure. "And the big deal, as you call it, is that whoever it is is looking for gold."

Laura's eyes popped open so wide she could feel the strain.

"There's gold there . . . ?"

"So you *do* know," he stated, his expression one of utter self-disgust.

"But I *don't* know," she protested. "How could I? I only arrived today." She frowned in concentration. "Besides, I understood that the little gold that was in these hills was exhausted by the miners who built that ghost town back there."

"Dammit, woman, I told you there is no ghost town in these parts," he barked. "Sage Flats is still full of those greedy, grubby castoffs and passel of outlaws, hanging around for the last of the pickin's." His full mouth curled into an unattractive sneer. "But I expect the filthy place *will* be a ghost town before too long, since the pickin's have just about run out."

Where in hell was the White Rabbit when a girl needed him? Laura thought, somewhat hysterically. For as normal as Jake Wilder looked, she feared she was dealing with a real nut case.

Mustering every ounce of fortitude she possessed, she managed to maintain a facade of composure, deciding to play along with him.

"So there are still miners living in Sage Flats, mining the surrounding hills?"

"You can quit the playactin'," he grumbled. "You know as well as I do that there are." A tiny, self-satisfied smile kicked up the corners of his tight lips. "That is, all except my hills, my mine. They don't know about that." His eyes narrowed and he gave her another piercing stare. "At least, up until a week or so ago, I *thought* they didn't know about it."

"I didn't tell anyone! I swear I did not know about the mine."

"Let's start again," he said, obviously not believing a word she said. "Why are you here?"

"I told you," she said, her low tone conveying her weariness. "I've always been interested in the Old West, and I wanted to see if there was anything left of it."

"The Old West?" The look he gave her said volumes, the pages of which Laura did not want to read.

"Yes, you know, the west of the 1800s," she felt compelled to explain.

"Lady, I warned you about taking me for a fool," he snapped. "This *is* the 1800s!" he shouted. "Eighteen-sixty, to be exact!"

4

1860!

Laura stared in sheer astonishment at the man seated opposite her, the man whose mental stability she now seriously questioned.

Pity, she mused, feeling disappointment. The man appeared to embody every quality she had always admired in the Western man. He was taciturn, cool . . . and ruggedly good-looking to boot. Too bad he was also apparently insane.

But the expression in Jake's dark eyes had more the look of sincerity than of madness. And that really scared her.

Wonderland indeed.

"Ah . . . Mr. Wilder," she began hesitantly, unsure how to proceed, "this time you really are amusing yourself at my expense . . . Right?"

"Why would I do that?"

"Boredom from being alone too long?" she hazarded.

He shook his head. "I'm not bored. I'll admit I'm getting a mite tired of this conversation, but I'm not bored. I'm never bored. I like being alone."

"But you believe it's 1860?" Somehow she managed to drag up a note of skepticism.

He was unimpressed by her derisive tone. Favoring her with a condescending look, he slid the newspaper from beneath the gunbelt and slapped it down on the table in front of her. "I *know* it's 1860," he retorted, stabbing a long forefinger at the date printed on the paper.

Laura stared and stared at the date displayed beneath the newspaper's banner, but no matter how hard she stared, the numbers didn't change. Nor did the newspaper appear old or yellowed with time.

She drew a slow, calming breath; it didn't work. She felt anything but calm. Niggling doubts nagged at her. There were the odd bits and pieces to be considered: the too-rustic appearance of the place; the crude, ancient-looking furnishings; the excellent condition of Jake's gun; the absence of electricity and the most basic refrigeration; and of course that awful privy.

Her breathing grew shallow. Her heart beat faster. And incipient panic now wrapped its choking hands around her throat.

"What year did you think it was?" he asked.

She tore her gaze from the newsprint to confront the mockery blazing in his eyes.

"Nineteen ninety-three."

He laughed in her face. "I knew there was something strange about you, with your odd clothes and all your talk about red Cherokee Indians with four wheels instead of legs and—"

"Dammit!" she exclaimed. "I'll prove it to you!" Shoving her chair back, she jumped up and looked around the kitchen. "Where's my backpack?"

"In the other room," he said, making no move to retrieve it for her.

"Thanks," she snarled, and dashed through the doorway.

The pack lay just inside the front door, on the

bare, rough-hewn floor. Why hadn't she noticed the floor before? she wondered.

Scooping the pack from the floor, she turned and marched back into the kitchen to where Jake lounged in his chair. He certainly looked bored now.

"You'll see, you'll see," she muttered.

"I can't wait," he drawled.

After opening the pack, she dug to the very bottom, grunting in satisfaction when her fingers curled around her wallet, the map, and the guidebook she had bound together with a rubber band.

She slipped the band from the packet and slapped the articles on the table in front of him.

"Official Nevada state map issued for the current year, 1993. A historical guidebook for Virginia City and environs—likewise for the current year, 1993."

Jake's bored expression became a puzzled frown, but she didn't give him time to respond. Flipping open her wallet, she pointed to the plastic window displaying her driver's license.

"Read it and reconsider your ridiculous claim, Mr. Wilder," she said, with more than a hint of self-satisfaction. "My Pennsylvania state driver's license, which you will note expires later this year, in November, 1993."

Jake looked stunned. Yet his obvious amazement only intensified Laura's uneasiness.

"Say something."

"I don't know what to say," he admitted, squinting as he peered down at the wallet. "Dammit, woman, I know what year it is, and it ain't 1993." He gave her a quizzical look. "What in hell is a driver's license, anyway?"

"A state-issued permit to operate a motor vehicle."

"And what in hell is a motor vehicle?"

"A car, an automobile," she said, her hand flailing, as if to pluck the answer from thin air. "You know, anything that runs on a motor."

"No, I don't know," he said, looking again at the wallet. "If I'm reading this little card correctly, you were born in the year 1962, which makes you thirty-one if this is 1993. Is that right?"

"Yes."

"Can't be."

"Why not?"

He snorted rudely, derisively. "Because you don't look a day over twenty-two, that's why."

As exhausted as she was, Laura blushed at the left-handed compliment, though in effect Jake had called her a liar.

"Thank you . . . I guess. But I assure you I am thirty-one years old."

"Then you must have had a damned easy life up to now." He still looked skeptical.

"Easy! I'll have you know I've worked hard for . . ." She broke off, struck by the pointlessness of the discussion. "What does my age have to do with anything?" she demanded, glaring down at him.

He shoved back his chair and slowly stood to tower over her. "It proves to me that, if you'll lie about one thing, you'll lie about another." He smirked. "And, lady, this ain't 1993, it's 1860, and I can prove it."

"How?" She jerked her head at the table. "With that paper? That doesn't prove a thing. You can buy a reproduction of one of those at any souvenir shop."

"Maybe so," he conceded. "But then, if the paper's a fake, maybe so are your map and your guidebook and that thing you call a license."

Laura angled her chin and scowled at him. "Look, buster, you don't have to prove a blasted thing to me. I'll show *you*. I'll take you for a spin in the Cherokee." She hesitated, biting her lip in consternation. "I parked it on the outskirts of town. Is it far to Sage Flats?"

"Not too far. Five miles, give or take."

"Okay, then. If you'll take me into town, I'll prove my case. Will you take me? Then we'll see who's right."

"Yes, we will. I was planning on taking you into Sage Flats." His upper lip curled. "We'll see what your friends have to say when they see you with me."

"I don't have any friends there. How could I? The place is a ghost town."

"Yeah, full of ghosts of two-bit miners, whores, and crooks," he retorted. "Which group of so-called spirits do you belong to, the soiled doves?"

"Soiled doves! That's a term used to describe prostitutes! How dare you? I'll have you know I'm a respected botanist!"

"Like I said, we'll see when we get into town."

"Good. When can we go?"

"In a week or so."

She started. "A week or so! Why not tomorrow morning?"

Jake merely smiled—a smug, infuriating smile—before replying. "Because I want to wait and see if your friends come sniffing around while they

think you're keeping my mind on other things."
He didn't need to elaborate on what those "other
things" were; the look he raked over her body said
it all. "Now," he said, turning away, "I've got
work to catch up on around here, and I have to be
up at first light."

"When is that?" she asked wearily.

He dipped his fingers into a small pocket near
the waistband of his pants, drew out an old-
fashioned timepiece, and glanced at it. "Coupla
hours."

Automatically raising her arm, Laura looked at
her watch. It read 3:18. No wonder she felt unequal to arguing in her own defense, she thought,
lifting her hand to muffle a yawn. She had been
up almost twenty-four hours, ever since her hotel
wake-up call had roused her at four yesterday
morning.

Life was just not fair.

"You look kinda funny." Jake's comment in-
truded into her thoughts. "Are you okay?"

"No." She blinked against a sudden sting in her
eyes. "I'm tired. I need some sleep."

"Well, damn, you don't have to cry about it."
He looked decidedly uncomfortable.

"I'm not crying."

Eyeing her, Jake appeared indecisive for a moment before his strong features locked into lines of
determination. Without a word he grabbed her
hand.

"Hey!" she cried. "What do you think you're
doing?"

"I know what I'm doing." He pulled her into
the other room and crossed to the far corner.

"Look, Jake, enough is en—" She broke off

when he stopped beside a narrow, metal-frame bed. Real fear sprang into her mind, leaped in her stomach. Was he going to throw her onto that bed and attack her? she thought, inching away from him. "Er . . . Jake, you wouldn't do anything rash now . . . would you?"

"What?" He looked at her as if she were insane. "What are you babbling about? And where are you slithering away to?" He frowned. "I thought you said you needed sleep?"

"Yes, but . . ."

"Well, there's the bed. Sleep. I'll get my bedroll and stretch out on the floor for a coupla hours."

"Okay," she agreed, relieved. "If you insist. But . . . I have nothing to wear."

He didn't respond, but sourly looked her up and down. As he turned away, she remembered a remark he'd made earlier.

"And what's wrong with my clothes, anyway?" she demanded, stopping him in mid-stride.

He slanted a sardonic glance over his shoulder. "A lady don't wear pants. Or loggers' boots."

"Doesn't," she absently corrected his grammar. "A lady doesn't wear pants."

"That's what I said."

"No, you said don't." She couldn't believe she was pursuing this line of discussion; weariness must have turned her mind to mush, she decided.

"Lady, you're loco," Jake said, walking to a chest of drawers near the front door. "Plain loco."

"I am not," Laura replied, dropping to the bed and bending to untie the boot laces. "And these aren't loggers' boots. They're hiking boots. Ladies' hiking boots."

"If you say so," he muttered in a tone of patent disbelief, as he yanked opened a drawer and pulled out a shirt. "You can sleep in this," he said, tossing it to her.

It landed on the floor near her feet. "You'll never make outfield for the Phillies," she said under her breath, reaching for the shirt.

"What?" He paused with his hand on the door and gave her a quizzical look. "What are you mumbling about?"

"Nothing. Thanks for the shirt. But another thing," she persisted. "Ladies do wear pants. At least in 1993 they do. All the time."

"Sure." He pulled the door shut after him.

"Smartass," she grumbled, making a face at the door. Then, realizing he probably wouldn't be gone long, she got up. She removed the bracelet and slipped it into the velvet bag, then stuffed the bag into the bottom of her pack. Within moments she was out of her clothes, into his shirt—the hem brushed her knees, and the sleeves hung below her hands—and beneath the bedcovers. And not a moment too soon. Jake entered the room as she was tugging the covers up around her throat.

"I heard that last remark," he drawled, crossing the room to drop his bedroll next to the opposite wall.

His voice was so dry that she couldn't keep from smiling.

"Damned if you're not even prettier when you smile," he said.

She almost responded to his compliment, when a thought occurred to her. "We forgot to clear off the table."

"Stay put. I'll do it."

"But . . ."

"I said I'll do it." He headed for the other room. "You get some rest."

"Okay, but there's one more thing I have to say."

"Yeah? What's that?" He stopped in the doorway.

"I'm not a soiled dove."

"I know. At least," he qualified, "I know you're not the run-of-the-mill, dirty-neck-and-feet kind."

"How do you know that?"

"I'm a smartass."

Laura almost laughed, but her frustration at his assumption of her identity squelched it. "Yes, you are."

"Uh-huh." He walked into the other room.

"And it is 1993," she called after him.

"Go to sleep," he ordered.

She willingly closed her eyes.

5

"Laura."
She came out of the depths of sleep to the soft sound of Jake's voice calling her name, the gentle nudge of his hand on her shoulder, and the delicious aroma of coffee tantalizing her senses.

"Is it first light?" she asked, blinking the cobwebs of forgotten dreams from her eyes.

"Long past. It's after ten." He removed his hand in a slow, almost caressing glide down her arm.

"After ten! I must have died!" Stifling a yawn, and a sensuous shiver in response to his touch, she sat up and stretched. "Why didn't you call me sooner?"

He turned abruptly and headed for the door. "You needed the rest," he said tersely. "But you'd better roll out now. Breakfast is ready."

Wondering what she had done to annoy him—or was he always grumpy in the morning?—she tossed back the covers and crawled out of bed. She ached all over from her tumble into that hole.

Pushing her fingers into her tangled hair, she turned to gaze out the small window above the bed. The unrelenting glare of the midmorning sun hurt her eyes and brought an old saying to mind: Things always look better in the light of day.

Wrong.

She shook her head, wincing as her fingers caught in her snarled hair. Things didn't look better at all; in fact, the view through the window looked pretty darned depressing.

Alternating sunlight and shadow played over the rock-strewn, craggy hills in the near distance. The terrain closer to the ranch house was somewhat level, with only an occasional series of rough-looking bumps. The landscape seemed dry, barren, and devoid of life, both animal and plant.

But Laura knew better, having tramped over that arid earth, those craggy humpbacked hills. The evidence of tracks and animal droppings, and the variety of plant life, had not surprised her. She had read books and watched several TV documentaries on the Western deserts and had expected it to *appear* barren, lifeless, and desolate.

No wonder Jake behaved a trifle off center, she

mused. Living alone in such a remote place would have had her climbing the walls.

"Rustle your rump, woman!" Jake shouted from the kitchen, ending her reverie. "Grub's on the table!"

Insufferable, arrogant . . . Breaking off the thought, she smiled and sauntered into the kitchen.

Raising his gaze from the cup he was filling with coffee, Jake started, then stared at her in stark amazement. The coffee ran over the sides of the cup and onto the table.

"Mr. Wilder, watch it!" Laura exclaimed, rushing forward.

"Dammit! Your fault," he growled. "What in hell do you think you're doing, woman, coming to the table dressed like that?" He indicated her appearance with a sweep of his hand.

She glanced down at herself, then back up at him. "It's your shirt. What's the problem?"

"It's indecent."

Laura's back went up. "I do beg to differ, Mr. Wilder, but I consider myself adequately and decently covered."

"I can see most of your legs."

"No kidding. So what?" She gave him a haughty look. "I've been told I have very attractive legs."

Her statement seemed to throw him into confusion. "Well, you do," he admitted grudgingly. "But dammit, woman, it's unladylike to show your legs to a man. The only women who do are the kind you claim you're not."

"Soiled doves?" She arched her brows.

"Yes."

"Oh, brother," she moaned, shaking her head in despair.

He slammed the coffeepot onto the table. "Since the food's ready, you might as well just sit down and eat. But as soon as you're done, you get yourself decently dressed."

"All right, I'll eat." She seated herself opposite him. "But before I'll even think about getting dressed, I need a shower."

"A shower," he repeated, his face blank. "We don't get much rain out here."

This was just too much. "I don't mean a rain shower, you nit!" she yelled. "I'm talking about a bath."

He shook his head like a punchy prizefighter. "Well, hell, why didn't you say so?"

"You have a bathtub?" she asked eagerly.

"No." He shrugged. "But I have my ma's old washtub. I can fill that for you."

"Wonderful," she muttered, picking up her fork and spearing a mouthful of scrambled eggs. "I suppose beggars can't be choosers. I'll take it."

"Thought you might." Jake scraped his chair back and got to his feet. "I'll have to put the water on the stove to heat."

"Figures," she said, heaving a sigh.

Laura caught herself sighing often throughout the following days.

She sighed in exasperation every time she prepared a simple meal for Jake on that impossible excuse for a stove. She sighed in frustration every time she had to drag the washtub into the kitchen and heat water for her bath.

She sighed with confusion at the excitement she

felt every time she made physical contact, no matter how slight and impersonal, with the solid masculine warmth of Jake's body.

And she sighed because he didn't trust her, and believed she was there to get information from him.

For Laura, it was a long and harrowing week, fraught with moments of dizzying delight . . . and unmitigated torture.

One evening as they dawdled over their after-supper coffee, Laura decided to try a little mining of her own, digging for personal information about her host.

"Where were you born?" she asked, not even trying to hide her curiosity.

"Here," he murmured, jerking his head at the doorway. "Right there in the bedroom."

Laura was appalled at the very idea of a woman giving birth under such primitive conditions. "In there?" she exclaimed in disbelief. "The same room I'm sleeping in?"

"In the same corner." A smile twitched the edges of his lips. "Of course, there was a double bed then."

"How utterly primitive."

"Hey," Jake objected. "The bed was handmade, and maybe a little crude, but it wasn't primitive."

She shot him an impatient look. "I meant the overall conditions, not the bed."

"Oh." He frowned. "I'm sure . . . I think my pa did wash his hands before helping to deliver me."

"Oh . . . well then . . ." Realizing it was useless to pursue the subject, Laura asked another question. "Then you've lived on this ranch all your life?"

"Yes." He nodded, then turned the tables on her.

"How about you? You live in Pennsylvania all your life?"

"Yes. I was born in Philadelphia . . . *in a hospital.*"

"That's nice." Jake shrugged off her verbal jab. "I've heard of hospitals, but I've never been in one. Don't want to, either. Heard they're nasty places."

Never been in one! Nasty places! Laura thought in astonishment, feeling a feathering of unease along her spine. Could Jake honestly believe he was living in the nineteenth century?

Naw. She rejected the idea as too farfetched. Ignoring the unsettling sensation, she again changed the subject. "What was it like growing up out here? I mean, well, in comparison to Philadelphia, or almost any city, this place is pretty deserted and remote."

"Remote . . . maybe." Jake smiled and turned his head to gaze through the one small kitchen window to the dusk-softened landscape beyond. "Deserted?" He turned back to her, his expression patient, tolerant. "No, ma'am. It's not at all deserted. It's teeming with life, maybe not human life, but real, breathin' life, sure enough."

"And you weren't lonely growing up?" Laura asked, recalling his telling her he never got lonely.

"No. I had my ma and pa, and the horses we ran." He frowned. "That is, until Pa got sick, and we had to sell some of the horses to keep going. Ma and I did the best we could to hang onto all the horses until Pa got better, but . . ." He shrugged. "I was only ten, and Pa didn't get better." Painful memories darkened his eyes. "Then he died and, over the years, some of the horses had to go. Most of them were gone by the time I was grown enough to take over running the ranch."

Jake fell silent, except for the soft sigh that whispered through his lips; then he gave a shrug, as if shaking himself free from introspection.

"You've had a hard life," Laura murmured, silently deriding herself for all the times she had thought she'd had it tough. Though she had worked hard to achieve her degree and her associate professorship, she had had the support of a loving and encouraging upper-middle-class family.

"No harder than most out here," he said. "But, then, God never did promise that life would be easy." He shrugged again. "Anyway, then I built the herd up again to what it had been when Pa got sick." A cynical smile flickered across his face. "I even got betrothed to the daughter of our nearest neighbor, a good half-day's ride east. Then Ma got sick and my girl didn't want to be saddled with a sick mother-in-law. She wasn't getting any younger, she said, and she broke the engagement. Two weeks later she married a dry-goods clerk she'd met during one of her family's trips into Virginia City for supplies."

"Oh, Jake," she murmured, impulsively reaching across the table to give his hand a sympathetic squeeze. A shock of awareness jolted through her, awareness of Jake as a man, of herself as a woman . . . alone together.

A fine tremor rippled Jake's flesh beneath her palm, giving evidence that he was also experiencing a heightened sensual awareness. He sliced a glance to her hand resting against his, then as quickly shifted a piercing stare to her, probing the depths of her eyes.

"Don't waste your pity on me," he said, his rough-edged voice betraying his reaction to their physical contact. "Turned out I got off lucky. Less than a year after she married the dry-goods clerk, she ran off to California with a gambler headed for the gold fields."

"And you never married?" For a reason Laura refused to explore, she held her breath waiting for his answer.

"No." He gave a brief, decisive shake of his head. "There aren't many marriageable females out here and, what with taking care of Ma, and running the ranch, I didn't have time to waste looking for a bride in Virginia City." He heaved a sigh. "Ma died just two years ago."

"I'm sorry," she said again, and would have continued with more questions, but he beat her to it.

"Thanks, but it was for the best," he said, accepting and dismissing her sympathy at the same time. "What about you? You married or anything?"

"No." Laura managed a weak smile as she carefully lifted her tingling hand from his. "I was too busy with my college and postgraduate studies even to consider marriage."

"But there must have been men in your life," he insisted.

"Well . . ." She hesitated, then, because he had been so forthright with her, went on. "I did have a brief, very brief, affair with an associate, a professor of literature."

"You went to bed with him?" Jake demanded, sounding positively Victorian in his shock.

"Once." Laura, who considered herself a self-confident, independent woman, had to swallow to moisten her suddenly dry throat. "Just once," she repeated. "He was a very nice man, a genuine gentleman, but there simply were no sparks, no sparks at all," she explained, annoyed at defending herself. "Going to bed with a man before marriage is common practice in 1993, you know."

"I told you before that I *don't* know," he growled. "I don't like it a damn sight, either."

Laura was well grounded in the precepts of equality, and could have retaliated with a crushing argument. But she didn't, wanting to maintain the fragile truce between them. She tried another topic, opting to dazzle him with her expertise in the field of botany.

Fortunately, Jake allowed himself to be distracted from the thorny topic of male-female relationships in the fading days of the twentieth century.

Had Laura believed herself less than a sensuous woman? After almost a week of experiencing the tingles evoked by the mere sound of Jake's rough velvet voice, and enduring the flames of desire set ablaze inside her by the lightest of Jake's touches, she was forced to revise her self-evaluation.

By the end of that week, Laura concluded that she was either intensely sensuous, completely bananas, or falling in love.

Seeking distraction from her disturbing thoughts, she came up with a positively brilliant idea, one that would serve her in several ways. Besides appealing to her interest in the Old West, it

could prove especially useful when she returned
home. That is, if she could get Jake to agree to it.

6

"**Y**ou want me to do what?" Jake asked, although he had heard her perfectly well.

"Teach me to shoot," she repeated.

"That's what I thought you said." Suspicion
sharpened his mind, tightened his muscles.
"Why?"

Laura lifted her slim shoulders in a light shrug.
"Well, I've been thinking for some time now about
getting instruction on the proper handling of a
handgun, because of the prevailing conditions today, you know."

Jake refrained from reminding her that he did
not, in fact, know. Instead, frowning, he asked,
"The streets back East are dangerous for a
woman?"

"Not just for women, but for men, too, and even
children." She grimaced. "Come to think of it, I
could probably make good use of the proper handling of a weapon out here."

"How?" he demanded, his suspicion growing.
"In what way?"

"Self-protection," Laura said. "I get nervous every time I step outside the door." She gave him a
self-deprecating look. "Though I know it's irra-
tional, and I hate to admit it, I'm afraid of snakes."

Snakes! Jake resisted an urge to laugh, and gave her request serious consideration. He didn't trust her, though he strongly wished he could. Damn. Why did she have to be so innocent-looking, so pretty, so appealing?

"Will you teach me, Jake?" she said with quiet, beguiling entreaty. "Please?"

Jake fought the plea on her full, moist lips, in her soft eyes. Then he gave in, simply because he wanted to. The mere prospect of being close to Laura, touching her satiny flesh while he instructed her in the correct handling of the Peacemaker, sent a lightning bolt of excitement streaking through him.

"Okay, I'll teach you." His voice was rough-edged and abrupt in response to the conflict churning inside him.

"When?" Her voice was eager, her smile devastating.

Jake swallowed a sigh of surrender. "Tomorrow."

"Thank you." Laura's smile challenged the summer sunlight for brilliance. "What time?"

"Right after I finish the morning chores."

Which, Jake silently acknowledged, had been requiring less and less time as his herd had dwindled. The need to sell off two more horses had sent him to Virginia City the previous week. He only hoped he could hang on until the gold petered out in the hills around Sage Flats and the shanty town's ruffians drifted away in search of greener pastures. If he couldn't mine that rich vein of gold on his own property, and soon, Jake knew he would not only lose the few remaining horses, but his land as well.

* * *

Jake didn't dawdle with his chores the next day, or bide his time and struggle against temptation, as he had ever since Laura's arrival.

"We can begin your lessons as soon as you're done there," he said, ambling across the yard to her.

Laura looked up from the laundry she was pegging to the wash line strung close to the back of the house, and her eyes widened in surprise. "You're finished . . . already?"

"Yeah," he said, not about to offer an explanation. "You almost done there?"

"This is the last of it," she said, bending to pull two flimsy pieces of underwear—just two of the temptations tormenting Jake—from the wicker basket at her feet. "I'll be ready in a minute."

"I'll get the Colts," he said raggedly, turning his back to her.

"Colts?" Her voice stopped him in mid-stride. "As in more than one gun?"

"Yes." He shot her a wry look over his shoulder. "I'm not letting you play around with my special issue. I have an old Navy Peacemaker you can practice with."

That afternoon Laura proved to be a fast learner—much to Jake's disappointment. The first hour of her lesson had been sheer bliss . . . and pure physical torture.

Standing behind her, his body molded to hers, his right arm stretched alongside hers, his hand curled around hers as she gripped the smooth gun handle, had created a riot of sensations inside Jake's body the likes of which he had never before experienced.

It was both thrilling and disheartening. Thrilling, because he could feel Laura's involuntary response to his nearness, the fine tremor that quivered down her spine, her derriere, her long legs. And disheartening because he still couldn't trust her, couldn't accept the truth of her incredible claim of coming from the twentieth century.

Even so, Jake felt sharp disappointment when he moved away from her sweetly curved body to allow her to practice aiming and firing on her own.

When he called a halt after two hours, Jake was surprised at how well Laura had done. In all truth, he was amazed at her accuracy in hitting most of the targets he had set up.

"Well done," he praised her. "But that's enough for one day. Your arm's gotta be getting tired."

"A little," she admitted, turning the pistol to hand it to him handle first. "It was fun. Can you believe I hit almost all of those targets?"

"I suppose I must believe what I see with my own eyes," he said teasingly, suddenly feeling light-hearted, and more relaxed than he had in years. "I'd better be careful. A little more practice and you'll outshoot me."

Laura laughed in delight, sending his spirits soaring. She was so darned pretty. Swallowing with difficulty, he turned back to the house.

"Jake, wait," she said, reaching out to grasp his arm, causing the skin beneath his shirt to quiver and prickle, exactly as it had the evening she had reached across the supper table to cover his hand with hers. "There's a cluster of plants I'd like to examine near the far end of the corral . . ." She paused, then rushed on, sounding both breathless and anxious. "Will you walk over there with me?"

Jake hesitated, fighting his raging desire to be with her, and his nagging fear of the impact on his already diminishing self-control.

Uncertainty and trepidation were new and unwelcome emotions for him. His impatience with his apparent weakness settled the issue.

"Okay," he drawled. He gave her a crooked smile as he turned to walk beside her to the corner corral post. "Let's have a look."

By the time they returned to the house hours later, Jake was struggling with an even larger inner battle. He and Laura had laughed and talked together as if they had known each other for years . . . forever. He had even agreed to her last request to teach her to ride. But what bothered him most was the realization that Laura actually did know about plants, in many instances more than he himself knew, and he had spent his entire life on the ranch. The fact that she was so knowledgeable caused him to question his doubts concerning her explanation as to how and why she had fallen into his mine shaft.

7

If she had thought that learning to shoot and to ride, and doing the household chores, would ease her feelings toward Jake, Laura was very much mistaken. Being with him was enough to drive her to the point of rebellion. Telling herself her growing attraction to Jake was simply the result of proximity, and certainly not love, Laura was determined during the following week to prove her assertiveness by distancing herself from Jake's immediate presence ... by getting to Sage Flats and her Jeep.

She was beginning to feel desperate, especially since she had demanded several times that he take her to the ghost town and he had put her off with one lame excuse after another. During supper on the last evening of their second week together, she decided on a little casual probing so that she could plan her escape.

"Ah ... How far did you say it was to Sage Flats?" she asked offhandedly, pretending to be preoccupied sopping up her gravy with a slice of bread.

"Four, five miles or so," Jake said every bit as offhandedly, studying her over the rim of his coffee mug. "Why?"

"Just curious," she said, raising innocent eyes to his. "Due west, did you say?"

"Mm-hmm." He nodded and narrowed his gaze. "As the crow flies."

"You don't go there often, do you?" She kept her tone neutral.

"Not if I can help it."

"After what you told me about the place, I can't say I blame you." She raised her mug to her mouth to conceal the smile of satisfaction on her lips. "You did say you were going to take me in a week's time, but you haven't, even though I keep asking you to." She watched him carefully.

Jake didn't answer. She had not expected him to. If he thought she was in cahoots with someone in Sage Flats, he wouldn't want to give her a chance to meet her accomplice. Well, she'd make it to town on her own. Before first light, when Jake always left his bedroll, she would sneak from the house and head out—as the crow flies.

Laura didn't sleep a wink, and faking it wasn't easy—not with Jake asleep on the floor at the other end of the room. Listening to his slow, even breathing and an occasional gentle snore didn't make it any easier.

Then, at last, when her eyelids were beginning to droop, the faint pearl-gray of predawn smeared the eastern horizon. Stifling a yawn, afraid to breathe, Laura crept from the narrow bed and stealthily pulled on her clothes. With her eyes fastened on Jake's sleep-sprawled form, she clutched her hiking boots in one hand and her backpack in the other, poised for a tiptoeing flight. Still, she hesitated, her gaze resting on his sleep-softened face.

She wanted his mouth. The realization brought an ache to the pit of her stomach, and to other places as well.

Shaken by the depth and intensity of her feelings, she hastened to the door. It creaked. She froze. Jake slept on. She stepped into the other room, drew a deep breath, and quietly shut the door. She entered the kitchen, took the canteen from her pack, and allowed water to dribble into it. God, she hoped Jake wouldn't wake up!

She eased out the back door and, dropping to the hard ground, quickly pulled on her boots. She scrambled up, walked to the front of the house, and set off at a brisk pace, knowing she had to put as much distance as possible between herself and the ranch before Jake awoke and found her missing. Fortune must have been smiling on her, for luckily she happened upon rutted tracks leading west at the far end of the ranch yard.

Praying the parallel tracks would lead her to town, she followed them.

Although Laura stumbled occasionally on the uneven ground, the going wasn't too bad until the sun cleared the horizon behind her. Then it was just plain hot.

After hours that seemed more like days, her face and neck slick with sweat, her damp shirt plastered to her body, beads of salty moisture trickling between her breasts, Laura was on the point of admitting defeat. Her canteen was more than half empty, and she reasoned that if she turned back now, she might just make it back to the ranch.

Relief shivered through her, banishing all thought of giving up as, reaching the crest of a slight incline, she discerned a cluster of buildings in the distance.

Sage Flats!

Her purpose and energy renewed, she proceeded once more, only to come to an abrupt halt as she recalled the old Indian's advice to wear the bracelet for protection. Telling herself she was being foolish, she nevertheless dug the velvet pouch from her pack and clamped the cuff to her wrist. Then, allowing herself a sip of precious water, she strode forward again.

Her steps faltered as she drew nearer to town.

Finally she came to a complete stop, her eyes wide in disbelief at the sight that lay before her.

Sage Flats, the same town that just two weeks ago had been a ramshackle, rundown skeleton, a ghost town, now showed distinct signs of activity.

A queasy, sinking sensation overcame her as Laura stared in confusion and amazement at the obviously occupied community. The buildings now appeared more substantial, if not permanent. People, primarily men, roughly attired in the garb of a bygone era, moved along the dusty street, walking close to the buildings to avoid the traffic of horsemen and horse-drawn vehicles, mostly buckboards.

How could this be? Laura's rattled mind demanded, when just two weeks ago . . . Was it possible that Jake was right, and it really was 1860? But then, that would mean . . . time travel!

Feeling sick, Laura shook her head in denial of the proof before her eyes. Traveling through time was simply not possible, she assured herself.

Her Cherokee! She had parked the Jeep a little way outside of town. All she had to do was find it, her solid assurance of the twentieth century.

Swallowing the coppery taste of fear, she took off at a trot, skirting the town and heading for the spot where she had parked the Jeep. But when she arrived where she was sure she'd left the vehicle, there was no sign of it.

Squeezing her eyes shut, Laura sent up a fervent prayer for deliverance, then pried her eyes open again. Her prayer went unanswered. She saw only the nineteenth-century town and its scruffy residents.

Dazed and shaken, seriously beginning to question her grip on reality, Laura forced herself to walk on trembling legs into Sage Flats for a closer look at the town and its inhabitants. It was not a pretty or encouraging sight. In fact, it was plain godawful.

The men and two women were even more disheveled than they had appeared from a distance.

Stunned, she stood to one side of the saloon, staring, staring. A sharp tug on her backpack shattered her reverie.

"Hey, little gal, what ya got in that pack?"

The sneering voice, definitely male, outraged Laura. She did not need some hick Casanova accosting her.

"None of your damned business!" she said icily, yanking the pack away as she spun to face the man. He looked every bit as oily as he sounded.

Medium in height, he was thin, bordering on skinny. His long, narrow face was pockmarked, and his hair hung lank and greasy to his shoulders. His worn, dirty clothes seemed to have been of good quality at one time. A black string tie was crumpled against his shirt. But what caught Laura's gaze was the lethal-looking pistol holstered in the well-worn gunbelt around his waist.

"Now's that any way for a pretty little gal to talk?"

Panic-stricken at the threat underlying his jeering voice, she glanced around, hoping to find a champion, but the few people who were within view took no notice of her predicament.

"Ain't ya the prettiest piece I ever did see," her tormentor said.

"Go away and leave me alone," Laura said in a

hard-won tone of authority, taking a cautious step back.

"Cain't do that, pretty lady." The man smiled suggestively. "I'm plannin' on you and me havin' some real fun."

Fun! Certain she knew the manner of fun he meant, Laura nearly gagged. Terrified, and only vaguely aware of a tingling warmth encircling her wrist beneath the bracelet, she shook her head, clutched the pack to her chest, and took several more steps back into a narrow alley separating the saloon from the next building.

Then Laura heard the slow, muffled sound of approaching hoofbeats and Jake's low voice behind her.

"I'm coming up alongside you. Be ready to grab my hand and mount."

Even before he had finished speaking, Jake moved the horse forward, between Laura and her would-be attacker.

"Hey, what do you think you're doin'?" the man snarled, as Jake heaved Laura onto the horse behind him.

"I don't *think* I'm doing anything," Jake answered, moving his hand to the butt of the special-issue weapon strapped to his waist. "I'm *doing* it."

The heat coiling her wrist intensified, but still Laura gave it scant notice. Mesmerized, she watched the man stagger toward them.

"Well, if it ain't the two-bit rancher. Whatcha doin' off yer land? Got somebody keepin' an eye on that gold mine of yers?" he asked, a sneer twisting his lips.

"I should have known. It's Fancy Frank

Finnegan," Jake murmured, his slitted eyes glued to the other man as he approached Jake's horse.

"I know thar's gold on your land and I aim to find it. So ya better not sleep, Wilder, ol' boy."

"Really?" Jake drawled cynically, keeping his gaze steady on Frank's gun hand. "Well, I'm gonna tell you only once. Stay off my land, because if I catch you on it, you won't live to tell about it."

Frank's hand moved toward his pistol, and Jake said, "Hold on," then yelled, "Ya-hah," and slapped the reins against the horse's rump.

The horse leapt forward, and in the same instant, searing blue heat emanated from the turquoise stone in Laura's bracelet and shot out in a crackling, radiating arc at Fancy Frank. With a startled cry, he backpedaled in the dirt street in a frantic attempt to get out of the way of both the animal and the whiplike tongue of sizzling turquoise fire.

Jake kept the horse at a gallop all the way back to the ranch. Hanging on for dear life, her heart thumping in time with the horse's hooves, Laura was immune to the bouncing ride.

"Goddamn!" Jake turned to stare at her the minute he brought the horse to a shuddering stop in front of the house. "What in hell happened back there?"

Shaking, Laura gasped for breath before trying to answer. "I don't know," she finally managed to reply, and raised her arm to stare in fascinated amazement at the bracelet. "The Indian told me this would protect me, but—"

"I thought you said the Cherokee wasn't a person, but a wheeled vehicle."

"Not the Cherokee," she said, shaking her head. "That *is* a vehicle. But on my way here there was an Indian with a stand by the side of the road selling hand-crafted jewelry. I bought this bracelet from him. He said it possessed magical powers. I—I didn't believe him."

"And now you do?" Skepticism laced his voice and stamped his face.

"I . . ." She shifted a quick glance from him to the bracelet, then back to him. She swallowed, then blurted out, "I don't know. After what happened back in town, and two weeks ago, after I fell into that hole, I—I just don't know what to believe."

"Wait a minute." He held up his hand. "What do you mean?"

She frowned. "I don't know how to explain it. It was so strange." She ran a hand around the back of her neck; it came away wet with sweat. "Look, could we go inside, out of this heat? I need a drink."

"Yeah, sure. You go on in," he said, dismounting then turning to help her. "And sit down before you fall down again. I'll be in as soon as I take care of the horse."

Laura was seated dejectedly at the kitchen table, staring fixedly at the bracelet, when Jake entered through the back door.

"Is it possible, Jake?" she asked in a tremulous whisper. "I mean, what that Indian said about the bracelet having magical powers? Could something like that really be possible?"

"I don't know, and right now I don't much care," Jake said in a hard-edged voice. "What I want to know is what you were doing in Sage

Flats, and what you and Frank were cooking up together."

"Cooking up?" Laura blinked. "What are you talking about?"

"You know damned well," he shot back. "Were you giving him directions to the mine entrance?"

"No!" she cried. "I couldn't have even if I wanted to. I don't know where it is." She paused, taking a shuddering breath, then rushed on. "Jake, will you think! You saw the situation when you arrived. I was terrified of that man. Besides, if I was in league with Frank, wouldn't the bracelet have zapped you instead of him?"

"Well . . ." Jake frowned and stared into her eyes. He sighed. "I suppose so. But that doesn't explain what you were doing there."

Laura inhaled deeply. "I went looking for my Jeep so I could go home. But it wasn't there. It's disappeared."

He gave her a searching, wary look. "Are you really who you say you are?"

"Yes, Jake," Laura answered wearily. "I really am. Do you believe me now?"

"Don't know yet," he muttered, turning toward the sink. "I just don't know what to think anymore."

She trembled, and gratefully accepted the cup of water he got her from the tap. Though it quenched her thirst, it was ineffective against the chill permeating her overheated body. She began to shake in delayed reaction to the recent shocks to her system: her tumble into the hole; her subsequent rescue and surprise at the primitive house; the sexually and emotionally tense, altogether wonderful two weeks she'd spent with Jake; and then the ultimate shock of the town and that crude bully, or gunslinger, or whatever that awful man was.

"Laura?" Jake came around the table to stand beside her. Bending, he stared into her face with concern-filled eyes. "You're as white as a ghost. What's wrong?"

"I'm scared," she whispered. Panic curled through her, bringing a wail from the depths of her being. "I don't belong here. I'm a botanist, not a pioneer! What am I going to do?"

He pulled her from her seat and into his arms. He stroked her back in a gesture meant to calm her, but it only intensified her shivers.

She raised her head from his chest to peek up at him. "Do you enjoy holding me like this?" she asked, really needing no answer, for she could feel the bulge pressing against her lower abdomen.

"Yes," he said, meeting her wide-eyed gaze with an expression of heavy-lidded desire. "Unless you tell me no and push me away right now, I'm going to kiss you, Laura."

She chose not to heed his warning. Instead, filled with her own desire, she boldly parted her lips in blatant and hungry invitation.

Slowly, enticingly, he lowered his head to touch his hard male lips to her soft female ones.

Never before had she felt anything quite like the riot of feelings exploding inside her. She wanted, needed, ached for . . . Jake. She made a moan of protest when he lifted his mouth to look down at her.

"Sparks?" he asked in a tone laden with hope.

"No." She shook her head.

"No?" His frown was fierce.

"A raging inferno," she confessed, parting her lips to be consumed once more.

A growl of satisfaction rumbling deep in his throat, Jake lowered his mouth.

Clinging to him, returning his ardor in equal measure, she purred acceptance when he swept her off her feet and carried her into the front room, to the bed. Then, feverish with a raging desire she would not have previously believed herself capable of, she reciprocated in kind when he began to remove her clothes.

Her senses on fire, fanned by flames of need, she caressed his muscle-ridged body as he lifted her onto the narrow bed and eagerly parted her legs.

Not once did she give thought to the wantonness of her response to him, or to the fact that he was still a stranger. Entering her, possessing her, Jake didn't feel like a stranger to her, he felt like a part of her, an integral part that had been missing all her life.

As his gliding hands learned all her curves, and his lips fed greedily on the tightening crests of her breasts, she forgot all her fears and concerns about being in the wrong time. For the moment, time stood still, as she explored the hard angles and hair-roughened textures of Jake's body.

And all the while, Jake thrust into her, igniting within her a fiery tension that grew steadily until it snapped, flinging her into a world that knew no time at all.

8

The desert's cool night air drifted through the window and feathered Laura's exposed back, waking her. She curled into Jake's warmth.

"Cold?" He drew her closer.

"Ummm." She nodded and rubbed her cheek against his chest.

"We're lying on top of the blanket," he said, reminding her of their avid rush to make love.

"I know."

"Are you sorry?" A hint of worry shaded his tone.

"Sorry? For what, lying on top of the blanket?"

"For what we did . . . on top of the blanket."

"No." She craned her neck to look at him. "Are you?"

He smiled; and though it was all the answer she needed, he replied anyway, if wickedly. "I'd be happy to play stallion any time and keep you warm by covering you with my body."

His teasing renewed her desire, and reminded her of something Fancy Frank had said.

"Jake, are you what that dreadful man called you, a two-bit horse rancher?"

"For now, yes," he answered, obviously not bothered by the question.

"For now? I don't understand."

His smile held equal parts shrewdness and loving concern for her.

"For the present, it suits my purposes to let that no-account bunch in town believe I'm nothing more than a flat-busted, down-at-the-heel horse rancher."

"But you're not?"

"Well, I'm not exactly rich." He smiled at her. "But the little money I have I keep in a bank in Virginia City, away from the prying, avaricious eyes of the local crook who calls himself a banker. And, while I'm waiting, I keep tending my small herd of horses, trying to make a go at ranching."

Laura pushed herself up onto her elbow to look at him. "Waiting for what?"

"For the inferior-grade gold to peter out in those half-assed mines they're working." He sneered. "When they leave off drinking long enough to work."

"But I don't understand," she said, her brow wrinkling. "What happens when the gold does run out?"

"Why, honey, those scum-of-the-earth claim jumpers will clear out in search of better pickin's, and Sage Flats will become the ghost town you said it will."

"Jake, really." She rose to a sitting position, just so she could glare down at him. "I don't care what happens to them, or to that ugly town. I was asking what will happen to you when the gold runs out."

His smile grew blatantly smug. "I'm gonna be a very rich man, because there's gold in my mine, and it won't peter out for a good, long time. I'm just waitin' for them to go before I start mining it."

Her eyes grew wide. "There really is gold in that hole in the ground I fell into?"

He nodded. "A wide, deep vein of almost pure, high-grade gold. And that mine is on my land."

"Geez!"

"Yeah. And now I think we should get dressed." He sat up beside her. "I don't know about you, but I'm hungry enough to eat one of my own horses." He grinned, rising from the bed.

As he dressed, Laura felt a grumbling in her stomach. She could eat *two* horses, she thought as she got up and pulled on her clothes.

While she and Jake were clearing away the supper dishes, they discussed Jake's plans to eventually begin his own mining operations. But Laura couldn't help remembering that nowhere in her historical guide had there been so much as a passing mention of a rich vein of gold being discovered, let alone mined, anywhere near Sage Flats.

Which suggested that Jake never did get to mine the gold on his land, and the reason was Fancy Frank.

Jake's life was in danger. He would die before the town did.

"No!" she cried.

"No, what?" Jake asked, turning from the sink to frown at her.

"Er . . . No, you don't have to wash the dishes," she said, pulling herself together. "I'll do that. I'm sure you must have some chores to see to outside."

"Sure," he said. "But I don't mind washing up."

"No, you go on." She made a shooing motion

with her hand while nudging him away from the sink with a sideways swinging of her hips.

When he had finally left, Laura's mind raced. She frantically searched for a way to prevent Jake's death. But all she concluded was that panic was not conducive to clear thinking.

And time was of the essence; she felt it in every cell of her body. The very air around her seemed to vibrate with approaching danger.

She longed to go home to the more familiar dangers of the late twentieth century. And she wanted to take Jake with her.

Now, she mused, making short shrift of the dishes, all she had to do was figure out a way to get herself and Jake out of there, before danger descended upon them.

Just past dawn, Laura came awake to the sound of a taunting call, and the certainty that time had run out for her and Jake.

"Hey, Wilder," Fancy Frank called from somewhere beyond the side of the house. "Come on out with yer hands up and bring that gal with ya. You're gonna show me where that mine is or I'm gonna burn ya out." His laughter rang harsh and nasty on the morning air. "If ya don't give me no trouble, I might just let ya live to watch me have some fun with yer pretty piece."

The bedsprings squeaked as Jake rolled off the edge. "Go to hell, Finnegan!" he shouted, stepping into his pants. "Laura, are you awake?"

"Yes," she answered, scrambling off the bed to stand trembling and uncertain beside him.

"Get dressed and get your things together. I want you ready when I return."

"Return?" She grabbed his arm. "Where are you going?"

"To get our horses. We won't escape on foot." Jake didn't pause in stuffing his shirt into his pants.

She shuddered, and not just at his words. He was strapping on his gunbelt.

"What are you going to do with that?"

He flashed her a determined look. "Defend us, if I have to. Now get ready, I'm going for the horses." He strode out of the room. In another second she heard the outside kitchen door open and close.

Laura stood immobile for a moment, frozen with fear for his safety. Then another jeering call came from outside.

"Hey, Wilder, git yer and that gal's pretty rump movin', or you're gonna fry."

Laura hurriedly got dressed. Slinging the backpack over her shoulder, she grabbed the Peacemaker, then ran for the back door. Flinging it open, she ran toward the lean-to and nearly collided with Jake and the horses.

"Are you all right? Think you can ride?" he demanded.

Breathless, she nodded and took her horse's reins from him.

"Okay," he said shortly. "Let's move. We've got to ride hard and fast to get the jump on him."

"I understand," she said, mounting with his assistance.

At Jake's signal, she snapped the reins and followed him as they galloped away from the back of the ranch house.

They had not been riding long when Laura

turned to glance behind them and saw a cloud of dust rising in the distance. "He's coming, Jake!" she screamed above the thundering of the horses' hooves.

Jake didn't answer, but urged his horse on to even greater speed. Then, to Laura's amazement, he pulled back on the reins, bringing the animal to a shuddering halt. She followed suit.

"Jake, what—"

"Don't ask questions." He dismounted and helped her off her horse. "Run for that pile of brush over there, and take another tumble into that hole in the ground."

"But . . ."

"Dammit, woman, we gotta move!" As he barked the order, Jake slapped both horses on their rumps. The animals took off at a gallop, and grabbing Laura's hand, Jake dashed for the mine entrance.

They plowed into the brush, and all at once the earth disappeared under Laura's feet. She dropped several yards into the hole, landing on her backside on the hard ground. Only this time she wasn't alone in the dark.

"He'll . . . find us," she said, panting for breath. "We must have made a gaping hole in that brush."

"Maybe not. Maybe he'll be too busy following the horses to notice." But even as he spoke, they heard the unmistakable stomping and whinnying of a horse being brought to a halt.

Without thinking, and grasping his hand, Laura drew Jake into the bright shaft of morning sunlight streaming down through the mine opening.

"Laura . . ."

"Quiet," she whispered. "He's coming. Listen, I

can hear . . . Thank God! It's working," she cried, watching wide-eyed as crackling blue light radiated from the bracelet. The light swirled out, coiling around their bodies from head to foot.

"What in hell!" Jake said, jolting back.

The light intensified, then as quickly dissipated and disappeared. When it was gone, neither the sound of a horse nor Fancy Frank's footfalls disturbed the early-morning peace.

And suddenly Laura knew. Shaking, certain, yet afraid she might be wrong, she turned to Jake.

"Can you get us out of here?" she said with barely suppressed excitement.

"Are you crazy, woman?"

"Jake, listen, do you hear anything?"

"No . . . but . . ."

"Frank and the horse are gone," she said with more conviction than she actually felt. "I'm sure of it. Now, can you get us out of this damned hole?"

"Yes, of course, but . . ."

"Please, Jake, don't argue. Just do it."

Though he looked doubtful, he turned to walk farther into the mine tunnel. He returned moments later carrying a rough-hewn, ricketylooking wooden ladder. "Damn," he muttered, "this thing looks as old as hell all of a sudden." He gave her a wry look. "All you had to do before was explore a little."

"Why didn't you tell me it was there when you found me?"

"I didn't know who you were. If I'd told you where the ladder was, you would have known this wasn't just a hole. I'll go first," he said, stepping around her and placing the ladder against the rim of the hole. Then, slowly, cautiously, he climbed the rungs and peered over the edge of the opening. When he turned to gaze down at her, he looked absolutely dumbfounded.

"You were right. Frank and his horse are gone." He shook his head as if trying to clear it. "Come on up."

Anxious but eager, Laura slung her pack over her shoulder and carefully climbed the ladder. The instant she was above ground, she grabbed Jake's hand and began walking.

"Laura, where are you heading?" Jake asked, bringing her to a halt when he stopped dead. "My house is that way." He pointed in the opposite direction.

"Come with me. I want to show you something that will blow your mind."

"Blow my mind?" he muttered, frowning at the unfamiliar expression. Nevertheless, he allowed her to lead the way.

When they arrived at Sage Flats, Jake stared in stunned silence. His head turning from side to side, his eyes wide with wonder and sheer disbelief, he docilely followed as Laura marched through the ghost town and directly to the vehicle parked beyond it.

"And that," she announced in a voice tremulous from relief, "is the red Cherokee."

Jake looked at the Jeep, then back at her, then back at the Jeep once more. Finally a slow grin curved his lips.

"Damned if it ain't."

Epilogue

"**N**ow that's the way to start the day," Jake said, repeating a slogan he had heard on TV, as he often did. "Just go for the gusto," he went on, repeating yet another one. Smiling, he turned his head on the pillow to look at Laura. "You are beautiful after making love, woman."

"Jake Wilder, how many times do I have to tell you not to call me woman?" But Laura's voice held too much satisfaction to carry any weight.

"But you are a woman," he murmured, rolling on his side to caress her naked thigh. "You're my woman. Mrs. Jake Wilder. I like the sound of that."

Her smile was misty. "I would think you'd be used to it by now."

"Yeah," he agreed. "It's been almost a year since you dragged me into the twentieth century." His hand stroked up her thigh to settle on the slight mound of her belly. "And only five months to go till the Wilder heir makes an appearance."

"And the heir to a sizable fortune, to boot."

"Yeah," he said proudly. "I told you that vein of gold was pure and deep."

"Yes, you did," she said, moving sensuously in response to the hand he slid up her body to cup one breast. "And it was very accommodating of the government to take the mine off our hands when we reported the find after legally buying your abandoned ranch."

"Yeah." His laughter rippled with pure delight. "I would never have thought a person couldn't own the gold he found. But it was a generous offer the government made, and the money will give me time to build that plant nursery you said you wanted. It's something we both can work at. Think of all the fun we'll have traveling around the country looking for specimens."

Laura shivered when he rubbed the tight crest of her aching breast. "Jake, you must stop," she protested, making not the slightest move away from him.

"I love touching you, loving you." He inched closer to nip her ear, and laughed softly when she moaned. "I love you, my beautiful woman."

"And I love you, you teasing devil." She turned to brush her lips over his stubbled jaw. "But I have to go to work."

"Only one more week," he said, removing his hand from her body with gratifying reluctance, "then we'll be on summer vacation, free to make love and roam at will."

"Roam?" Blinking the clouds of sensuous arousal from her eyes, she stared at him in confusion. "Roam where?"

"Wherever." Rolling away, he leaned over the side of the bed. When he turned back to her, he held a small midnight-blue velvet pouch. "What century would you like to visit?"

"Jake Wilder, put that away at once!" She dived for the pouch dangling from his fingers. "It's dangerous."

Laughing, he held it just out of her reach. "I'll put it away on one condition."

"What's that?" she asked suspiciously.

He shook his head. "You gotta promise."

"Okay, okay, I promise. What's the condition?"

A blatantly sexy smile crossed his face. "You cut your first class and make love with me again."

Her smile was every bit as sexy as his. "You drive a hard bargain, Mr. Wilder, but since I'm your woman, I suppose I'll have to agree."

"You will?" he asked with endearing eagerness.

"Damned if I won't," she taunted, curling her arms around his neck. "Now stash the pouch and come here."

Joan Hohl

JOAN HOHL sold her first novel, a category romance, in 1979. Since then she has had forty-three books published—category romances, single-title contemporary women's fiction, historical romances, futuristic romances, and . . . time-travel romances.

"Turquoise Yesterdays" is Joan's fourth time-travel story, but the first set in the mythic Old West. Like the heroine of her story, Joan has always been fascinated with, and felt an affinity for, the American West.

Forever

Bobby Hutchinson

1

May 16, 1939

"Excuse me, is this seat taken?" Elizabeth Porter smiled down at the portly middle-aged woman in the flowered hat.

She'd had to change trains at Springfield, Massachusetts, and there was only one empty seat in this coach.

The woman beamed and shook her head, her faded blue eyes full of welcome. "Not at all, dear. I'm traveling alone, I'd be right glad of the company."

Elizabeth tucked her overnight bag into the luggage rack and smoothed the skirt of her new rose-colored summer suit before she sat down.

The older woman waited until Elizabeth was settled before she spoke again.

"Lovely day, not too hot yet. June is the best month, isn't it?"

Elizabeth agreed that it was.

"I'm going to visit my son, lives up near Framingham? They've had a new baby, a girl, my first granddaughter. They're naming her after me, I can't wait to see the little tyke."

Elizabeth returned the woman's smile. It was obviously going to be a talkative trip, but Elizabeth didn't really mind. She felt at ease with older people, aware that they were often lonely and liked to chat.

"My name's Florence, Florence Sprague."

"I'm Elizabeth Porter, how do you do."

Florence smiled and nodded, the crimson rose on her hat bobbing. "Nice to meet you, I'm sure. Are you going far, Miss Porter?"

Elizabeth shook her head. "Only as far as Bolton."

Florence indicated with raised eyebrows and a shake of her head that she'd never heard of Bolton.

"It's a small town just across the Massachusetts border, in New Hampshire."

"Ahhh. You have family there, I suppose?"

"No." Elizabeth hesitated. "I think my grandmother used to work there, a long time ago."

It was hard to mention Ann, even to this stranger. Her grandmother's death had been devastating for Elizabeth, particularly because Ann had been both mother and father to her, raising her after her parents' death twenty-three years ago when Elizabeth was only three.

As if she sensed Elizabeth's feelings, Florence was quiet for a time. Both women looked out the window as the train began to chug slowly. Soon the grimy outskirts of the city gave way to green, rolling countryside, and it wasn't until the conduc-

tor had come and taken their tickets and gone
again that Florence tapped the window and gestured out at the newly planted fields of a small
farm.

"My husband John and I used to have a little
place like that. Then John was killed in the Great
War, and I moved into town. I couldn't work the
farm by myself, so I had to get a job to support my
son, Sam." She was quiet a moment, remembering.
"I did housework for a real nice family, they were
good to me, but I never got over missing John."
She frowned and shook her head. "Now there's all
this talk about that Hitler fellow in the papers and
on the radio. Makes me right sick when I think
about another war coming. See, my Sam's the
right age, he'd have to go, he's twenty-five." She
glanced down at Elizabeth's gloved hands. "You
look about the same age as my Sam. You married,
dear?"

"No. No, I'm not married, not even engaged."
She didn't add that she was also one year older
than Sam. "Some of my friends have told me I'm
too fussy when it comes to dating," she confided.

Florence gave her an appraising once-over.
"With your looks, you can wait and take your
pick, I'd say. When you stopped to ask to sit here,
I thought, oh, my, that's the most beautiful girl
I've seen outside the picture shows, that shiny
black hair, those cheekbones and those great big
brown eyes, long lashes, skin like cream. Why,
dear, I thought for sure you must be an actress or
something."

Elizabeth flushed, embarrassed by the woman's
effusive praise. "Thank you, but I'm just a secretary, for Chantelle Cosmetics in New York."

Florence's eyes sparkled with interest. "My, that must be a glamorous job all the same."

"There was a time," Elizabeth said, thinking out loud as much as answering Florence, "when I thought the cosmetics industry was glamorous. I'm afraid I don't anymore."

Now, secretary to the president of Chantelle, she was disillusioned with her job, had been for months. "It seems so . . . meaningless somehow, frivolous even, to worry about—oh, shades of lipstick, or the effectiveness of some night cream, when—when a man like this Adolph Hitler is terrorizing half of Europe."

Florence nodded agreement, her face grave at the mention of Hitler and war.

"In fact," Elizabeth blurted, "I've been thinking of changing jobs, maybe working for New York's social services department, or something of that sort."

"Social services? Oh, I'd give that some careful thought, dear, before you go quitting your nice job." She eyed Elizabeth's expensive suit and cream silk blouse. "What would your family think about you working with that class of people, probably earning less money than you do now with twice the headaches?"

In spite of herself, Elizabeth had to smile at the inverted snobbery apparent in Florence's obvious disapproval of her idea, but she sobered as she answered her seatmate's question. "My grandmother died three months ago. She was the only family I had, so I guess it's up to me what I do with my life from now on."

Ann had left everything she owned to Elizabeth—the comfortable brownstone in Chelsea, her sizeable, valuable jewelry collection, and a generous amount of cash. Elizabeth didn't have to worry too much about money, and she had a feeling her grandmother would understand perfectly if she decided to work at something less lucrative but more meaningful.

Florence reached out and patted Elizabeth's hand. "You poor thing, losing your granny so recently. How old was she? What did she die of?"

"She was eighty-nine." Elizabeth felt the familiar tightness in her chest that came whenever she talked about Ann. "She was my friend as well as my grandmother. She was a wonderful woman, always very cheerful and healthy, at least until the last year of her life. She had a stroke, you see. It left her partially paralyzed and it affected her speech." The stroke had changed Ann emotionally as well as physically, and at the time, Elizabeth thought it likely that her grandmother's mind had been affected as well.

Elizabeth would often come home from work and find Ann in tears. At first, when Elizabeth begged Ann to tell her why she was so unhappy, the old woman would only shake her head, unwilling or unable to explain. But as the months passed she began to mumble disjointed phrases, meaningless words that puzzled Elizabeth. "Had to go, loved him, loved him," her grandmother would say repeatedly, and cry bitterly, tearing at Elizabeth's heart. She'd assumed Ann was talking about Elizabeth's grandfather, and she'd tried to sympathize. But Ann had shaken her head in vehement denial.

"Brent," she'd insisted, her impaired speech almost impossible to decipher. "Brent. Didn't want to leave. Never stopped loving Brent." Her once-beautiful brown eyes would stream with tears.

Elizabeth had been baffled. She'd never heard of anyone named Brent. Her grandfather, long dead by the time she came to live with Ann, had been named Robert.

"It's right hard, losing someone you love," Florence said now, her gently wrinkled face filled with compassion. "And I sure understand why you're going to this Bolton town where your granny worked. After my John died, I used to take Sam and get on the bus sometimes, just ride out to the farm, look around for an hour, ride back again. Made me feel closer to John, somehow."

Elizabeth nodded, unwilling to explain her real reasons for using her precious vacation days to visit a town she'd never even heard of until two weeks ago, when she'd finally faced the heart-breaking task of disposing of Ann's clothing and possessions.

In a box in the back of a closet, she'd found Ann's diary. Reading it, she had discovered things her grandmother had never hinted at, romantic secrets so intriguing that Elizabeth had felt an over-whelming urge to uncover even more of her grandmother's mysterious past.

"Framingham, next stop," the conductor called, swaying with the movement of the coach as he ambled down the aisle. The train was slowing down, the outskirts of the small city already visible outside the windows.

"Goodness, here we are already, this is where I get off." Florence, excited now and a little flustered, stood and pulled several packages from the overhead rack, piling them on the seat for a moment so she could offer a work-roughened hand to Elizabeth.

"It's been lovely visiting with you, Miss Porter, and I hope you find whatever it is you're looking for."

"Thank you. Good-bye, and congratulations on your granddaughter's birth."

Elizabeth watched through the window as, a few moments later, a tall, redheaded man and a small boy came hurrying along the station platform. Florence held out her arms, the rose on her hat in a perfect frenzy, and scooped up the running child a moment before she was enveloped in the man's arms.

They were a family.

Watching them, Elizabeth felt her eyes mist, and she wondered if the day would ever come when there'd be a tall man, children, a family of her own. Most of her friends had married long ago, and sometimes she despaired of ever meeting a man she could love without reservation for the rest of her life.

The way her grandmother must have loved Brent Hollis.

Elizabeth sat back in the seat, closed her eyes, and thought about her grandmother's diary.

In 1867, her grandmother had left home to work as a maid in the village of Bolton, and there she'd fallen in love with wealthy, twenty-five-year-old Brent Hollis. An extraordinarily handsome man, he had noticed the beautiful young maid serving dinner at one of the season's numerous parties.

Engaged to a girl from a family as rich and influential as his own, he courted Ann secretly, then broke off his engagement, vowing he would marry

Ann instead. His stern father, Alexander Hollis, was horrified at the idea of his only son marrying a lowly maid.

Terrified at the thought of defying a man as prominent and powerful as Alexander Hollis, Ann nevertheless agreed to marry Brent. It seemed that Brent, too, was afraid of his father, but his love for Ann overpowered his fear.

Reading what her grandmother had written, Elizabeth felt outrage that anyone would think her dear, beloved grandmother hadn't been good enough to marry, but she realized that in 1867, social standing was a major issue, and marriage often a matter not of love but of powerful alliances between important families.

Ann hadn't gone into detail in the diary, but it seemed that Brent's first engagement had been the result of just such an alliance.

Brent had shown a considerable amount of backbone, from what Ann wrote. Alexander tried threats, bribery, and every other method at his disposal to force his son to call off his engagement to Ann, but Brent held fast.

He said to me today, "Imagine, my father thinking money could be as important to me as you are," Ann had written.

Brent sounded strong and wonderfully romantic, and Elizabeth had fallen a little in love with him herself when, a little further on, Ann reported that he was even building her a house.

Using money his father had endowed on him at birth, Brent built a magnificent manor on a cliff in Bolton, overlooking a lake. Close to the house, he built a small chapel, surrounded by rosebushes and topped by a bell tower, and he put a gazebo on the cliff where he and Ann could look out over the lake in the valley.

We are to be married in the chapel, and Brent insists that the chapel bell is not to ring until our wedding day, Ann confided to her diary.

Elizabeth had sat far into the night, turning the pages of the old book with eager anticipation, enthralled by the powerful tale of romance. But soon after writing about the chapel, Ann had abruptly stopped making entries in her diary. Disappointed, Elizabeth was left with nothing except blank pages and unanswered questions.

What had happened? What catastrophic occurrence had kept Ann from marrying Brent? The questions nagged at Elizabeth during the days that followed her discovery of the diary.

Until after the stroke, her grandmother had never once mentioned Brent Hollis. She'd obviously come to New York and, at the age of thirty-two, married Elizabeth's grandfather. They'd had Rosemary, Elizabeth's mother, and lived a sedate and comfortable life in Manhattan's fashionable Chelsea area, in the brownstone Elizabeth had now inherited.

What had become of Brent? Why, at the end of Ann's long life, had she wept, not for her dead husband with whom she'd lived for years, and who'd fathered her only child, but instead for a man she'd loved and lost so many years before?

Elizabeth had become obsessed with Ann's unfinished story until at last she'd decided on a course of action.

During the past week, she'd done research and verified that the town of Bolton was in New Hampshire. Armed with this information, her grandmother's maiden name, Merrill, and the haunting story of the house and chapel that Brent Hollis supposedly built, Elizabeth had bought a ticket and boarded a train.

She must have dozed off, lulled by the warm sun coming through the window and the rocking motion of the coach.

The next thing she was aware of was the conductor's gentle hand on her shoulder, his smiling face looking down at her.

"Next stop Bolton, miss. I thought you'd like to know."

Elizabeth's heart lurched and then began to pound as if something momentous was about to happen, an unreasonable yet overwhelming sensation that she'd arrived at the beginning of Ann's story.

2

"**I** wonder if you could help me." Elizabeth smiled at the tiny apple-cheeked woman behind the low counter in the post office. "I'm new here and I'm staying at the Greenbrier Inn. I've spent several hours just walking around, admiring your beautiful town. When I was down by the lake a few minutes ago, I couldn't help wondering about that old, deserted house. Up on the cliff?"

"The old Hollis place." The short, round woman

nodded her head. "Been there since long before I was born." Behind her steel-rimmed glasses, she winked one roguish blue eye at Elizabeth. "Heaven knows, that's a good long stretch, gettin' longer all the time." Laughter seemed to bubble up from somewhere near her toes.

Hollis. The name was right. A tingle of anticipation ran down Elizabeth's spine, and she tried to remain calm as she said, "There seem to be two buildings. The smaller one looks as if it's almost on the edge of the cliff."

The postmistress nodded. "The old chapel, yes. Quite a story to that. Don't know it it's true or not, mind you. It's sort of a local legend in these parts. A real romantic story, miss. They say back in the 1860s or thereabouts, this Brent Hollis fellow, well-to-do he was, too, built both the house and the chapel for this girl he was dead set on marrying."

Elizabeth felt short of breath, and her voice wasn't quite steady. "Do you know what her name was, this girl Brent Hollis wanted to marry?"

The woman shook her head. "No one hereabouts seems to know her name anymore, but it's said she was common, not his type at all, just a maid for one of the local families."

It had to be Ann. It was disconcerting to hear her regal grandmother dismissed as a common maid.

The postmistress was enjoying her role as storyteller. She leaned her ample bosom on the counter and folded her arms. "He planned on them being wed in that chapel, poor man. They say he wouldn't let anybody ring the chapel bell. He vowed it would ring only on the day he married his sweetheart."

She paused dramatically. "Then would you believe, two weeks before the wedding, didn't that maid run off with some local boy more her station, and never was seen or heard from again."

Never stopped loving Brent. Didn't want to leave. Loved him. Had to go.

Ann's words echoed in Elizabeth's mind. "What . . ." Tears thickened her voice and she had to clear her throat before she could continue. "What became of Brent Hollis?"

"Well, they say he was right broken-hearted. Locked that chapel up tight as a drum, went off somewhere for months. But as you and I well know, miss, life goes on. Nary a one of us dies from a broken heart, do we, now? Brent Hollis came back a year later and married the girl his father had wanted him to marry in the first place. Probably for the best, like most things in life. They had a son, Jeremy."

"Did they—did they live in the house on the cliff?"

The woman nodded. "That they did, but to this very day, miss, nobody's ever set foot in that chapel. It's sat there just the way it was the day that maid ran off and he locked it up. And the chapel bell has never rung."

Somehow Elizabeth managed to thank the postmistress. Shaken, she made her way out the post office door, into the blinding sunshine of the glorious June day. The warmth didn't seem to help the cold chills running through her. She stood for a moment, gazing around at the old-fashioned shops and trim houses that lined Bolton's main street, seeing in her mind's eye a beautiful young woman standing in this exact spot, perhaps smiling the smile Elizabeth remembered so well, reading a love note from the man she planned to marry.

Elizabeth knew now that every word in Ann's diary was true. But what had really happened here to her grandmother? What was the rest of the story?

Elizabeth had known her grandmother better than she knew anyone else, except herself. She knew without a doubt that even at seventeen, Ann would never have betrayed someone she loved as much as she'd loved Brent Hollis.

There had to be a way to discover the truth. Ann's story had become an obsession for Elizabeth, and illogical as it seemed, she felt that Ann wouldn't rest peacefully until it was resolved. Elizabeth knew that the place to start was at the manor house on the hill.

There'd been a taxi stand beside the drugstore she'd passed earlier. She walked with brisk determination toward it.

"You sure you don't want me to wait, miss?" The taxi driver stuck his head out of the cab's window, his brow furrowed as he squinted up at Elizabeth. "This place's been deserted for years, nothin' here to see, sun'll be goin' down in another hour, hour an' a half at most. That there road we come up is full of potholes, could break an axle easy as pie, don't fancy drivin' up here a second time to collect you."

"I'm just going to look around, maybe—ummm, maybe sketch the old chapel. I'd really like you to come back for me at sundown, would you do that, please?" Elizabeth gave him her most appealing smile. It had always been effective, and it didn't fail her this time. He shook his head at such foolishness, but he promised he'd be back for her in under two hours.

She stood still, waiting until the sound of his tortured motor faded into the distance as he negotiated the turns and twists of the neglected roadway.

At last all she could hear was the buzzing of bees in the overgrown rosebushes, the constant chirping of birds in the thick growth of trees and underbrush that almost encompassed the ruined house.

Here, high above the lake, the air was hot and heavy, and a shimmering heat mist lay over the landscape below. From the village it had seemed as if the chapel stood close to the house, but now that she was here, Elizabeth realized it wasn't as close as she'd thought. She couldn't see it.

Shaking off her apprehension, and wishing she were wearing something more practical than her fashionable cream leather pumps, she began her trek toward the cliff.

The underbrush tore at her suit, and it wasn't long before her silk stockings were hopelessly snagged by the thistles that grew along the faint path she followed. She saw the gazebo through the trees, and all of a sudden the foliage parted and Elizabeth stared in awe.

Just ahead, almost obscured by rosebushes grown to the size of small trees, was the tiny chapel. The air was thick with the smell of roses and pine resin, and Elizabeth drew in a long, shaky breath, wondering if the heavy perfume was the reason for her light-headedness.

A little hesitant now, she moved closer to the quaint, weather-beaten stone chapel, huddled in its canopy of roses. She could see the heavily padlocked thick wooden door, graying with age. She gazed at it for a few long moments.

Brent Hollis had put that lock on the door. It seemed to Elizabeth only fitting that she, a descendant of his beloved Ann, should remove it at last.

She dropped her purse on the ground and looked around for a heavy stone.

The iron padlock was rusty and corroded, and still she had to hammer it. She hit her fingers twice, but the pain made her even more determined to succeed. Finally, she used a stick to pry it from the door, and the heavy lock fell to the ground.

Already sweating and puffing, she pushed the door. It stuck, and she shoved her body against it. Creaking and groaning, the thick wooden door at last gave way, and, her heart hammering from excitement as much as from her efforts, she stepped inside, leaving the door ajar.

It took several moments before her eyes adjusted to the dim interior. Small, leaded-glass windows on either side allowed in the small amount of light that filtered through the thick, overgrown rosebushes.

The small chapel smelled of dust, age, and dirt. As her eyes grew more accustomed to the gloom, Elizabeth could see a few rows of crudely built wooden pews, hung with cobwebs. At the front was a simple altar, and to her right, a narrow, winding staircase leading to what could only be the bell tower.

She walked down the dusty aisle. This was where Ann should have walked, going slowly up the aisle to marry her beloved Brent, coming triumphantly back, her white-gloved hand on his arm, her heart filled with love, joy, and anticipation for the years ahead.

Never stopped loving Brent.

Tears came to Elizabeth's eyes, and she fought the painful sobs rising in her throat as she mourned for the love that her grandmother had lost, and also for the love that she, Elizabeth, couldn't seem to find.

Her tears dried, and a sense of urgency propelled her forward. She turned to the steep stairs and hurried up them, shuddering at the cobwebs that clung to her face, the foul-smelling dust that sifted down on her head when she pushed open the small door at the top.

There were cobwebs here as well, but at least there was more light. She looked up, and gasped, for there high above her in the tower was a beautiful, carved bell, with a thick rope that hung almost to her feet.

Straining her neck, she could see engraved on the bell, "A+B."

Ann and Brent, forever entwined, on a bell that had never rung to signal their happiness.

It hurt to look at it, to remember her poor grandmother, struggling at the end of her life with her impaired speech to convey her feelings for a love she'd somehow lost.

With a choked cry, Elizabeth grabbed the rope and pulled with all her might, paying tribute to Ann and her long-ago love.

The first deep-toned peal made her jump as it

echoed through the tower and out over the valley. The sound was pure and sweet, and tears coursed down her face as she continued pulling the rope, sobbing for the woman who had never heard it ring.

Why? What tragedy had kept Ann and Brent apart? What could possibly have persuaded Ann to leave the man she adored, and never return to Bolton?

With each peal of the bell, the questions echoed in Elizabeth's mind. She rang the bell until her arms were aching, her face burning from her tears. At last, she allowed the rope to drop, and after a few last peals, the bell was silent once again.

Elizabeth looked down at her hands. They were fiery red and burning, and her carefully manicured nails were chipped and broken from her earlier efforts with the door. Her rose suit had a rust mark across the skirt, and she realized she was sweaty, hungry, and exhausted.

How long had she been in the tower? Perhaps the taxi had already returned and its driver, impatient, was waiting for her. Heavens, she hoped he wouldn't leave before she got outside. The last thing she wanted to do was spend the night in the chapel.

She descended the narrow steps, trying to hurry. When she reached the bottom, she stopped, bewildered, and looked around.

Somehow, the chapel was now bright with sunshine streaming through the windows. By some trick of the light, the small room seemed much less melancholy, less dilapidated and dirty.

Puzzled, anxious now to go out into the fresh air, Elizabeth rushed to the door.

It was closed. A frisson of fear ran up her spine as she remembered how difficult it had been to open. She was positive she'd left it open when she'd entered.

She grasped the knob, feeling a little frantic, pulling as hard as she could.

The door wouldn't budge.

Her heart began to race. She grasped the knob with both hands, using all her strength to open it, but it was as if someone had locked her in.

But how could that be? There wasn't another soul for miles around, and she'd already broken the lock on the door herself.

It must somehow have blown shut, and stuck.

Shaking, her hands gripping the back of a pew for support, she forced herself to calm down, to think.

She could break a window, she decided, looking around for something heavy.

" . . . rang the bell . . ."

" . . . inside? . . ."

Men's voices. They sounded alarmed. Elizabeth froze.

The bell, she realized. The ringing bell had probably brought men from a neighboring farm to investigate.

Relief flooded through her. They would get her out, they'd be able to push the heavy door open. She stumbled on her high heels as she hurried to bang on it with her fists.

"Help, help me, please. I can't get out. Open the door."

Male voices rose in excitement, and a moment later someone was wrestling with the lock.

A splintering crash sent Elizabeth scurrying,

and then the heavy door burst open and sunlight streamed inside, half-blinding her as she quickly walked out.

"Thank you so much. I don't understand how that darned door . . ." Her voice trailed off as she stared at her rescuers. Standing before her were two men, one who was distinguished-looking with a luxurious mustache and who seemed to be in his mid-fifties; the other younger, and what the stenos at Chantelle would have labeled a heartthrob. They wore dark, high-buttoned suits, high-collared, starched white shirts, bow ties, and rounded, small-brimmed hats. Their attire looked absurdly out of date, even for a village in New Hampshire. Heavens. This really was a long way from stylish New York.

"It . . . the door . . . must have blown shut. I . . . I'm very grateful," Elizabeth stammered.

The men were gaping at her. Self-conscious now, she straightened her jacket, settling her padded shoulders in place, and tugged at her knee-length skirt so it hung properly before she sneaked another glance at them.

They were still staring at her.

She reached up to touch her dark hair, piled on her head in a loose pompadour. She must look a sight, covered with dust and heaven knew what else. She probably didn't have a scrap of makeup left on. Her purse had a compact, with powder, lipstick, and a comb, but she couldn't at the moment see where she'd dropped it in the grass.

Oh, gosh, she *was* a mess. A quick glance down at her feet revealed dirt and scratches marring her cream pumps, and of course her silk stockings were ruined.

Well, there was nothing she could do about that until she had access to her overnight bag at the inn.

These men were making her decidedly nervous, and a disturbing thought struck her. Perhaps they owned the old manor house and the chapel, and she was trespassing. Heavens, she'd broken the lock right off the door. Were they upset about that?

Probably. Thinking fast, she improvised, smiling what she hoped was an ingenuous and ingratiating smile.

"I'm terribly sorry, you must think I'm dreadful, breaking into the chapel this way. I, ummm, I work for—for a museum in Boston, you see, and I'm, ummm, exploring the New Hampshire countryside for—for antique artifacts." She felt quite proud of her ingenuity. She'd feel a lot more relaxed, though, if only this—she searched for a term to describe the younger man and could only come up with glorious—if only this glorious-looking man would stop staring at her.

Seemingly in his early thirties, he was a whole head taller than the older man, which Elizabeth figured put him well over six feet. He had jet-black hair, not unlike the color of Elizabeth's, and it escaped from under his hat in gentle waves. His sideburns were unfashionably long, defining a strong jaw with a deep cleft in the middle of his chin. His dark, rather somber face was all planes and angles, with a slightly crooked nose that added a certain ruggedness to his features.

He was standing with his long legs apart, his hands thrust into the side pockets of his suit jacket, and his wide-shouldered body looked lean and hard.

Elizabeth was becoming more flustered by the second. "I didn't think anyone would mind if I looked around at the ruined manor house, or this old chapel." She gestured at the building behind her, glancing around at it, and realized the chapel didn't really look that old. The stone seemed far less weather-beaten than she'd thought. She turned and frowned at it.

What on earth was going on? Surely the rose-bushes hadn't been pruned back like that when she'd gone inside? The stained-glass windows now reflected the afternoon light, and the wood trim was a deep brown and not faded.

She glanced beyond the men, where the trees had grown thick and hidden the manor house. Her mouth fell open. She was looking at a well-groomed lawn, flowers and shrubs laid out in neat beds. Beyond it, in plain view, was the manor house, now a completely intact, meticulously maintained Tudor home.

Feeling more and more perturbed and a little frightened, Elizabeth again turned toward the men, who were still staring at her in a disturbing way.

Her throat was dry, and she had to clear it before she could speak. "I—I'm sorry, I should have introduced myself. I'm Elizabeth Porter, I—I hired a cab from Bolton to bring me up here a couple of hours ago. He really should be along any moment to—to take me back." She wished with all her heart that the grumpy taxi driver would roar up this minute and rescue her.

The two men exchanged glances. Then the older one stepped forward, bowed slightly in a courte-ous fashion, and said, very formally, "Good afternoon, madam. My name is Brent Hollis, and this is my son, Jeremy."

3

*B*rent Hollis?

If this man was Brent Hollis, he had to be a ghost. And his son—Jeremy?

For a moment, Elizabeth was sure she was going to faint, even though she'd never fainted in her life. But there were spots in front of her eyes and a buzzing in her head, and she felt dizzy and weak.

Jeremy Hollis moved to her, and Elizabeth was all too aware of his strong arm around her waist, supporting her, and of the sound of his deep, baritone voice far too close to her ear. "She's about to swoon, Father. Perhaps we should take her up to the house?"

The dizziness was passing, and Elizabeth moved a little away from him. "Thank you, I'll be fine now, it—it must have been the sun." She could feel perspiration on her forehead. She had a handkerchief in her bag, if only she could find it. She looked around, but her purse seemed to have disappeared.

"Have you lost something?" Jeremy was still staring at her, his intent blue gaze unnerving.

"My bag. I left my purse out here on the grass when I went inside the chapel, and now it's gone."

Both men looked around, but the cream leather purse was nowhere to be seen. And neither man seemed at all convinced that she'd ever had a purse, because they didn't spend much time looking.

Elizabeth was beginning to feel irritated.

"Perhaps you left your bag in the carriage, madam?"

Carriage? Elizabeth looked at the two of them, in their peculiar suits and stuffy vests and bow ties. There had to be a logical answer to all this. Her mind flitted from one outrageous idea to the next, at last settling on one that was logical.

"Is there a fair going on?" She knew that sometimes, during a fair, villagers reenacted earlier times, dressing up in period costumes. That had to be it. Relief flooded through her. These two were having a little joke with her, pretending to be the former residents of the manor. "You're teasing me, aren't you? There's a fair, isn't there, and you've dressed up for the occasion, pretending to be the people who used to live here. I'm right, aren't I?"

She was a little annoyed at them for the fright they'd given her, but it was a relief at least to know what was going on.

Again they exchanged glances. "I'm afraid not, miss," Jeremy said, shaking his head. "My father and I live in the manor house, and we were most astonished to hear the chapel bell ringing just now. The Bolton fair is in early May, Miss Porter."

Jeremy was using the gentle, patronizing tone he might adopt to soothe a lunatic, Elizabeth concluded—though the way he kept looking at her was anything but soothing. In fact, both men seemed to be paying an inordinate amount of attention to her clothes. Heavens, hadn't they seen a woman in a fashionable suit before?

"Where did you say you were from, Miss Porter?" The older Hollis gestured down toward Bolton. "If you're staying with friends in the village, perhaps we could give you a ride to their home."

Hollis sounded on edge, as if he wanted to get rid of her before she began frothing at the mouth or something. He kept staring at her, and his face was noticeably pale. "Jeremy, perhaps you'd go and ask Benjamin to get the carriage ready?"

There it was again, carriage. As in horse.

She had to get away from them both, back to the village. Perhaps her grandmother's death had affected her in some peculiar way, and she was hallucinating. She'd never been delicate, but she'd never imagined herself in a situation like this before, either.

"No, thanks all the same. I absolutely don't want a ride."

Jeremy was striding up the pebbled path toward the manor, but he stopped and looked back at her. Elizabeth made her refusal in as firm a voice as she could muster.

"I'll just walk to the village. It's a lovely afternoon and I'm sure I'll meet the taxi coming for me. I did make it quite plain that he was to fetch me." She gave them a little wave with her fingers and started walking toward the road leading down the hill. "You've been very kind, rescuing me and all that. I do apologize for trespassing. And, oh, if you should come across my bag—a cream leather one, sort of puffy—perhaps you'd drop it off to me. I'm staying at the Greenbrier Inn."

Feeling as if she'd like to break into a run, she

hurried away before they could protest, and she could feel their eyes on her back for the few hundred yards it took her to reach the first bend.

At that point, she couldn't stop herself from turning around and staring up at the house and the chapel. She fully expected the scene to have reverted to the way it had looked when the taxi first rounded this last corner a few hours earlier. But the well-kept manor and the manicured lawns were just as she'd left them moments before, and the two men hadn't moved. They were standing where she'd left them, gazing at her.

It was a long, weary walk back to the village. By the time she neared it, Elizabeth was cursing her high-heeled pumps and carrying her light suit jacket. No one had passed her on the way, and when at last the village neared, she felt profound relief. She'd pondered her experience all the way back, and she'd almost decided she'd hit a time warp up there on the hill.

She couldn't wait to reach the inn, have a cool bath, and change her clothing. She was hungry, confused, and tired.

Losing her purse was upsetting, but at least she'd paid for her stay at the inn in advance, and tonight's dinner as well as tomorrow's breakfast were included in the price.

Her return train ticket was in her bag, however, as well as her wallet, and undoubtedly it was too late to visit the bank and ask the manager to arrange for funds to be transferred from her account in New York. She'd have to do it in the morning.

She was on the outskirts of the village when she realized how strange everything looked. The paved streets she'd wandered up and down were now cobbled. The shops looked different, smaller, and the merchandise in the windows was nothing short of antique.

A horse-drawn carriage clattered past, and the couple inside stared at Elizabeth as they passed her, their heads turning so far around it seemed they were on a pivot.

When another woman came walking toward her, dressed in an ankle-length blue cotton dress and a ridiculous feathered hat, Elizabeth felt the stirrings of hysteria. Laughter and tears battled within her as the woman stopped and gawked at her, horror and shock evident on her plain face. Neither of the women she'd seen had been wearing even a trace of makeup.

Almost running now, Elizabeth reached the street where the Greenbrier Inn had been that morning. A livery stable was there instead. She stood on the wooden sidewalk and swallowed hard, struggling to control her panic.

A young boy came hurrying along the sidewalk, and Elizabeth stopped him.

"Excuse me, I—I seem to have, to have—gotten lost. Could you show me where the Greenbrier Inn is, please?"

The boy was staring at her clothing, his mouth agape. It took him several moments to answer, and Elizabeth was already certain of what he'd say.

"Ain't never heard of no Greenbrier Inn, miss."

"Are you sure?"

He looked up into her face at last and shook his head, his eyes round and earnest. "Ain't no inn by that name in this whole town."

Elizabeth held onto her self-control with all her

might, because she was beginning to believe something preposterous had happened to her.

Absurd, incredible, unbelievable as it seemed, she'd somehow gone back in time. Dressed as she was, in the height of 1939 fashion, she was causing a sensation on the streets of Bolton.

Women walking past were giving her a wide berth, and men leered at her legs in their torn hosiery. She began hurrying along, avoiding the curious and scandalized looks directed her way.

The shops were still open, and she'd almost passed the bank before she realized what it was.

Money. She needed money.

She opened the door and went inside. A buzz of shocked voices greeted her appearance, and a line of customers turned to peer at her.

Elizabeth was barely aware of them, because shock waves were running like icy water up and down her spine.

Above an ornate writing desk, a boldly lettered sign read, "TODAY IS JUNE 16, 1899."

The sign as well as the townspeople's reactions and dress confirmed exactly what she'd suspected. Elizabeth collapsed into one of the wooden chairs against the wall. She trembled, her heart hammering so hard she thought it might pop right out of her silk blouse.

She tried to draw in deep breaths in an effort to calm herself. What had happened to her? How had she gotten here, and why? The chapel bell flashed into her mind. Her predicament must have something to do with her ringing the bell in the chapel. It was after that that everything had changed.

She'd have to go back there. She had to get

home, to her own time. But if Brent and Jeremy Hollis caught her trying to get into the chapel again . . . She'd have to wait until she ran less risk of being seen, perhaps at night.

Another frightening realization struck her as she sat watching the people making deposits and withdrawals. There wasn't any way she could withdraw money from an account that hadn't existed in 1899.

Intense fear gripped her. What if she couldn't get back? How would she survive here, even for a short time, with no money, nothing but the clothes on her back? Her appearance had caused such a sensation among the bank's customers that, right at that moment, a formally dressed young man with a pompous air was bearing down on her, his mouth pursed tight in disapproval even as his hot eyes traveled boldly over her legs and breasts.

"The manager has asked me to inform you that no loitering is allowed on these premises," he announced with a sniff. "I must ask you to leave immediately."

He was looking at her, staring at her as if she were . . . Elizabeth swallowed. She'd seen prostitutes on the streets of New York. This clerk was giving her the same look she'd seen on men's faces when they looked at those poor women, a look of both contempt and desire.

All at once Elizabeth's fear subsided and anger took hold. How dare this arrogant idiot speak to her like that, look at her as if she were a piece of merchandise? It wasn't her fault she'd ended up in the wrong century, for heaven's sake.

She shot to her feet, tilting her chin in the air and glaring at him, her voice icy. "Don't you speak to me like that. I'd like to remind you that this is a public place, and I happen to be a customer. In fact, I'd like to see the manager this instant. Take me to him, if you please."

Her aggressive behavior took the clerk by surprise. His face turned scarlet, and he glanced over his shoulder. The customers and even the clerks were silent, shamelessly eavesdropping.

The man hesitated, glanced at his audience again, and then turned. He led her to a door behind the tellers' cages.

"Mr. Bartholomew Isaacs, Manager," was emblazoned on the glass.

Elizabeth gave the clerk one last glare and then swept past him and marched into the manager's office, banging the door shut behind her. Her anger was fading fast, and an idea was forming.

Perhaps this had happened for a purpose. Perhaps she was meant to find out what had really happened to her grandmother in Bolton. And what better way of finding out than being here, investigating the secrets that Ann had taken to her grave?

But in order to do that, Elizabeth needed to survive, and she couldn't do that without a job. She only hoped the bank needed a new clerk.

The room was small and the air was thick with smoke. A fat, florid-faced man sat behind a wide desk puffing on a cigar, and he looked up in amazement when Elizabeth barged in. He shoved the cigar in an ashtray and got to his feet with some difficulty, his mouth opening and closing again, his eyes riveted on Elizabeth's outfit. "What—who—I told young Metcalfe—"

Before he could say more, Elizabeth began talking fast. She'd decided she was going to throw herself on this man's mercy, and she only hoped he had more of it than showed in his self-indulgent features. A bank manager in a small town wielded a lot of power, and she was counting on using that to her advantage.

"Mr. Isaacs, I desperately need your help," she began, staring him straight in the eye. "My name is Elizabeth Porter, I'm from New York, and I've ended up here under the most distressing circumstances." That was an understatement, if ever there was one. "My bag, with all my money, has disappeared, along with my luggage. I have nowhere to stay, and no relatives or friends in town. In fact, I'm quite alone in the world." The melodrama was perhaps a bit overdone, but the quiver in her voice wasn't contrived in the least. "My grandmother, my only living relative, died recently." Elizabeth stopped to take a deep breath, putting all the urgency she could muster into her next sentence.

"Mr. Isaacs, I need a job."

4

Working as a maid at a boarding house wasn't exactly what Elizabeth had envisioned, but there had been no openings at the bank and this was a job, she reminded herself two days later as she plumped the pillows and drew the sheets tightly over a horsehair mattress.

"Poooorterrr!" The shrill tones of her employer echoed up the stairwell and into the bedroom where she was working.

Elizabeth rolled her eyes. "Yes, Mrs. Decker?"

"When you finish the bedrooms, come down to the kitchen and peel the dinner vegetables."

Mr. Isaacs had told Elizabeth that Hannah Decker was his sister-in-law who'd recently been widowed, and to support herself, she'd turned her large house just off the village green into a boardinghouse. The bank manager had indicated his eagerness for Hannah's business endeavor to succeed, and Elizabeth suspected he feared having to support Hannah himself if it didn't.

He'd introduced Elizabeth to Mrs. Decker two days before and they'd all agreed that Elizabeth would work as a maid in return for room and board and a small wage.

Elizabeth went back to work, swiping at the sweat trickling down her forehead and cursing her hot, cumbersome ankle-length serge skirt, her high-necked, long-sleeved blouse, and the bulky petticoat that Hannah Decker had insisted must be worn at all times under everything. At least she was wearing her own underwear, washing out her silk bra and panties every night and hanging them over the end of her bed to dry, using her garter belt to hold up the black-ribbed cotton hose Hannah had insisted upon.

Elizabeth had seen the current underwear alternatives—camisoles, bloomers, and corsets—and she'd vowed to avoid them at all costs.

Hannah had been scandalized by Elizabeth's

clothes and had insisted that Elizabeth dress as a proper maid should. From somewhere she'd produced two blouses, a navy serge skirt, and a petticoat, adding that the cost would be deducted from Elizabeth's wages. The clothing fit well enough, but shoes were a problem. Finally, after much hand-wringing and a written IOU, Hannah had given Elizabeth an advance on her first week's pittance, so she could purchase a sturdy pair of buttoned-up boots from the shoemaker down the street. They were easier on her feet than her pumps, but they took an inordinate amount of time to lace every morning.

Refilling the china pitcher on the washstand with water from the bucket she'd carried upstairs, Elizabeth had an attack of the homesickness she experienced often in this strange place and time.

She missed her brownstone's indoor plumbing and her own comfortable wardrobe. She even missed her secretarial work, the job she'd been so dissatisfied with, and once again she had to close her eyes and fight the tears burning at the back of her eyes. She was exhausted from this grueling physical labor and the long working hours.

"Pooorterrr, what's taking so long up there?" Mrs. Decker's irascible voice echoed up the stairwell.

Grandmother was a maid, Elizabeth reminded herself, squaring her shoulders and wiping away her tears with her sleeve. *If she could do this, so can I.*

"I'm just finishing up, Mrs. Decker," she called, giving the blue china basin a quick swipe with a towel instead of the careful scrub her employer had insisted was necessary. She was going to have to learn to cut corners to get through the work

Hannah expected of her, and still have time to do the investigating she was determined to do.

Wasn't it a shame that her grandmother had never given her any tips on being a maid?

Down in the steamy kitchen, Elizabeth peeled the mountains of potatoes, turnips, and carrots. Hannah was rolling out pastry for pies.

"I met Mr. Brent Hollis and his son Jeremy, who live up in the manor house on the hill," Elizabeth remarked. Hannah liked to gossip, and Elizabeth was counting on getting some information from her. "I heard a strange story about Mr. Brent Hollis, that he was engaged to a maid at one time, years ago. Could that possibly be true?"

"Hmmph." Hannah nodded, her lips pursed into a prim knot. "True as I'm standing here. Brent Hollis's whore. I heard all about that carry-on from my mother, must be thirty some years ago it all happened. Ann Merrill, the maid's name was, worked for the Thornburgs, old Dr. Thornburg and his wife."

Elizabeth's knuckles were white. She clutched the potato she was peeling and struggled with an overwhelming urge to hurl it at Hannah for calling her grandmother a whore.

"That Merrill baggage was traipsing around, puttin' on airs, walking out with Brent Hollis, even gettin' engaged to him, and all the time she was keeping company"—Hannah's voice was filled with insinuation—"if you know what I mean, with some young man from the village. Don't know who he was. Seems to me he worked as a stableboy over at the Blue Swan Inn. If you're finished with the vegetables, start on these apples, Porter."

"The inn that's near the church?" Elizabeth reached for an apple, trying her best to sound nonchalant, even though she was seething inside at Hannah's implications.

The other woman nodded, too intent on her pastry and her story to notice how agitated Elizabeth was. "Same one, been there long as I can remember." Her voice dropped to a near whisper. "See, it was plain as the nose on your face that this maid, this Ann Merrill, had got herself up the creek by that stableboy, probably used her condition to make him run off with her." She shook her head. "Imagine one of the Hollises falling for a maid, and asking her to marry him."

She clucked her tongue and flipped the pastry shells into a row of pie plates. "Why, Brent Hollis even built the manor house and that there chapel for the Merrill baggage, my mother told me. And old Alexander just beside hisself over the whole thing, and rightly so. The Hollises are quality. It was old Alexander's father, y'know, who first started the Hollis Mill over in Lowell that's made the whole family rich. Cut those peeled apples up into pieces."

Since she'd arrived, Elizabeth had heard much of the cotton mills in nearby Lowell, Massachusetts. At one time Lowell had been the largest industrial center in America, producing huge amounts of cotton cloth, but now, in the late 1800s, the mills were apparently experiencing severe labor problems.

"Talk around town," Hannah confided, "is young Jeremy Hollis wants to make big changes in the family business, better working conditions, maybe higher wages. But old Brent, he's got no such ambitions. He's like his father, is Brent, thinks only of profit." She blew a strand of pepper-and-salt hair out of her eyes and dusted the flour off her hands. "Funny thing is, they say he was once just like Jeremy. They say when Brent Hollis was young he fought with Alexander to change conditions at the mill. Funny how people change as they get older."

She plopped three of the finished pies into the oven. "When you get done with cleaning up here, you can start setting the tables in the dining room. And be sure to turn the cloths over and put something on top of that gravy stain Kennedy made, clumsy old fool."

That evening, when the dishes were finally done and she was free, Elizabeth hurried along the twilight streets to the Blue Swan Inn.

Jennie Roston, the cheerful middle-aged woman who, with her husband Albert, owned and operated the inn, listened to Elizabeth's queries about Ann Merrill and the stableboy, then shook her head.

"It's my da, Tom Gunn, you'd be wanting to talk with. He ran the inn back in those times. He lives here with us since we took over. He's upstairs in his room. Has the rheumatism bad and can't get out of bed most days. Go right on up. He'd be glad of the company."

The old man's hands were gnarled and nearly useless, but his mind was alert and his bright black eyes sparkled when Elizabeth asked her questions.

"Ann Merrill? Sure, and I remember her well. Didn't she throw over hoity-toity Brent Hollis to run off with Sam Turner, my stableboy and bartender?" He cackled as if it had been a fine joke. He gave Elizabeth a lewd wink. "Sam and that maid would go for long walks in the woods after their workday was finished, two, three times a week. Shoulda known what would come of that carry-on, Sam should."

Elizabeth was getting better at hiding her feelings, because with each derogatory comment about her grandmother, she became more determined than ever to uncover the truth and clear Ann's name and reputation.

"Did Ann or Sam ever return to Bolton?"

The old man shook his head. "Disappeared without a trace, the both of 'em. Right smart of 'em, too, because that there Brent Hollis was right out of his mind over losin' that slip of a girl. No tellin' what he mighta done if he'd a gotten his hands on young Sam." The old man leaned forward, his black eyes studying Elizabeth's features. "Now why's a pretty thing like you askin' all these questions, I wonder? No chance you're maybe related to that there Ann Merrill, is there? You favor her, come to think on it. She was a beauty too, same dark hair, same brown eyes you got, miss. You say yer workin' as a maid for Hannah Decker?"

Elizabeth nodded, relieved when he didn't expect answers to his own questions.

"Don't you let that old biddy work you too hard, now. You have problems there, you come over and see my Jennie, she'll give you a job here at the Blue Swan." He winked, a lecherous wink for one so old. "Put you in the tavern downstairs.

That pretty face'll sell whiskey hand over fist, I'll be bound."

It had been ten days since the afternoon Jeremy Hollis unbolted the chapel door for the strange woman who called herself Elizabeth Porter.

During those ten days he'd tried and failed to get her image out of his head, and now it seemed that everywhere he turned, he was hearing about her as well. Townspeople who worked at the mill, even his own servants had found occasion to tell him Elizabeth Porter was snooping all around the town, asking questions about his father and the Hollis family history.

Jeremy'd thought of little else all day, and by evening he'd had enough of it. He had Benjamin saddle his stallion, Lucifer, and as he galloped down the road to the village he was determined to confront the young woman whose face and slender figure had haunted his dreams every night since he'd first laid eyes on her.

He'd question her and get some honest answers, he vowed, and then he'd lay down the law, making it crystal clear her behavior wouldn't be tolerated.

Undoubtedly, Miss Porter fitted his father's view of a great many females: a gold digger, intent on destroying the family's solid reputation with some trumped-up scandal unless she received a princely sum for keeping quiet.

She'd lied in the very beginning, telling him she was working for some museum in Boston, and then telling Bartholomew Isaacs at the bank that she was destitute and needed a job.

Leaving the horse at the nearby livery stable

and telling himself he had every right to be indignant, Jeremy strode up the walkway to Hannah Decker's boardinghouse and hammered on the door.

Elizabeth, wearing a snowy cotton blouse, a proper dark skirt, and a maid's apron and cap, opened the door. Her brown eyes—even darker than Jeremy remembered—opened wide when she recognized him.

"Why, Jeremy Hollis. Hello, come on in."

From somewhere behind her, Mrs. Decker called, "Who is it, Porter?"

Elizabeth rolled her eyes heavenward and shocked Jeremy when she whispered, "Damn, I keep forgetting." In a louder voice, with a trace of mischief in her eyes, she said, "Good evening, Mr. Hollis, won't you come in? Mrs. Decker's in the parlor."

She was beautiful, there was no denying it. Breathtaking. It put Jeremy in an even worse humor than before. He'd been hoping that his eyes had deceived him that other afternoon, that her skin wasn't as fair, her midnight hair not so luxurious. He'd hoped that her figure was skinny rather than slender, that her breasts under the pristine white bib weren't as rounded as he remembered.

"It's you I've come to see, not Mrs. Decker," he snapped. "I should like to talk to you privately, if you please."

"There's no one in the small parlor, I guess we can talk in there. I'll go tell Hannah it's me you want instead of her. That'll put her in a temper." She left him standing just inside the door and disappeared into one of the rooms off the hallway.

Jeremy fumed. The silly wench didn't even understand a maid's duties. She hadn't taken his cape or his riding crop, or seen first to his comfort, the way any proper maid would have done. It irritated him that he couldn't stop himself from admiring the provocative sway of her hips as she walked away from him.

A few moments later he was sitting in an armchair in the small parlor, and she was perched on a sofa a few yards away, her legs tucked up under her in a most unladylike fashion.

Jeremy cleared his throat and tried not to remember how bare and shapely those legs had looked the day he'd first met her.

"It's come to my attention, Miss Porter, that you've been making inquiries about my family. The day we met, you lied to my father and me about who you were and what you were doing on our property. I must warn you I won't tolerate such behavior. You will stop asking questions of the townspeople, and I would like an explanation as to who you are and what you're doing in Bolton."

Her cheeks had turned from pink to scarlet as he spoke, and her relaxed posture disappeared. She drew her legs from under her and got to her feet, her hands on her hips, glaring down at him.

"Oh, you'd like an explanation, would you? Well, Mr. Jeremy Hollis, you can just whistle for one. Who do you think you are, storming in here like this and treating me like—like some servant, for heaven's sake?" Her dark eyes were shooting sparks at him.

Jeremy stared up at her, flabbergasted at her audacity. She *was* a servant, and as for his position

. . . Why, no one in Bolton would think to question his authority.

A tiny part of him had to admire her audacity, her courage. Anger suited her—the high color in her cheeks, the sparkle in her eyes. Against his will, he imagined her beneath him in a tumbled bed, knowing she'd look much the same overcome with passion. It was a vivid and most unfortunate image; he was wearing close-fitting riding breeches and it meant that for a few moments, at least, he had to remain seated, thus giving her the moral advantage of looking down on him.

"If it's blackmail you're about, miss, I warn you, it won't work." He made his tone ominous.

"Blackmail?" She sounded flabbergasted. "Blackmail! Well, I simply don't believe this. You, Mr. Jeremy Hollis, have an evil mind."

He raised a cynical eyebrow. "Ah, but I'm not the one telling lies and disrupting the village with nonsensical questions, am I?" At last he was able to get to his feet, moving close to her, half wanting to intimidate her, but also wondering what it would be like to take this fiery woman into his arms and kiss some sense into her. "Whatever scheme you've concocted, miss, is not going to work. So I suggest you pack your bags and go back where you came from. Boston, didn't you say? Or was it New York? Or do you keep track of all of the lies you invent?"

She stood her ground, her hands on her slender hips, her chin tilted at a defiant angle. "You can forget about scaring me off, you—you bully. I'm free to ask whatever I please, go anywhere I choose, do whatever I like. You, Mr. Hollis, would do well to mind your own business."

With that, she turned and marched out of the room, slamming the door so hard that the pictures on the walls rattled and a porcelain figurine on the mantel tumbled to the floor and shattered.

Jeremy stood staring at the door. He knew he should be righteously outraged, but instead of anger he was struggling with fascination and desire, and even amusement at her brash manner of speaking, her outrageous behavior.

Elizabeth Porter was the most intriguing young woman he'd ever met, and one way or another, he was going to get to know her better. His eyes narrowed. The thing to do with Elizabeth Porter, he concluded, was to win her trust, pretend to tell her his family's history, and in the process, learn who she really was and what she was up to.

What was the old saying? "You catch more flies with honey than with vinegar."

5

The large male hand came out of the darkness and clasped Elizabeth's arm just as she closed the back door and stepped onto the porch. She jerked away and opened her mouth to scream.

Before she could, a deep voice spoke from the shadows on the back porch.

"Hush, Miss Porter, it's Jeremy Hollis. I apologize for frightening you. I thought you could see me here, the moon is so bright tonight."

Elizabeth had to wait until her pounding heart subsided enough so she could speak. "What on earth do you think you're doing, scaring me half to death?" she sputtered. "And what are you doing skulking around on Hannah's back porch, anyway?"

Four days had gone by since her last encounter with him, and she didn't relish the idea of another battle with the arrogant heir to the Hollis fortune. "Let me guess." Her voice was dripping with sarcasm. "You've had a new by-law passed that forbids me to take a walk after dark without your permission, is that right, Mr. Hollis?"

His white teeth flashed, and she was certain he was smiling.

For heaven's sake. She hadn't seen pompous Jeremy Hollis come anywhere near a smile until now. "Have you been drinking?" Suspicious, she leaned over and sniffed in his direction.

The unbelievable happened, and he actually laughed. He had a good laugh, too, deep, hearty, and contagious. Elizabeth couldn't suppress a small smile of her own.

"I assure you I'm quite sober, Miss Porter. I've come to beg your forgiveness. I was rude the other night. Will you accept my apology by taking a stroll with me in the moonlight? Bolton is much enhanced by moonlight, and we could walk along the lakeshore."

Elizabeth hesitated. His suggestion was exactly what she'd planned to do on her own, in spite of Hannah's dire warnings about going out alone at night. But what were his real intentions?

Well, perhaps the best way of finding out was to take a chance and accept his invitation.

"I would appreciate an opportunity to make amends for my ungracious words the other night, Miss Porter." He sounded both sincere and contrite, and she gave in.

In spite of her misgivings, Elizabeth was acutely aware of Jeremy's size, his dark good looks, the warmth of his skin beneath his coat when she placed her hand on his arm as they walked.

He also had a sense of humor under his stiff facade.

"What exactly were you planning to do over at Hannah's?" She was curious about his appearance there. "You could hardly have known I was going to come outside tonight."

"After the fiasco the other night, I thought you'd refuse to see me if I asked for you at the door, so I thought I'd creep up the back stairs and try to figure out which room was yours. I was on the porch when it began to occur to me what dreadful ramifications might result should I hammer on Miss Penelope Thurgood's door instead of yours." He gave an exaggerated shudder. "It's well known that she keeps a blunderbuss loaded and ready for just such an intrusion."

Elizabeth giggled. "Penelope has the room directly under mine. I go to sleep each night to the sound of her snoring drifting up through the floorboards."

Elizabeth had learned from Hannah that the six-foot, three-hundred-pound Penelope Thurgood was the town's librarian. Fifty or thereabouts, she was a spinster and a self-pronounced manhater.

"I'll try not to lose my way, should I decide to burglarize Mrs. Decker's house in the future," he remarked dryly.

"Oh, you never know about Penelope," Elizabeth teased. "Maybe she'd drag you inside and keep you a love prisoner until you agreed to marry her. Maybe all her rantings about men simply hide a romantic soul."

"May God spare me." Jeremy clutched at his heart, and they both laughed.

At ease together, they finally addressed each other by their first names, and Jeremy related some intriguing facts about Bolton's history. Then they talked about books. Jeremy had read and enjoyed Arthur Conan Doyle's *A Study in Scarlet*.

Elizabeth, also an ardent fan of Sherlock Holmes, immediately said, "Oh, that was wonderful, but have you read *The Hound of the Baskervilles?* I think it's Doyle's masterpiece."

"I've never heard of it. You're certain it was by Arthur Conan Doyle?"

Too late, she realized that the story probably hadn't been written yet. She gave Jeremy a spirited account of it anyway, thinking mischievously how surprised Mr. Doyle would be to hear her summary of a story he wouldn't get around to writing for a few years.

She asked him about his work. One of the boarders had a niece who worked in the Hollis Mill, and from what she'd overheard, it sounded as if working conditions there were terrible. Of course she didn't say that to Jeremy, but she asked dozens of questions about the nearby industrial town and its predominantly female labor force.

"It's difficult to describe Lowell," he finally said. "Perhaps you'd like to visit our mill one day soon. I'd be happy to give you a tour."

"I'd like that very much."

When they arrived back at Hannah's rear gate, Elizabeth was almost sorry the evening was ending. Jeremy was actually fun to be with, and they'd talked nonstop for a full hour without touching once on her reasons for being in Bolton or her invasion of the Hollis chapel.

"Good night, Elizabeth." He lifted her hand and kissed the back of it. The gesture sent a thrill coursing through her, and she could imagine all too vividly how it would feel to have those hard, warm lips covering her own. She withdrew her hand, grateful that, in the moonlight, he wouldn't know she was blushing.

"May I call on you again?" His voice was deep, soft, and sensual.

"Yes. Yes, of course." She tried, without success, to sound nonchalant. "I'd like that."

She could feel his eyes on her as she climbed the porch stairs. She opened the door and turned, and he lifted a hand in salute.

There was a lamp lit and voices in the parlor, but Elizabeth crept up the narrow stairwell to her room, hoping no one would see her. She wanted to be alone. She felt a little giddy at the thought of Jeremy taking her out again, and happier than she'd felt for a long while.

"Well, Porter." Hannah was on the tiny landing, and she looked self-satisfied and smug.

Elizabeth felt suddenly wary. "Hello, Mrs. Decker." She tried to pass, but Hannah blocked her way.

"I saw you just now, out there in the backyard with Jeremy Hollis," Hannah said with a sneer. "Well, the apple never falls far from the tree, is what I always say."

"What's that supposed to mean?" Elizabeth's tone was sharp.

"Don't get uppity with me, young lady. Remember your place. What I'm saying is, here you've been asking me about Brent Hollis and the scandal years ago with that maid, and here's Jeremy out flirting with you tonight. Brent was already engaged when he got tangled up with *his* maid, and so is Jeremy. Like I said, the apple never falls far from the tree."

Elizabeth wasn't sure what Hannah was getting at. "What do you mean, so is Jeremy?"

Hannah gave a mean little chuckle. "Engaged, you silly girl. Jeremy's engaged to Clarissa Darwell, has been these past two months. Clarissa's a lovely girl, daughter of Henry Darwell, don't ya know, the mayor of Bolton." Hannah was studying Elizabeth with her beady eyes, gloating at the effect her words were having.

Elizabeth was taken aback and tried to hide her reaction, with little success. She had to get to her room and think about what Hannah had just said.

Hannah stood aside finally and allowed Elizabeth past, but she called out, "Like father, like son," just as Elizabeth finally reached her own door.

Elizabeth lit a candle and sank down on her bed. She was confused and curious. They had spent the evening talking about various subjects, so why hadn't Jeremy said one word to her about being engaged? Surely it would have been the proper thing to do. He seemed to be a respectable gentleman.

And Hannah Decker had a definite nasty streak,

that was certain. *Mean old gossip*. But Elizabeth had to admit that Jeremy's behavior was suspicious.

Damn him anyway. Damn his father, too. If it weren't for Brent Hollis, Elizabeth would be soaking in a scented bubble bath this minute, safe in her Chelsea brownstone, instead of sitting in this barren room feeling unnerved by Jeremy Hollis. She'd be thinking of what to wear to work tomorrow instead of pretending to be a maid in some godforsaken village in New Hampshire, trapped in the wrong century.

Annoyed and feeling unaccountably disappointed, she unlaced her hated boots and tossed them into the corner, then got to her feet and stripped off the cumbersome layers of clothing. She filled the china basin on the washstand and shivered as she scrubbed her body with the tepid water.

One thing was certain, she vowed as she tossed and turned later in the lumpy bed. She'd been correct in suspecting Jeremy's motives. She wasn't going to trust that scoundrel one bit from here on in. Oh, she'd take him up on his invitation to see his mill, all right. Perhaps she'd get some information about his father and her grandmother out of him.

But a peculiar sadness filled her, because she'd really liked Jeremy Hollis tonight, and she wanted to believe he'd been sincere.

She blocked out of her mind the fact that she'd also longed to have him take her in his arms and kiss her.

The following day was Saturday, and after the heavy noon meal was served and the dishes were done, Elizabeth had the afternoon off. She raced through the washing up, eager to be outside. It was a beautiful day, sunny and hot, without a cloud in the sky.

Hannah always napped after lunch, and Elizabeth didn't want to disturb her. Her employer had a nasty habit of finding just one more thing to do before her maid was finally free.

Elizabeth crept upstairs and washed quickly, then put on a new dress she'd bought, pale pink cotton with white lace ruffles. She tore off the black boots, determined to wear her own cream-colored pumps. She tied her hair up with a ribbon, coaxing tendrils down around her ears, and carrying her shoes, she crept back down the stairs.

She was at the bottom when there was a knock on the door, and she cursed under her breath, wondering if she dared to sneak out the back door without answering it.

The knock came again, and with a sigh she unlocked the door and swung it open.

Jeremy stood there, a top hat in his hand. He wore well-tailored cream trousers and a brown jacket, with a yellow waistcoat over his pristine white shirt. Behind him Elizabeth could see a carriage at the gate, harnessed to a beautiful black horse.

He looked at her, and she could see admiration in his eyes, and amusement as well when he noticed the shoes in her hand.

"Elizabeth, good afternoon. I wondered if perhaps you'd like to put on your shoes and come out for a ride. There's a country fair in a small town a few miles away. I thought you might enjoy it."

A welter of emotions coursed through her. His

black hair gleamed in the sunlight, tumbling over his forehead, and his long sideburns emphasized his strong jaw and rugged features.

Damn him, he was attractive. But what kind of game was he playing with her? She fought the urge to ask him where Miss Clarissa Darwell might be this afternoon, telling herself that here was an unexpected turn of good luck. She wouldn't have to wait now for their trip to the mill to learn about her grandmother. If she played her cards right, perhaps she could learn something today.

"Well, I just happen to have the afternoon off," she said in a flippant tone. "A country fair sounds like fun." She put down her shoes and stepped into them, and he held her elbow, steadying her.

Heavens, why did his slightest touch excite her? Why couldn't she have felt like this about one of the men she'd dated in her own time?

As they rode to the fair in the open horse-drawn carriage, Elizabeth couldn't help smiling with pleasure at the wonderful smell of the country air, and the view of fields and streams and small cottages along the lanes. She was all too aware of the narrow seat, and the fact that Jeremy's hard thigh was pressed against hers, and she could feel every movement he made as he held the reins and controlled the spirited horse.

He pointed out landmarks, a certain tree that had been struck by lightning, a covered bridge, a place along the stream where he'd fished as a child.

"What was your childhood like, Elizabeth?"

She tensed, instantly on guard. Careful to omit anything that would date her recollection, she told him of being raised by her grandmother, and of always feeling a little old-fashioned in her thinking because of it.

He turned and gave her an incredulous look. "You're the most outspoken young woman I've ever met. There's not a single thing old-fashioned about you, Elizabeth. Quite the contrary." He gave her a teasing grin. "You look very modern and outrageously pretty and quite harmless, but I've learned you have a wicked tongue when you're annoyed, Miss Porter."

He sobered and gave her a long, intense look that made the blood pound in her temples. "There's also an air of mystery about you that quite intrigues me," he added in a quiet voice. "I warn you, I intend to unravel it."

There was something ominous about his words. But before Elizabeth could confront him about them, he shook the reins and the horse broke into a gallop, and in another few moments they entered a tiny hamlet.

At the fair, Jeremy engaged in arm wrestling as Elizabeth cheered him on. But he lost to a massive young farm boy with wrists like fence posts. He won at hammer throwing, however, and bowing low, he presented Elizabeth with the ribbon and a garland of roses that were his prize.

He broke off a rose and wound it into her hair, and Elizabeth looked up at his dark, handsome face and heard Hannah's voice echo in her mind. "He's engaged. The apple never falls far from the tree."

He took her hand, and she pulled away from him, reminding herself of her vow not to trust him, but to remain friendly enough so that he would open up to her.

But on such a beautiful, fun-filled day like this it was difficult for Elizabeth to keep her mind on the reason she'd agreed to accompany Jeremy to the fair.

Jeremy bought hot meatpies for their supper, and enormous scarlet strawberries for dessert, with thick yellow cream to dip them in. Together, they toured the booths, admiring the jars of fruit and loaves of bread and knitted socks and scarves the farm women had brought to sell, and they laughed together as young boys tried to catch a greased pig.

At last, weary of the noise and commotion, they walked along the stream that wound through the village, and sat down on a rustic bench beneath a willow tree.

Elizabeth was pleasantly tired, and she leaned her head back and closed her eyes.

When Jeremy drew her into his arms, her eyes flew open. His arms were strong, holding her against his chest. She could feel his heart pounding. His mouth covered hers, and for a long moment, she hadn't the strength to resist. His tongue teased her lips apart, exploring her mouth, and deep inside of her, desire spread its petals like a flower striving to bloom. She kissed him back, pressing herself against him, when reason finally asserted itself.

He was engaged to another woman, just as his father had been engaged when he had courted Ann.

It took immense effort to push him away, because in spite of everything, some traitorous part of Elizabeth didn't want the kiss to end.

Because of that, she was furious with him, with herself. She tilted her head back and met his hot, questioning gaze.

"What would Clarissa think of this, Jeremy? I understand you're engaged to marry her." She was trembling, and she struggled for control of her voice. "Is—is unfaithfulness something you learned from your father?" She drew in a deep, shuddering breath and let it out with a whoosh. "Deceit must run in the Hollis family."

He was still for a long moment, and then, his hands like steel clamps on her shoulders, he pushed her away from him. His eyes were shuttered, his expression cold. He got to his feet and waited until she was also standing before he said between gritted teeth, "And is blackmail something you learned from your family, Elizabeth?"

He quickly strode toward the carriage, Elizabeth angrily trailing behind him. Once seated, Jeremy urged the horse to an all-out run, and Elizabeth clung to the side of the carriage, unnerved by the wild swaying and bouncing.

She'd rather have bitten her tongue off than ask him to slow down, even though at times she was certain he was going to upset the carriage and kill them both.

Well, let him. She had no intention of ever speaking to Jeremy Hollis again, dead or alive.

6

During the following week, Jeremy tried everything to get Elizabeth out of his mind.

He arrived at the mill early and stayed late, and by the third day everyone was avoiding him because of his volatile temper.

A few moments ago, his scowling father had asked what ailed him and Jeremy snapped at the older man for the second time within ten minutes.

Jeremy apologized, and then stalked back to his own office and slammed the door nearly off its hinges. Although it wasn't even noon, he took the bottle of whiskey he kept in the cupboard and poured himself half a tumblerful, tossing the drink down as if it were medicine.

The liquor burned like fire, but instead of dulling the images of Elizabeth that plagued him, it made them more vivid.

He was attracted to her, he admitted that much.

Thunderation! He threw the glass against the wall and grimaced as it shattered into a million shards.

He wasn't just attracted to the maddening woman. He wanted her with a violent, unreasonable need that gnawed at his guts and interrupted his sleep, that drove him to behaving like a tyrant and wishing to God he weren't engaged to Clarissa.

Clarissa. He groaned and shook his head, rubbing his forehead. He'd never loved her, but in all his thirty-two years, he'd never loved anyone else, either. But they got on well enough and being the only son and heir, he had to perpetuate his family line, so the engagement and marriage to Clarissa had seemed a good idea. He knew it had pleased his father a great deal. A union between Clarissa's family and his own made good business sense.

Now, God help him, Jeremy knew exactly what was missing between him and Clarissa. He'd never burned and ached to hold his fiancée in his arms. He'd never imagined stripping off her clothes, plunging into her and making her his own, as he imagined doing with Elizabeth.

And as if that weren't enough, he couldn't trust Elizabeth, no matter how much he wanted her. He'd meant what he'd said about her being mysterious. The question was whether she was also dishonest, whether she intended in some way to hurt his father and their family name.

He could delude himself into believing that the best thing to do was to get to know his enemy, and use that as the reason for having to see her again. But in his heart he knew it was more than that. It was because he couldn't bear the thought of *not* seeing her again.

Hannah had run out of flour in the middle of baking bread, and Elizabeth was hurrying back from the grocer's carrying the heavy sack when Jeremy's buggy pulled up and stopped beside her.

It had been just over a week since the fair, and although her temper had cooled, she was still annoyed with him.

"Elizabeth, may I offer you a ride? I'd like to talk to you."

She didn't answer him, tilting her chin up and ignoring him as she kept walking. But he refused to take the hint. He held the horse to a snail's pace beside her, talking all the way, drawing curious stares and amused grins from passers-by.

"I want to apologize for my behavior at the fair, Elizabeth. You were quite right to be insulted. My only excuse is that you are a beautiful woman, and I lost my head for a moment. If you could find it in your heart to forgive my rash behavior, I thought perhaps you'd like to accompany me to Lowell one day this week and see the mill. I did promise I'd take you."

Damn him and his pretty words. Why did he still want to take her to Lowell? She was more suspicious than ever of his motives. He didn't trust her; he'd accused her of blackmail, for heaven's sake.

Well, she didn't trust him, either, so that made them even. And, she reminded herself, there was still the chance he'd tell her something about his father that would provide a key to what had happened to Ann in this town thirty-two years ago.

After the disastrous occurrence at the fair, Elizabeth had decided not to pursue Jeremy for information, but to try to find other sources. Why, just last night she had returned to the Blue Swan to talk again with Tom Gunn, hoping the old man might have remembered something more. But although he was willing to help her, he could only repeat the story he had told her the first time she'd visited him. And when she asked him if there were other people who might know more, he said he'd have to think on that. So it seemed for now as if she had come to a dead end.

"Elizabeth." Jeremy sounded as if he was fast losing his patience. "Would you get in this buggy and allow me to give you a ride? I feel ridiculous, trying to carry on a conversation in this manner."

The flour was getting heavier by the moment. She stopped and allowed him to take the bag and help her into the buggy. Though she had already made her decision, she wouldn't tell him—yet. Jeremy Hollis brought out what Gram had labeled "Lizbeth's stubborn streak."

"I have a half day off on Wednesday," she finally told him in a haughty voice fifteen minutes later when he dropped her at Hannah's gate. "Pick me up at one."

The Hollis Mill was a huge red-brick fortress, covered, like everything else in Lowell, by soot and grime from the coal-burning steam engines that powered the numerous factories.

Jeremy gained them entry through the locked gates and they rode past railroad tracks and carts of baled cotton. Elizabeth had been aware of a low, steady humming in the air since they'd arrived in Lowell, and as Jeremy stood back now to allow her through the factory door, the hum turned to a deafening roar of whirring, clacking machines spinning raw cotton into thread and then into miles of cloth.

The noise was deafening, reverberating through Elizabeth's body as she followed Jeremy up a narrow flight of stairs and into one of the spinning rooms.

Here, thirty or forty women worked at ma-

chines, spinning thick white ropes of cotton onto
tall bobbins. Girls who looked as young as eight or
ten ran collecting the filled bobbins and replacing
them with empty ones. The air was thick with lint,
the room unventilated and so hot Elizabeth almost
gagged at the smell of unwashed bodies, overheated machines, oil, raw cotton, and something
that smelled moldy. Some of the women glanced
up and smiled at her in a friendly fashion, but
their attention returned immediately to the mael-
strom of bobbins and frames in front of them, and
the overwhelming noise made it impossible to say
anything, either to them or to Jeremy, who was
looking at some papers the foreman had produced.

Elizabeth's eyes and nose began to tickle, and
even in her pink cotton dress she was hot and uncomfortable. She knew that these women worked
here for ten hours a day, six days a week, with ri-
diculously short breaks for meals. They lived in
boardinghouses run by the mill owners, and they
were forced to abide by the rules those owners demanded or lose their jobs.

Elizabeth had now been in the spinning room
for less than ten minutes, and she could barely re-
strain the urge to run from this hell of noise, dust,
odor, and monotony.

A vivid image of her desk at Chantelle came
into her mind, and she remembered that she'd
once considered the quiet hubbub of lowered
voices, ringing phones, and typewriters noisy, her
own eight-hour days with an hour for lunch stren-
uous, and she felt ashamed. Even her job as a
maid for Hannah Decker was child's play compared to these conditions.

After what seemed an eternity Jeremy smiled at her and gestured toward the door. He led the way to his office, a pleasant room where the noise of the machines was muted and the wide window overlooked the Merrimack River. Jeremy told his secretary to bring them coffee, and when the small, bespectacled man laid the tray down and scurried out, Jeremy handed a steaming china cup to her.

"Well, Elizabeth, what are your impressions of the Hollis Mill?"

It was the trace of pride in his voice that made Elizabeth throw caution to the winds. Her cup clattered in its saucer, and her voice filled with indignation. "The working conditions here are nothing short of atrocious. You're employing children who ought to be in school, and how those people stand the noise, the smell, the endless hours of work, is beyond me. As far as I'm concerned, Jeremy Hollis, you and your father ought to be ashamed of yourselves, allowing fellow human beings to slave like this so that you can—can live in your mansion in luxury."

Jeremy first looked shocked and then exasperated. "Elizabeth, our mill is one of the most lenient in Lowell," he insisted hotly. "We are one of the few to abide by the ten-hour workday. These girls and their families depend on us for their livelihood. Why, three generations of Hollises have lived and prospered according to this system, and we abide by the law."

Elizabeth snorted. "*Hollises* have prospered, certainly. You may have kept to the letter of the law, but believe me, you are guilty of exploitation." She was fuming. "I don't know how you can sleep at night, Jeremy Hollis."

Jeremy looked at this delicious, impossible woman, her lovely face flushed and her brown eyes spitting fire at him.

He wanted to tell her that he *couldn't* sleep at night, and it wasn't due to the mill at all, but to her. With a low exclamation, he stood up and lifted her into his arms, stifling the protest on her lips with a kiss that in a moment had her arms twining around his neck, her body molded to his. He cupped her silken head in his hand, drinking in the taste and feel of her, using his mouth and body to convey his desperate longing for her.

Lost in the embrace, Jeremy did not realize that his father was in the room until the older man cleared his throat and coughed.

Elizabeth made a small, embarrassed sound, but Jeremy refused to release her, keeping his arm around her waist.

"Yes, Father?"

Brent Hollis gave Jeremy a disapproving glare, barely glancing at Elizabeth, not recognizing her. "Madam, why are you not at your loom? I suggest you return to work this instant," he snarled. "Jeremy, I should like a word with you."

Jeremy felt Elizabeth's body stiffen, and her chin came up in the manner he was all too familiar with.

"I'm not one of your poor overworked employees, Mr. Hollis. I'm here as Jeremy's guest." She pulled away and sashayed to the door, holding her skirts as if brushing against Brent would dirty them. "Jeremy, I'll wait for you in the carriage.

Good day, Mr. Hollis." She closed the door softly behind her, and Jeremy felt like applauding.

Whatever else Elizabeth Porter might be, she was brave.

His father was furious. He turned on Jeremy, his face scarlet. "Well, who is she?" he demanded.

"Elizabeth Porter, Father. You met her when I did. She'd somehow become locked in the chapel."

Recognition dawned on Brent's face. "She said she worked for a Boston museum. I was struck by her resemblance to—" He cut off whatever he'd been about to say, puffing up again with indignation. "I shouldn't have to remind you, Jeremy, that you are engaged to Clarissa. This—this cheap dalliance could jeopardize your marriage, and with it Darwell's decision to invest in our mill. You know some of our equipment is worn out. How can you be rash enough to endanger the business over some—some cheap little trollop from God knows where?"

"You will not speak of Elizabeth in that way, Father." Jeremy's tone was icy, and Brent's gaze fell under the impact of his son's anger.

Jeremy *was* angry, but he was also painfully aware that the old man hadn't once considered anything other than the financial aspects of the proposed union with Clarissa. Painful memories flooded through Jeremy, scenes from his childhood, memories of his mother weeping because of his father's coldness, and Brent's oft-repeated cruel remarks in front of her that women were nothing but gold diggers.

Jeremy knew Brent had acquired his attitudes from his own father. Grandfather Alexander, a dour old man, had warned the young Jeremy many times about women and their duplicity.

Jeremy had grown up distrusting women because of their attitudes, he realized now. Was his own life fated to be as loveless and bitter as his father's had been? His mother had died twelve years before of tuberculosis, and even when she was dying, Jeremy had never seen his father show her honest affection.

A thought that had been slowly building for the past week became a decision. "I intend to break off my engagement to Clarissa, Father. I don't love her, and I don't want her as my wife. I refuse to marry a woman simply because of some business deal. And I must warn you that I care deeply for Elizabeth."

Brent's mouth opened and closed several times before he could get a word out. "Have—have you gone entirely mad, Jeremy? I absolutely forbid—"

Jeremy was already halfway out the door. "I'm thirty-two years old, Father," he reminded Brent in a quiet voice. "I think it's rather late to forbid me to make up my own mind, don't you?" He closed the door behind him, feeling as if a ton had been lifted from his soul.

Elizabeth was waiting. Jeremy had expected her to be angry with him again for kissing her, but she was silent as the driver of the closed hired carriage drove them away from the mill.

Halfway to Bolton, Jeremy decided the time had come to tell Elizabeth he planned to break off his engagement to Clarissa.

She gave him a long, level look out of those remarkable brown eyes. "Are you telling me the truth?"

The woman had the ability to infuriate him with one single sentence. "Damn it, Elizabeth, why would you suspect I was lying about a matter as important as this?"

"Because you didn't see fit to tell me of your engagement until I confronted you with it. For all I know, you're keeping Clarissa and me on a string and making us dance like puppets for your pleasure."

He cursed under his breath and pulled her roughly into his arms. "If words won't convince you, maybe this will," he ground out, and his lips clamped down on hers, hard and searching, savage in a demand for her response.

After a moment's struggle, she melted, returning his kisses with equal passion. His hands cupped her breasts, feeling the nipples harden at his touch, and it was all he could do to keep from ripping off her clothes.

Clinging to the last vestiges of control, he at last released her, his heart pounding, his body aching with his need for her.

Her face was flushed, her breathing as unsteady as his own, but her expression was furious instead of loving.

She shouted to the driver to stop the carriage, wrenched open the door, and jumped out into the dusty road.

Jeremy got out. He argued, ordered, pleaded with her to get back into the carriage, since they were still several miles from Bolton, but to no avail. Elizabeth stomped along with her nose in the air, ignoring everything he said.

At last, he picked her up, tumbled her into the carriage, and slammed the door. He then shoved a handful of bills at the bemused driver and ordered the man to take her to Hannah Decker's boarding-house.

Jeremy walked the long, hot miles into town, arriving late in the afternoon, sweaty, dishevelled, and covered in dust. He headed straight for the tavern at the Blue Swan Inn, aware that for the first time in his life he understood what really drove men to drink.

7

"**A**le, Albert. A jug of your best." Jeremy sank into a chair, and the owner of the Blue Swan was back in moments with a brimming pitcher. He poured the foaming liquid expertly into a mug and said in a quiet voice, "I'd like a word with you, Mr. Hollis, if it's convenient."

Jeremy had tipped many an ale with Albert Roston. He liked the big, slow, good-natured man, and although at the moment Jeremy would have preferred solitude, he invited the other man to join him. They talked about the weather and the crops, and then Jeremy said, "What's on your mind, Albert?"

Albert's brow furrowed in a frown. "See, Mr. Hollis, it's this maid the widow Decker's hired, name of Elizabeth Porter."

Jeremy groaned inwardly and drained half his mug, waiting for Albert, who sipped his ale, to continue. A sense of foreboding overcame him. What had Elizabeth been up to now?

"See, Mr. Hollis, a while back she come here askin' Jennie about your da and some maid used to work here in Bolton years ago, name of Ann Merrill. Jennie sent her up to talk to old Tom. Seems he filled her head with tales better forgotten, you ask me, but you know how the old man likes to gab. Anyways, she went away, but then she come back again t'other night, askin' more questions and listenin' all over again to Tom's story, quizzin' him, like. And asked if he knew other folks she could talk to."

"And what was this story Tom told her?"

Albert's face reddened. "I only ast Tom to tell me so's I could pass it on should you ask," he explained. Haltingly, Albert related the story of Jeremy's father and his courtship of the maid, including every detail of the whole affair. When he finished, Albert shook his head and took a long draught of his ale.

"Doesn't seem right to me, some stranger askin' all those questions about personal matters. Thought mebbe you should know."

Jeremy thanked Albert and left the Blue Swan without finishing his drink. He felt sick at both Tom's story, which he didn't believe for an instant, and Elizabeth's pursuing some twisted plot behind his back. What hurt most was the fact that not once had she confronted him directly with her questions—not that he'd have confided much to her. He hadn't even been aware of the gossip Albert had related, much less other details of his father's early life. Brent had never been a communicative man.

The fact was, Elizabeth didn't trust him even enough to ask him. Not, he had to reluctantly admit, that he'd yet done anything to win her trust.

He retrieved Lucifer from the livery stable and rode back to the manor house as if all the demons in hell were on his trail.

His father wasn't home, which was a relief. Another confrontation with Brent was more than he needed today. But all through his bath and a dinner he left half-eaten, Jeremy's thoughts were in turmoil.

Elizabeth's actions angered him. Having her ask questions of other people instead of coming to him was humiliating, and he intended to tell her so as soon as possible.

He also must inform Clarissa the wedding was off. Her father had planned an engagement ball to be held soon, and Jeremy had to break it off before then. He decided that this distasteful task was his first priority, and there was no better time to do it than the present. It was still early, barely eight o'clock.

In a few moments, he was once again on Lucifer's back galloping toward Bolton, rehearsing what he'd say to Clarissa, dreading the encounter but eager to have it behind him.

It was anticlimactic to arrive at the Darwell mansion and learn that Clarissa was out, attending a ladies' get-together at a friend's home. Jeremy cantered down the darkening streets, and he was in the alley behind Mrs. Decker's boardinghouse before he realized where he'd been heading all along.

He reined Lucifer in and sat staring at the house for several long, thoughtful moments. The last thing he wanted was to barge in old gossipy Decker's front door and demand to see her maid. He must talk to Elizabeth in private.

He remembered Elizabeth's telling him she was in the room directly above Penelope Thurgood's. He looked up at the third-floor windows. Which one was hers?

For half an hour or more he watched as lamps were lit and shades lowered in the various rooms. Lucifer grew restless, snorted and whinnied, and Jeremy dismounted, leading the horse up and down the dark alley, watching.

When he was about to give up, a lamp was lit in a second-floor window, and for a moment before she drew the shade he saw Penelope Thurgood's immense frame silhouetted against the faint light.

It took only a few moments to ride Lucifer to the hitching rail and water trough outside the Blue Swan. Jeremy watered and tethered the horse, and made his way swiftly and silently back through the alleys, praying that Hannah Decker hadn't taken to locking her back door.

The door was open. He slipped like a shadow up the dark stairwell and tapped at the door he fervently hoped was Elizabeth's.

The day had been long and exhausting. Elizabeth had taken off the layers of petticoats and the cumbersome dress, washed herself in cool water, and put on the long white cotton nightgown she'd bought at the dry goods store. It was pretty and feminine, with lace and ribbons, but best of all, it was thin and cool. Her third-floor bedroom was usually stifling after the day's heat.

She frowned at the tap at the door. She was

Hannah's only live-in servant, so she was alone on this floor, and no one ever visited her.

She drew a shawl around her nightgown and undid the door catch.

Jeremy's strong hand covered her mouth before she could do more than stutter his name, and he was inside with the door latched behind him before she could speak. Her shawl slipped to the floor and his fingers bit into her shoulders through the delicate fabric of her gown. He scowled down at her.

"Damnation, Elizabeth, are you trying to ruin my family's name?" He gave her a little shake, his blue eyes smoldering with anger. "Everywhere I go I'm told that you're asking questions about my father and this—this Merrill woman, encouraging people to gossip shamelessly about my family. Why do you persist in this prying, woman? I asked you once before and I want an answer now. Are you thinking to blackmail my father by inventing some ridiculous scandal about him and some—some cheap trollop who I doubt even existed?"

Elizabeth's hand connected hard with his cheek, and she wrenched herself out of his grasp. "Don't you dare use such language about my grandmother," she spat at him. "Gram was no trollop, she was a fine lady." To her horror, her eyes filled with tears that began streaming down her cheeks, and sobs rose in her throat.

The mark of her hand blazed red on Jeremy's face, but he ignored it. He stared at her, shock and surprise mingling on his dark features. "Your— your grandmother? This Ann Merrill was your grandmother?"

Elizabeth nodded, scrubbing at her tears with her palms. "She—she was a wonderful woman, she raised me and I lov-loved her so much." She hiccupped and gulped. "And—and she loved your father, he was going to marry her, but something—" she struggled for control— "something happened, and Ann left here without a word to anyone." She was crying in earnest now, her face screwed up and tears wetting the front of her gown. "They say she ran off with a stableboy, that she made your father the laughingstock of the entire village. She'd—never have—have left like that unless something, something—terrible happened. My grandmother was an honorable, honest woman, and she was always conscious of others' feelings. She'd never have hurt your father that way, running off with someone else just before the wedding." She sniffed. Her nose was running.

His gentle hands came to rest on her shoulders, drawing her into an embrace that brought on a new flood of tears, because she didn't have the strength or the desire to resist him any longer. Being in his arms felt safe, secure, comforting. She'd been lonely for so long. She so wanted him to hold her. She didn't care about anything except being in his arms.

He drew a huge pristine handkerchief out of his pocket and mopped at her face, clumsy, endearing, tender.

"Dear Elizabeth. My dear, beautiful Elizabeth, please don't cry." His voice rumbled in her ear, pressed as it was against his white shirt front, which was now soaked with her tears.

"Blow." He held the handkerchief to her nose, and like a child, she did as she was told. He stroked her hair, and her hands snaked up and wrapped around his neck.

She wasn't certain just when comfort became hunger. She became aware of her breasts against his chest, her nipples hard and aching. She shivered at the thinness of her nightgown beneath his stroking hands. She felt the evidence of his desire pressing against her abdomen. Breathless, aching, she tilted her head up, shamelessly begging for his kiss.

With a groan, he enveloped her, lifting her against him, his mouth crushing down on hers in a fiery kiss that had her arching against him.

"God, Elizabeth . . ." He reached over to the dresser and turned down the wick in the small lamp until only a pinprick of light remained in the room. He picked her up and put her on the bed, and then his trembling hands were stripping off first his clothing and then her nightgown. The bed sank beneath his weight as he lowered himself beside her.

Her breath caught as his naked body came in contact with hers. His broad chest had soft dark hair, delightfully rough against her sensitive skin, and she felt enveloped in heat as his strong arms drew her against him.

"Beautiful girl," he whispered, kissing her lips, her throat, and then taking her nipple in his mouth and suckling until she writhed beneath him.

He was far more experienced than she. He knew where to kiss, how to touch, paying rapt attention with his lips, teeth, and tongue to every inch of her until at last she could only whisper his name, begging him for release from the sensations that overwhelmed her.

His hand slid between them, and for a moment she was poised, aching, trembling. Then, in a rush of overwhelming pleasure, she cried out.

In that instant, Jeremy entered her, and the moment of intense pain she felt was swiftly gone, lost in the rapture of his loving.

He was braced above her on his elbows, and he took her face between his palms, forcing her to look into his eyes as he moved with increasing urgency within her.

"Mine," he ground out. "Mine, Elizabeth. I love you. You're mine now, forever." Even as paroxysms of delight began to convulse him, he looked into her eyes, sharing his very soul until at last he could no longer control the ecstasy ripping through him. His head reared back, and his eyes closed. His body shuddered; then he held her, caressing her, murmuring words of love and praise.

Even drugged with pleasure, something bothered her. She had to know, she had to be certain. "What about Clarissa, Jeremy?"

He crushed her against him. "It's over, Elizabeth. It was a mistake, but how could I know what I was missing until I met you?"

His solemn intensity erased the last of her doubts. With a bleary smile, she slipped into sleep in his arms, and woke with a start only when she realized she was alone in the bed.

It was long past midnight. Jeremy was dressing in a pool of moonlight, careful to make no sound. He pulled on his waistcoat, clutching his boots in one hand, and stepped over to the bed, leaning down to kiss her lips, tucking the sheet up around her shoulders.

"Sleep, my love," he whispered in her ear. "It's late. I'll call on you tomorrow evening, at the front door this time. I love you, Elizabeth."

Like a shadow, he opened the door and slipped through it.

Elizabeth listened anxiously, but all she heard was the single creak of a stair as he made his way down and out of the house. A part of her insisted she should be worrying over what had just happened, but she couldn't bring herself to begin. She slid back into sleep, dreaming of Jeremy cradling her in his arms.

The next day was laundry day, and although Hannah hired a woman to come in and help, Elizabeth was expected in the late afternoon to bring the dry, sweet-smelling sheets from the line in the backyard.

She was thinking of Jeremy, reaching high up to the clothesline, when a man's voice sounded from behind her.

"You be Elizabeth Porter?"

She whirled around, dropping a handful of pegs.

"Sorry, ma'am." The man was middle-aged but looked older, his back twisted in some permanent curve, and he bent with difficulty to recover the pegs. He handed them to her, his pale eyes intent on her features, his hat held against his chest.

"By gum, old Tom was right, you're the very spittin' image of her," he muttered. "Tom Gunn, over at the Blue Swan? He's who told me I should come to talk to you," he added as Elizabeth stepped back nervously, wondering just who this apparition was. "Brought a load of wood down, like I do every month or thereabouts. Went up to have a jug and a jaw with Tom. He and my da were good friends."

Elizabeth now saw the team of horses and the wagon in the alleyway. "You're a woodcutter?"

The man nodded. "Like my pa 'afore me." He was still staring at Elizabeth and shaking his head. "Don't that beat all, you and her both pretty as pictures, same black hair and brown eyes, same look to both of ya."

Elizabeth's eyes widened. "Are you talking about Ann Merrill?" Her heart hammered when he nodded.

"Run off with a stableboy over thirty years ago, ne'er been heard from since, either of 'em." He reached up a hand to scratch his head. "Peculiar, that whole thing. Like I was tellin' Tom, me and my pa saw her two weeks before she was s'posed to marry young Hollis. Same day she ran off with Sam."

"You saw Ann that day? Where?" Excitement filled Elizabeth, and she waited impatiently for the woodcutter to continue his story.

"We was up the mountain, Pa and me. Felled a right big log and was cuttin' it up. Had a good view of the Hollis place, up where we was. Old Alexander was there, just settin' in that there gazebo, lookin' out over the lake. Brent was livin' there in the manor house already, see. Then we noticed this Ann Merrill, walkin' up the road. Had on a blue dress, she did. Pa and I was right surprised when she went on past the house, to where the old man was. Seemed as if she'd come to see him, 'stead of Brent."

"What happened next? What else did you see?" Elizabeth felt like shaking the slow-speaking man to hurry him on, but he wagged his head.

"Nothin'. Pa and me loaded the wood on the wagon and we left right then. She was still there when we passed, still talkin' to Alexander. And that very night, she was gone. I heared next time I come to town she'd run off with that there Sam that very same night." He cocked his head. "Seems peculiar, don't it, that a girl pretty as that would choose Sam over Brent Hollis? No accountin' fer it, I always did say."

Elizabeth trembled with excitement. It seemed that finally she had a chance to find out what had happened to Ann. Jeremy's grandfather was the key to the mystery, she was certain of it. She couldn't wait to confront him.

"Tell me, does Alexander Hollis still live in Bolton?" Jeremy had never mentioned where his grandfather lived.

The woodcutter shook his head. "Nope. Lives down Boston way. Moved there when young Brent took over the mill."

Elizabeth thanked the woodcutter and hurried into the house.

Hannah had the vapors when she realized there were still sheets on the line and no one except herself to serve the dinner, but Elizabeth's mind was made up. Within an hour she was at the railroad station, and in another hour she was boarding the afternoon train to Boston.

She'd scribbled a note to Jeremy and left it with Hannah, hating having to rely on the nosy woman but not knowing what else to do. She'd thought of waiting until she saw him tonight, of asking him to come with her, but she remembered all too well his fury at her digging into his family's past. She couldn't afford to have him try to stop her, not when she was so close to getting the answers she so desperately wanted.

All the same, her heart ached and she wanted him beside her when at last the train pulled slowly out of the station.

8

"Ann Merrill's granddaughter?" The human skeleton in the wheelchair cackled, but there was no real amusement in his laughter, and the eerie sound sent chills up Elizabeth's spine.

"You're lying, miss. You can't be Ann Merrill's granddaughter."

"Why do you say that?" Elizabeth tried to keep her voice from revealing her antipathy to this old man who looked as if every breath might be his last.

It had been a struggle to convince the sour-faced housekeeper even to let her into the dark mansion on Louisberg Square where Jeremy's grandfather lived, surrounded by a battery of servants. Elizabeth had finally told the woman to mention her grandmother's name to Alexander Hollis, and at last she'd been escorted into a musty parlor. A gaunt male servant had wheeled Hollis in and stood behind his chair, glaring at Elizabeth as if she planned to do his master bodily harm.

Perhaps she *was* doing him harm, through no fault of her own. Alexander Hollis kept staring at her, his wrinkled face ashen, his breathing stertorous.

"What makes you so certain I couldn't be Ann Merrill's granddaughter?" she demanded again, but Hollis just shook his head and wouldn't answer. He went on staring at her, though, his rheumy blue eyes as shocked as if he were seeing a ghost.

"Mr. Hollis, I know the whole story of my grandmother and your son and how opposed you were to their marriage. The only part I don't know is what happened on the day my grandmother disappeared, and I think you do. Someone saw you with her that afternoon, in the gazebo. Won't you please tell me what happened?"

Hollis again shook his head, motioning to the servant to wheel him away. They were halfway to the door when Elizabeth jumped up and blocked the opening with her body, her arms on the doorjamb.

"Remove her from my house," Hollis ordered, and the servant hurried over and took Elizabeth's arm, trying to drag her away.

She fought him off, rushing over to grasp the arms of the wheelchair. "You're dying," she cried, holding his gaze with her own. "You're dying, but don't you see, you still have this chance to make peace, with yourself, with—with God."

She drew a shuddering breath and went on, trying to convince him. "Whatever you tell me will remain between us, Mr. Hollis. I won't repeat it, but—but if you won't tell me now what happened to my grandmother, I swear I'll—I'll convince Jeremy, and Brent as well, to come here with me the next time." It was a desperate threat, but he had left her no choice.

There was fear on the old man's face at the mention of his son and grandson. He hesitated, and then gruffly ordered the servant out. When the door closed behind him, Alexander Hollis seemed to crumble. He buried his face in his hands and began to sob.

Elizabeth had to lean closer to hear his muffled words.

"I never meant to kill her, but I couldn't let some—some penniless maid, some laborer's daughter, marry my only son, could I?"

Her eyes widened and utter horror filled Elizabeth, as she straightened and stepped back from the old man. Even though she knew that what he said hadn't really happened, knowing that this man had tried to kill her grandmother filled her with outrage, with such anger that she wanted to attack him herself. It took extreme effort to control her reactions, to keep her voice steady. "Tell me what happened."

As if the words had been dammed up too long, they came bursting out of him with all the force of a gale. "Nothing I said or did had any effect on Brent, so I turned to her. At first, I tried to bribe her." His eyes were fastened now on Elizabeth's face, as if he was begging her for understanding. "She threw my money in my face. I threatened her, but she laughed at me, insisting Brent would protect her." Even now, so many years later, he sounded flabbergasted at his failure to frighten or coerce Ann, and fierce pride at her grandmother's indomitable spirit brought sudden tears to Elizabeth's eyes.

"So I sent her a note, saying that we should meet, that we should make peace between us." The quavering old voice had taken on a monotonous quality, as if in his mind Alexander had covered this part of the story innumerable times.

"That's why she came to the gazebo that afternoon," Elizabeth whispered.

He nodded. "I offered her a great deal of money, a king's ransom it was for the likes of a maid, if she would agree to leave Bolton forever. She wouldn't touch the packet. She tipped her chin up and asked in a quiet voice if I hadn't yet learned that nothing would prevent her from marrying Brent, because she loved him."

Alexander was trembling now, his twisted hands moving restlessly on the tartan blanket that covered his legs. "I lost my temper. I grabbed her by the shoulders, but she twisted away and ran." He made an agonized sound in his throat and smacked his fists down on his useless legs. "I was young and strong then. I could still run. I caught her. She fought me like a wildcat, but gradually I forced her to the edge of the cliff." His breath came and went in short, sharp bursts. "I threw her over the edge and she fell down into the lake." He was silent for a long time. Then he added in a sly tone, "I was lucky, because her body was never found."

Elizabeth felt sick, even though she knew that Ann had survived the fall. She must have swum to shore and then fled for her life, aware at last that

Alexander would stop at nothing to keep his son from her. The anguish, the terror, she must have felt made Elizabeth wrap her arms around herself, barely able to control the grief and pity she felt for the frightened girl her grandmother had been that fateful day.

"Then I had to invent a story that would explain her disappearance," Alexander was saying now. "So I paid a stableboy, Sam Turner, the same money I'd offered Ann, on the understanding that he'd leave Bolton and never come back. He was a simple lad and she'd befriended him. There'd been gossip about them in the village, so I dropped a word here and there that they'd run off together." He shook his head. "It was so easy, in the end. Even Brent came to believe it as time went on." His eyes lifted and he stared at Elizabeth. "I've tried to forget it, and at times I've almost succeeded. But when I saw you today it all came back. You're very like her."

Elizabeth's fists were clenched in an effort to stem her tumultuous emotions his revelation had created in her. With all her will, she spoke in a civilized manner, telling him Ann did not die that day. It gave her great pleasure to add that her grandmother had lived a long and privileged life, that she'd died a wealthy woman.

"And you're her granddaughter?" Alexander was frowning now, confusion evident on his cadaverous face. "When exactly did Ann Merrill die? How old are you, Miss Porter?"

The past hour had drained her, and she had no desire to confide in this man who'd tried to kill her grandmother. Besides, explaining how she'd arrived in 1899 was more than she could manage at this moment.

Repeating her promise that she'd keep Alexander's part in the story of Ann's disappearance confidential, she ignored his questions and found her way out of his house. She'd taken a room for the night in a small hotel near the railroad station. The train to Bolton didn't leave until late the following afternoon, and it seemed an eternity away.

At last she had the answers to the questions that had haunted her ever since she'd read her grandmother's diary. But instead of feeling peaceful, she was plagued more than ever with uncertainty.

Alexander had gone to murderous lengths to keep his son from marrying a woman he considered unsuitable. Would Brent do the same if he learned that Jeremy and Elizabeth were lovers? And now that her mission was fulfilled, there was nothing stopping her from trying to return to her own time—nothing, except that she didn't want to go.

She'd fallen in love with Jeremy Hollis.

"Clarissa, I've come to tell you that I cannot marry you. I realize how terrible it is of me to do this the day before our engagement ball, and of course I expect to inform everyone the decision was yours." An immense weight seemed to lift from Jeremy's shoulders when he finally was able to say the words he'd rehearsed all day.

He'd just spent two hours—a veritable eternity—making polite conversation with Clarissa's parents and wondering if he would ever be granted a private moment with the cool blonde.

Now he braced himself for a nasty scene.

Clarissa raised her eyebrows and said in a condescending tone, "I suppose this nonsense is all because of that scullery maid. You know, Jeremy, you really should be more circumspect. A little bird told me you'd been seen with her." She moved closer to him, putting one dainty hand on his sleeve and looking up at him through her lashes.

"Silly man, it's honorable of you to want to protect my reputation this way, but there's no need to go to extremes. Of course I'll forgive you. I'm innocent but not entirely stupid, Jeremy. I do understand a tiny bit—" she blushed and simpered—"about men's baser needs. And I won't allow you to sacrifice our marriage because of a silly little mistake in judgment."

Jeremy could feel sweat popping out on his forehead. This was a hell of a lot worse than he'd even imagined it would be. It was also giving him a horrifying glimpse into the mind of the woman he'd almost married, and he shuddered to think of the colossal mistake he'd nearly made. Baser needs, indeed. A vision of Elizabeth, naked, passionate, and vulnerable, flashed in vivid detail across his mind.

"Clarissa, listen to me and try to understand. This isn't a matter of honor, it's a matter of love. I don't love you, Clarissa." He thought of his parents and their wretchedness. "I've seen the unhappiness of a loveless marriage. I won't do that to you, or to myself, either. Our engagement is over."

She looked at him in shocked disbelief, and now the tears that he'd expected earlier came with a vengeance. She fell into his arms, sobbing and clutching him around the neck with surprising strength.

"The ball, Jeremy. You—you can't do this to me on—on the very eve of my—my engagement ball."

Damnation. He'd given little thought to the bloody ball, and he had no real idea how to deal with a woman's tears. Panic stricken, he tried to extricate himself gently. Her sobs increased, and he had visions of her parents bursting into the room at any moment.

"Clarissa, try to control yourself. It's not the end of the world. Some other man much worthier than I—"

"Please, please tell me you'll wait until after tomorrow, Jeremy." There was very real terror in her high-pitched voice. "Jeremy, please—please don't do this now. All—all the food is prepared, my dress . . . Everyone is coming. Everything is—is ready."

He realized suddenly that Clarissa wasn't bemoaning the loss of his love at all. It was having to cancel the ball that bothered her.

"Jeremy, no one will believe this was my de-decision, not now, just before the ball. Oh, Jeremy, please, please say you'll wait until after tomorrow." Her pale eyes widened with horror and fear. "I'll—I'll be the laughingstock of the entire village. I—I can't bear it. Please say that you'll wait. A few days after the ball I can let it be known we had a quarrel . . ."

Remembering something Elizabeth had said made him give in. "Grandmother would never have hurt your father that way, making him a laughingstock in the village by running off with someone else just before their wedding—"

Jeremy's heart sank. The villagers *would* talk. Clarissa was right. Some of them would take great delight in the thought of the rather haughty Clarissa Darwell being jilted the night before her engagement ball. Surely he owed her the right to save face. After all, he would have to continue this charade for only a few days.

"Very well, Clarissa. I'll go through with the ball tomorrow night, but by the end of the week I expect you to make it known that our engagement is over."

The tears stopped, and Jeremy frowned, wondering if he'd really caught that glimpse of shy triumph in her expression just before she gave him a tremulous smile. "Oh, thank you, Jeremy. I'll do just as you say."

He was immensely relieved to escape from Clarissa at last, and it was only just past nine o'clock. He rode Lucifer to the boardinghouse, tied him to the rail, and hurried up to the front door.

When Mrs. Decker answered his knock and handed him an envelope, it was obvious that the old biddy had steamed it open and then clumsily reglued it. As he opened it, she made pointed references to Clarissa and the engagement ball. There was little he could do except give the nosy chattering hen a look guaranteed to make her shut her mouth and quake in her high-laced boots.

The message was short. "Gone to Boston to talk with your grandfather. Will explain when I get back. Yours, Elizabeth."

He crumpled the note in his fist, more disappointed than he cared to admit at not being able to see her tonight. And what in God's name was she up to now? What could she possibly hope to learn by bothering his grouchy old grandfather? God, but she infuriated him. She was the most unpredictable, ungovernable, impetuous, irritating woman he'd ever come across.

Yet he couldn't wait to see her again, to hold her in his arms, to claim her as his own.

9

"You're fortunate even to have a job left, Miss Hoity-Toity, gallivanting all over the country, coming and going as you please. Now go put these on. I've agreed that you'll work as one of the maids for the Darwells' party tonight, starting in an hour."

Hannah thrust a bundle at Elizabeth. "This is what you'll wear. Mrs. Darwell wants all the maids dressed the same. And not a word out of you about it, either. What with the inconvenience you've put me to the past two days, you're lucky to have any job."

Elizabeth had half-expected to be fired when she arrived back at the boardinghouse late that afternoon. She'd rather looked forward to the confrontation; Hannah Decker had become one of her least favorite people. She frowned down at the elaborate maid's uniform, mystified.

What exactly was her employer up to, hiring her out to the Darwells, of all people? Not that she'd go, of course. She was going to find Jeremy. There was so much she had to tell him, so much about herself she still had to explain. After that, she'd make plans regarding the rest of her life.

"What's the party for, Mrs. Decker?"

"Why, surely Mr. Jeremy has told you, what with you being such close friends and all?" Hannah was all but rubbing her hands with malicious glee, and Elizabeth suddenly felt uneasy.

"It's the social event of the season," Hannah announced, her beady gaze intent on Elizabeth's face. "It's the formal announcement of Mr. Jeremy's engagement to Clarissa Darwell. Funny he didn't tell you, isn't it? Everyone in town's been talking about it for ages. Hurry up and change. There's a carriage coming to pick you up in less than an hour."

He'd lied to her. He'd told her the engagement to Clarissa was over, and like a fool she'd believed him.

Elizabeth's chest felt as if an iron band had closed around it, stopping her breath, choking the very life from her. There was no way to hide the effect of Hannah's words.

"Not going to swoon, are we?" Hannah's voice was full of viciousness, and it brought Elizabeth's chin up. She wouldn't let this nasty woman get the better of her, no matter how devastated she might feel at Jeremy's treachery.

She wanted to run, to hide and cry until she had no tears left. She wanted to hurry to the chapel, ring the bell, and try to go back to her other life, to a place where she might in time forget that Jeremy Hollis ever existed.

She couldn't. Not quite yet. In a flash, she understood what she had to do, the final confrontation that would at last afford her grandmother's memory dignity and peace.

Brent Hollis must know the truth.

She summoned up the strength of will she'd inherited from Ann and gave Hannah a long, cool look.

"Swoon? Not at all, Mrs. Decker. I'll be ready." She turned on her heel and, keeping her shoulders erect and her back ramrod straight, climbed the stairs to her room. But every muscle in her body ached at Jeremy's duplicity.

"... and so it gives me immense pleasure to announce the engagement of my precious daughter, Clarissa May, to Mr. Jeremy Hollis."

Mayor Henry Darwell raised his glass in a toast, and cheers erupted from the crowd in the great ballroom. The orchestra began to play a waltz, and Clarissa, gripping Jeremy's reluctant hand, pulled him out into the center of the room.

At that moment, it would have given Jeremy immense pleasure to strangle her. He was disgusted with himself for allowing her to talk him into going ahead with this sham of a celebration, and it was all he could do to control the anger he felt toward the cloying woman who was now giving him vapid looks from her treacherous pale eyes.

Clarissa had done her level best to double-cross him tonight, to trap him into marrying her after all. But the moment he got her alone, he would relish telling her that her ploy hadn't worked, that nothing on God's green earth could ever induce him to make her his wife.

He'd just spent the past half-hour closeted in the

Darwell library with his father. Clarissa had taken Brent aside earlier in the evening and tearfully told him that Jeremy had broken their engagement, and expected her to make the announcement by the end of the week. Of course, Clarissa had sobbed, she'd have to tell her daddy about Jeremy and that maid, that Elizabeth Porter, and then it would be out of the question for her father to loan Brent any money for his mill, wouldn't it?

Jeremy had never seen his father in such a state. He had raged, pleaded, and threatened, his face nearly purple, the veins standing out on his temples until Jeremy feared he might have a stroke. But it was the torment in Brent's eyes that was the worst, that made what Jeremy had to say the hardest.

"Father, I agreed, as any gentleman would, not to humiliate Clarissa tonight in front of the entire town. But I meant what I said to her. The engagement is off."

Brent had seemed to wither, to become an old man.

"If you do this, we will lose the mill. The situation is desperate, worse even than I've told you. But quite apart from the money, you're making a horrible mistake with this—this Elizabeth Porter. Believe me, I know. I almost ruined my own life over a woman in this very same fashion, and I can't stand by and see you do the same."

It hurt to stand firm, to deny the naked appeal in Brent's eyes. In some strange way, Jeremy had felt closer at that moment than he'd ever felt to the aloof, secretive man who was his father.

He'd clasped Brent's shoulder, his voice rough with emotion. "I know that what I'm doing is

right, Father. I'm in love with Elizabeth, and I plan
to marry her. Somehow I'll raise the money to
make the necessary changes at the mill. I promise
you."

He'd left his father there in the library, and he
hadn't seen him since. As soon as this cursed
waltz was over, he'd go and find him, make sure
the older man was all right.

"You—Parker, or whatever your name is. Take
this up to the buffet tables, and see you get back
down here right smart. And straighten your cap,
girl. It's crooked."

Elizabeth picked up the heavy platter, grateful
for the opportunity to escape from the sweltering
downstairs kitchens where she'd been frantically
ordered to do one job after another ever since
she'd arrived. The cooks and the entire staff were
in a frenzy, trying to get the elaborate buffet ready.

She made her way up the narrow stairs, through
a door, and into another world, one of laughter,
the murmur of genteel conversation, the sound of
music far down the hall.

She dumped the platter on the nearest available
surface, determined to somehow find Brent Hollis
and insist that he listen to what she had to say. But
how to find him in a crowd like this, in a house as
large as a New York museum, for heaven's sake?
And she didn't want to lay eyes on Jeremy or
Clarissa, either, which made matters much more
difficult.

She avoided the ballroom, looking into one
room after the other along the hall, ignoring a
brusque request to bring someone a napkin, as

well as another order from a liveried butler to make herself useful in the dining room.

Passing a room with a half-closed door, she caught a glimpse of candlelight, a huge fieldstone fireplace, and walls of books. She hesitated, and then jumped and cried out when a man's hand came down on her shoulder, shoving her into the room.

"You." Brent Hollis reached behind him and slammed the door.

Elizabeth whirled to face him, alarmed at the enraged look on the man's face, the agitated tremor in his voice.

"What are you doing here? How dare you show your face here, you—you scheming tart? You've been the ruination of my son, and my business as well, and now you're planning to cause still more trouble tonight, aren't you?" He was shaking, and Elizabeth could smell alcohol on his breath. She had no idea what he was raving about, but they were alone in the room, and terror gripped her as she remembered that this man's father had done his best to murder her grandmother.

"Jeremy may be taken in by you, but I'm not, Miss Porter." His voice was filled with contempt. "I know your kind, tempting a man with your beauty, laughing at him all the while."

He came close to her, his breathing uneven, his eyes narrowed, and Elizabeth moved away from him, putting a large oak desk between them.

"It's the devil's work that you should resemble her so strongly. You're nothing but a gold digger, spreading old gossip about me and some—some slut I once knew, dishonoring my dead wife's name. How much is it going to cost me to see the

last of you? How much to make you leave Bolton
and never come back? Name a sum, and by God,
I'll pay it."

Ever since she'd arrived, Elizabeth had heard
nothing but insults about her grandmother and accusations about herself. Hearing them now, from
this man, enraged her. "Don't you dare try to bribe
me, you wicked man." She lifted a heavy book
from the desk and hurled it with all her strength.
It missed him, and she was sorry. The stupid
maid's cap tipped forward and she ripped it from
her hair and flung it at him as well.

Brent Hollis stared at her in amazement. Elizabeth stormed toward him, and he actually backed
up, shocked by her fierceness.

"You—you pompous idiot," Elizabeth raged.
"How dare you call my grandmother a slut! Ann
Merrill loved you, she loved you until the very
day she died." Elizabeth's voice rang through the
room. "Why on earth she did, I'll never know, because you Hollis men have no honor, no loyalty."
Her hands on her hips, she confronted him. "I'll
have you know I spoke to your father yesterday."
She drew in a breath, aware that she mustn't be-
tray the old man's confidence, yet determined to
make Brent Hollis face the truth at last. "He admitted to me that on the day my grandmother disappeared, he did exactly what you've just done to
me. He offered her money to leave Bolton forever,
and she refused it. They argued, and all I can tell
you is that my grandmother didn't leave Bolton
willingly. Your father forced her to leave, and he
invented that ridiculous story about her running
off with Sam Turner." She snorted. "If you'd been

half the man Ann believed you were, you'd never have fallen for such—such awful crap!"

Brent Hollis's face had gone from red to pasty white. He lowered himself into a chair and sat there, staring at something invisible. At last he looked up at her, and Elizabeth could see him struggling, part of him wanting to believe her, part of him holding fast to his bitterness toward Ann, toward all women.

"I can't believe my father would be so cruel," he finally said in a strained voice. "I loved Ann, you see. I—" He swallowed, the admission almost more than he could bear to make. "I suppose I've always loved her, in spite of everything."

"Then you understand, Father, how I feel about Elizabeth." Jeremy's voice startled the other two as he emerged from the shadows near the door to the room.

When she turned and looked at him, Elizabeth had to admit grudgingly that Jeremy was incredibly handsome in his white tie and tails, his dark coloring and athletic body set off to perfection by the formal clothing. But her pain became unbearable when she thought of the reason for his elegant attire.

"Jeremy, how can you lie like this?" Her voice shook. "How can you stand here at—at your engagement party and pretend to have any real feelings for me?"

She wouldn't cry. She wouldn't give either of these men the satisfaction. But her heart felt as if it were shattering. "You know, even in my time it's considered despicable to make love to one woman and marry another." Her voice broke and she turned away.

His arms were around her before she realized he'd even crossed the room. She resisted, but he turned her around with ease and forced her to look up into his face.

"I've told Clarissa I won't marry her, Elizabeth. I agreed to this charade only because she begged me to go through with the ball so as not to embarrass her in front of the entire town. My father can attest to that fact. My engagement to Clarissa is over. She'll announce it in a few days. I love you, dearest one. It's you I want to marry."

She went very still in his arms. The words were like balm, soothing the raw pain in her soul and fanning the dying embers of hope in her heart. She looked into his face and knew that she wanted this man more than she'd wanted anything in her life. But she was also aware that there were things she hadn't told him, extraordinary things such as where she was really from.

How would he react?

She drew away a little. "Jeremy, I—I need to talk to you."

From somewhere behind them, Brent Hollis groaned. "That's it, then, Jeremy. If you marry this woman instead of Clarissa, the mill and all we stand for are doomed. We'll be bankrupt in six months."

They turned on him, both having forgotten that Brent was even in the room. "What do you mean, Mr. Hollis?" Elizabeth demanded.

"Just what I said." In a few words, Brent spelled out what Clarissa had threatened. "Darwell will be furious at Jeremy for jilting his daughter, and he'll make certain that no bank or other investor in town will loan us the money we require."

"Then we'll get it elsewhere, Father." Jeremy's arm was around Elizabeth's shoulders, holding her close to him, but his eyes were on his father and his voice was stern. "I heard what Elizabeth said a moment ago, about you and Ann Merrill. Surely you should know that a marriage should never be simply a matter of convenience, made for financial reasons."

Brent looked at his son, and his face seemed to crumble at the mention of Ann's name. "Can you tell me what became of her?" he asked Elizabeth.

The time had come to tell these two men not just about Ann, but also about herself, Elizabeth realized.

This wasn't the place, however. The Darwell mansion was filled with people, and it was a wonder they hadn't been interrupted already. "I will tell you, but not here," Elizabeth insisted.

"She's right, Father." Jeremy took Elizabeth's arm and motioned to the door. "Come, let's slip out the back way. I'll get our carriage and horses from the stable, and we'll all go home."

Their departure was accomplished easily, and soon the Darwell mansion, its windows ablaze with light, was far behind them. Jeremy clucked to the spirited team, and the carriage rolled quickly out of the village and up the winding road that led to the manor house at the top of the hill.

10

"**N**ow, Miss Porter, tell me what became of my Ann."

The three of them were seated in a spacious sitting room, Jeremy close beside Elizabeth on a small settee, Brent facing them in an armchair. A lamp on a lace-covered round table cast a pool of light, leaving the corners in shadows. The house was still, a welcome silence after the noise of the ball.

"I'll do my best to explain." With her hand clasped tightly in Jeremy's, Elizabeth began, telling them first of Ann's illness, of the love for Brent her grandmother had expressed with such difficulty. She told them of finding Ann's diary after her death and traveling to Bolton, and finally of visiting the chapel.

"Grandmother?" Brent interrupted, his brow furrowed. "You keep saying Ann was your grandmother, that she died a very old woman, but how can that be? She was younger than me by some years, and you're too old to be her granddaughter."

Elizabeth swallowed and took a deep breath. "I'll try to explain. It all happened when I visited your chapel. I rang the bell, and it acted as some sort of time portal. You see, I'm not from your time. I came here from 1939, forty years in the future. I'm twenty-six years old. I wasn't even born until 1913."

There was total, shocked silence, and then Brent slammed his hand down on the arm of his chair. "Lies!" he roared. He got to his feet, overturning his chair and waving a trembling finger a bare inch from Elizabeth's nose. "It's all lies, part of this cruel hoax you're playing on both Jeremy and me. You're not simply dishonest, madam." He bent over her, his whiskered face close to Elizabeth's. "You're insane," he hissed.

"Father. Enough!"

The stark warning in Jeremy's voice as he looped a protective arm around Elizabeth's shoulder was enough to stop Brent's tirade. But when Jeremy met Elizabeth's eyes, she could see by his expression that he, too, had his doubts about her claims.

Their attitude made her determined to convince them once and for all that she was telling the truth.

"Remember the day I arrived? How do you imagine I got into the chapel in the first place? It was locked from the outside, if you recall. And you must remember my clothes. You both stared at my suit and my shoes. Did you ever find my purse?" When neither of them answered, she looked around the room, searching for examples that might persuade them once and for all she was telling the truth. "In my time, we no longer rely on lamps like these for light. Each home has electricity, indoor plumbing, central heating." She picked up a pen. "We have portable typewriters to write upon, we ..." Her voice trailed off. Brent Hollis clearly didn't believe her, and even Jeremy looked skeptical.

Agitated, Elizabeth released Jeremy's hand and rose. "What in heaven's name would it take to make you believe me?" She directed the question to Brent.

She was determined to clear her grandmother's name but she also knew that if she were to marry Jeremy, there must be honesty and trust among the three of them. She couldn't come between father and son and be happy.

"Elizabeth, there's no need to prove anything to me." Jeremy was glowering at his father, but Brent ignored him.

"The diary. You said Ann kept a diary. I want to see it. And I once gave her a brooch, a small ivory and seed-pearl brooch."

Some part of her had known it would come to this.

"Very well, Mr. Hollis. If—if that's what it will take to convince you, I'll bring you the proof you need."

Elizabeth was out of the room and through the manor door before either man had a chance to react. The moon was bright, and holding her long skirts high, she raced for the path that led to the chapel.

Jeremy, my dearest love, will I ever see you again?

The manor door flew open and she heard Jeremy's frantic voice.

"Elizabeth, come back. Elizabeth, I love you . . ."

There has to be trust, there has to be honesty—

She started to cry and she stumbled, careening until she regained her balance, running as fast as she could with tears streaming down her cheeks, making the path difficult to see.

If Jeremy caught her, she'd never have the will to try again—

She could hear him, closer now, as she reached the chapel. The lock on the door was still broken. She fumbled for an instant and then shoved the door wide, blinded by the deeper darkness inside.

"Elizabeth, stop. For God's sake, stop."

I have to go, my love. I have to—

She stumbled toward the stairs to the bell tower, gasping, pain in her chest. She was halfway up when Jeremy burst through the door. He couldn't see her, and he paused for a moment, listening.

"Elizabeth . . . ?" His agitated voice rang through the chapel.

She scampered up the remaining stairs, shoving at the door, the sobs hurting her throat.

She heard Jeremy close behind her, taking the stairs in great leaps.

"Elizabeth, I beg you—" He was at the top and through the door, but her hands were already on the rope. She pulled with all her might, and as the sound of the bell echoed in her head, Jeremy seemed to waver and fade.

The last thing she saw was the face of the man she loved, his arms outstretched in frantic appeal, as the bell tolled again and again.

An impatient male voice was calling up the stairs. "Hey, lady. Lady? I been waitin' half an hour already. You wanna ride or you gonna stay here all night? Cause I'm leavin', can't spend any more time waitin' fer ya."

Trembling, Elizabeth brushed at the tears on her

cheeks. She released the bell rope, opened the tower door, and looked down.

In spite of herself, her heart sank.

She was back in 1939. The stairwell was filled with cobwebs, the air in the chapel dusty and dank. The taxi driver who'd brought her here from Bolton—how long ago?—was frowning up at her.

When she started down the stairs, holding her long skirt up to keep from stumbling, the driver stared up at her in open-mouthed astonishment, taking in her voluminous skirts, her petticoats, her high-laced boots.

"What the ... You playin' dress-up or somethin'?"

She'd been away weeks, and yet here, only hours had passed. She searched for an explanation that would sound logical.

"I—I found an old trunk in the manor house and tried on some things because—because my suit got ripped by thorns. I'll have to wear this back to the inn."

He eyed her suspiciously. "You're lucky I came lookin' fer you. There's somethin' downright spooky about this place. I don't like it one bit. Let's get outta here."

Elizabeth followed him through the chapel door into the fading sunlight. She dared a glance toward the manor house, where just a moment before ... But the neat hedges, the trim lawns, were gone. Thick foliage obscured all but the ruined chimneys, and wild grass covered the lawns. A sob tore at her throat.

Jeremy, my dearest love, will I ever see you again?

She had to believe she would. She had to, or she couldn't bear to live.

"This your purse? It was on the ground over there." The driver held out her cream leather bag, and Elizabeth took it. Inside was her return train ticket to New York.

The faster she got back there and found the diary and the brooch among the jewelry her grandmother had left her, the faster she could return to this chapel, and ring the bell, and . . . perhaps go home to Jeremy.

One week later, Elizabeth stood once again in front of the chapel and listened to the sound of the taxi driver's cab fading into the distance.

"Bloomin' nutcase," the driver had grumbled, dumping her at the top of the hill by the ruined manor. "I ain't comin' lookin' fer ya this time, neither. You can find yer own way back."

Her heart was beating as if it were about to leap out of her chest. She shifted the bag she carried from one hand to the other and made her way through the door.

Inside the chapel, nothing had changed. The air was thick with dust and mold, and the spiders had already replaced the webs she'd disturbed.

She put her bag on a dusty pew and undid the zipper closure on her fashionable short skirt, letting it slide down and off. She took off the matching jacket, unbuttoned her blouse, stepped out of her shoes, and reached into the bag.

She'd found the dress at a costumer's on Fifth Avenue. It was watered silk, a deep shade of blue. The high collar had bands of delicate ecru lace, as did the huge leg-o'-mutton sleeves and the tea-colored silk petticoat.

She smoothed the garment in place. It hugged

her waist and fell gracefully, covering her medium-heeled black pumps. She had no mirror, but she knew she looked both proper and attractive, dressed in the height of style for 1899. And— please let it happen—Jeremy would be the only other one to see the layers of wicked French lingerie and sheer hose she wore underneath this decorous exterior.

Her hands were shaking as she folded her suit and laid it on the seat of the pew. From the bag, she took a drawstring pouch containing Ann's seed-pearl brooch, as well as the rest of the valuable jewelry Elizabeth had inherited.

She planned to sell the jewelry and give Brent and Jeremy the money for their mill. They would be upset when they learned that Elizabeth also planned to become an active partner in the mill. There was a great deal to be done if working conditions were to improve for their female employees, and she was determined to make those changes.

She drew the pouch over her hand and hugged Ann's diary and another thick volume to her silk bosom.

This simply had to work, because she'd burned all her bridges. She'd quit her job. She'd contacted Ann's lawyers and instructed them to sell the brownstone and donate the money to a home for indigent women. She'd signed all her money, which would be useless in 1899, over to an orphanage, and given her clothes to a women's shelter. All she had left in the world was in her hands.

Her stomach in knots, she climbed the stairs to the bell tower. She put her free hand on the rope, and with a heart-filled, whispered prayer, she closed her eyes tight and pulled.

The pealing of the bell awakened Jeremy, and for a moment, he thought perhaps he was dreaming. He'd fallen asleep in one of the pews, as he'd done more than once in the weeks since Elizabeth had disappeared.

He was heartsick, utterly devastated at losing her. He'd raged at his father, blaming him for Elizabeth's leaving.

Brent had finally wept and begged Jeremy's forgiveness, confiding in his son for the first time, telling him the entire story of his love for Ann Merrill and his own irreconcilable grief at losing her. A bond formed between the two men, and for the first time in his life, Jeremy felt he was beginning to know and like the man who was his father.

It didn't assuage his terrible longing for Elizabeth, however. He'd tried, again and again, to follow her by ringing the infernal bell himself, but nothing had happened.

Now, he got quickly to his feet and hurried to the stairs, afraid even to hope. He climbed them in three long leaps, and the door at the top opened just as he reached for the handle.

"Jeremy!" Elizabeth cried his name and threw herself into his arms, almost sending them both tumbling back down the narrow stairs.

"Elizabeth. Elizabeth, my darling." He wrapped her in his arms and half-carried her down, afraid to relinquish his hold for even a moment lest she disappear again. When they were safe at the bottom of the stairs, he kissed her, claiming her mouth with savage hunger. The books she held slipped to the floor, and she wound her arms around his neck, the pouch dangling from her wrist, and hung on until they were both half-drunk with kisses.

"I'm never allowing you out of my sight again," he growled at last, looking down into her magnificent brown eyes. "I forbid you to go anywhere near that bell tower. I'm having this damnable chapel demolished, and that bell melted down."

"Surely we could make better use of it than that, Jeremy?"

He gazed at her lovely face and knew she was right. The chapel had been built expressly for a wedding, and by God, there'd be one, as soon as it was possible to get a minister. Unless, of course, she needed a dress and all that folderol.

Elizabeth bent over and picked up Ann's diary and the other book. She removed the pouch from her wrist and handed it to him. "I brought this to help you and your father with the mill. The brooch is in there, and here is the diary." She gave it to him. "But this is just for you."

He took the book from her, opened it to the title page, and was instantly reminded of that first moonlit night he'd walked and talked with her.

"*The Collected Works of Sir Arthur Conan Doyle*, born 1859, died 1930."

"It's time you read *The Hound of the Baskervilles*, Jeremy."

Three weeks later, the two lovers were wed in the chapel Brent had built for Ann so many years before. The bell tolled and tolled again, its pure, sweet song ringing out over the lake and the village.

Perhaps it was only the shimmer of joyful tears in Elizabeth's eyes that made her think her grandmother was standing at Brent's side in the front pew, both of them smiling as she and Jeremy made their way down the aisle in these first moments of their life together as husband and wife.

Perhaps it was only the echo of the bells that sounded like Ann's voice, whispering in her ear.

"Forever, Elizabeth," it said like a benediction. "True love is always forever."

Bobby Hutchinson

BOBBY HUTCHINSON says she's never really sure what day it is—or what year, for that matter, so writing time-travel stories makes perfect sense to her. Born in the Rocky Mountains of British Columbia, she lives with her husband, Alan, in Winfield, B.C., on ten acres of land overlooking a lake. Their six children are grown, and Bobby and Alan have six grandchildren. Bobby believes that human nature is constant, transcending time, and that love is eternal. She's certain that in the not-too-distant future, taking a trip back to 1899 to find out what really happened to Grandma and the man she loved and lost will be quite feasible. And if, like Elizabeth, the traveler falls in love in that other time—well, any romantic knows that where there's a will, there's a way.

Always Paradise

Evelyn Rogers

1

"Painkiller not working this afternoon?"

Stirred from her reverie, Beth Dixon glanced up at the handsome, fiftyish gentleman she'd seen dancing nightly in the cruise ship lounge. Usually suit-clad, he looked equally at home in shorts and a knit shirt here on the stretch of Caribbean beach.

And, she thought without pleasure, much too eager to talk.

She sat straight in her chair, which she'd dragged into the shade of a palm tree, away from the water and the crowd of her fellow passengers. "I'm sorry," she said, "I didn't catch what you said."

The man's kindly blue eyes twinkled as he stared at the plastic glass in her hand. "The Painkiller there. Doesn't seem to be doing much to take the worry lines from your brow. Too young to sit off by yourself like this and not get in on the

187

fun." He gestured with his matching drink toward the revelers along the shore.

Beth's gaze followed his gesture to the steel drum trio pounding out a calypso tune a few yards from the surf. A dozen couples swayed to the beat, and a smaller group of brave souls lined up near the water's edge for the upcoming limbo contest.

In this isolated bend of land known as Smuggler's Cove, at the western end of the island of Tortola, capital of the British Virgin Islands, the sand was white, the water turquoise, the balmy air sweet with scents of salt and sea and a thousand brilliant flowers. A low-hanging sun sparkled on the waves and cast a golden glow. Remembering that back in ice-bound New York the temperature was ten degrees, Beth wished she could be caught up in Tortola's charm.

At least, she thought with a sigh, she ought to be affected by the island's famous concoction. Rum and a mixture of tropical juices, the Painkiller came from Pusser's Outpost in Road Town, the heart of Tortola. Might as well be plain pineapple juice, as far as she was concerned.

"Would you care for a turn around the sand?" the gentleman asked with a gallant bow.

"Oh, no," she said hastily. "I'd rather watch."

He grinned as if they were in a conspiracy. "A wise decision. Do you mind if I join you?" Before she could respond, he dragged a folding chair beside hers and settled his angular body comfortably.

"Roland Boldt's the name. Cruise line provides my passage in exchange for squiring the single ladies around the dance floor, but I guess you already figured that out, smart-looking young woman like yourself." He shook his head. "No way the deal includes bending these old bones under a limbo pole."

He stretched his legs out in front of him, his white shorts ending at a pair of knobby knees, and revealing his thin calves thick with gray hairs. His sockless feet were thrust into a pair of leather deck shoes, and his pewter hair, usually carefully combed, was ruffled by the wind coming off the water. But as he sipped the Painkiller, he didn't seem to notice.

Beth glanced at her own getup, which a New York salesclerk has assured her would be perfect for a winter week in the Caribbean—a fuchsia halter, a floral sarong brushing against her thighs, thong sandals, even an ankle bracelet. Her auburn hair was bound at her nape by a matching floral scarf, and she wore a pair of very uncharacteristic parrot earrings that dangled almost to her shoulders. More comfortable in a business suit, she felt like a refugee from an old Dorothy Lamour movie. She'd refused to wear so much as the bracelet until this shore excursion came along.

"Island apparel, please," the brochure had read, and this was as close as she could get. She wouldn't even be here except that when her parents had given her the vacation as a combination Christmas and birthday present, she promised to participate in every festivity and not sit on deck with a lawbook in her hand.

She hadn't promised to enjoy anything, however, and it was a good thing, since she kept remembering the work piling up on her desk, work that needed to be done before the end of February.

She sipped the Painkiller and tried in vain to recall the particulars of a few accounts. Maybe the rum was working just a little bit after all.

Sighing, Beth traced the outline of a flower on her skirt. Details of work might blur, but her heart knew that a dozen Painkillers couldn't erase the loneliness and emptiness Michael's death had left in her life. Nor was a change in her surroundings sufficient to raise her spirits, no matter what her parents had hoped.

She saw the truth clearly now, although over the past two years she'd fooled herself into thinking her job would sufficiently fill her days. Funny how sometimes it was necessary to get away from something to put it in perspective.

"New Yorker," her persistent companion continued, "getting close to thirty, unmarried, recently divorced, is my guess. A professional of some kind, lawyer maybe."

Despite herself, Beth dragged her thoughts from the old sorrow and truly heard what Roland Boldt said.

"Could be in stocks," he continued with indefatigable cheer, "but you don't have that furtive, nervous look that comes with trading on the Big Board."

She looked at him in surprise. A lock of hair, pulled free by a gust of wind, brushed against her cheek. "How did you know?"

"My business. Doesn't take Sherlock Holmes to figure you out, my dear. Your accent, the way you isolate yourself, the books you carry on deck. Age was the toughie. Sometimes you look as old as the ocean—no insult intended, just meaning the solemn cast to your eye—and sometimes I'd swear you were no more than a girl. A well-formed girl, you understand," he added, his eyes again twinkling as he glanced quickly at her halter. "Again, no insult intended, Miss—"

"Dixon. Elizabeth, please," she said, then amended it to the preferred "Beth." She hesitated a moment. "I'm not offended. And you're right about several points." She leaned back in the chair, bemused to find herself willing to speak. "I plead guilty to the New York lawyer charge. Worse, I'm also an accountant."

"My goodness, sounds like a tax attorney."

"Afraid so," she said. "And I just celebrated my thirtieth birthday yesterday."

"Alone? A pretty woman like you? Always said New Yorkers were crazy. Now I'm sure of it. From South Carolina, myself. Lots of Southern charm. It's a commodity upon which I trade, like your knowing the law, only let me assure you that I enjoy people. And I haven't enjoyed seeing you always alone."

She opened her mouth to defend herself, but he hurried on. "We've been on this cruise for five days now, and you haven't struck up a conversation with anyone for more than a few minutes. I know. I've been watching."

She dug the heels of her sandals into the soft sand. "I just don't have much to say."

"What about the divorce part? Was I right about that?"

She looked toward the waves dying in the curve of beach behind the limbo pole. "I've never been married."

"Don't mean to pry." He smiled guiltily. "At least not so that it hurts."

"I'm not searching for a man, if that's what you're wondering about. I was engaged once, and that was enough."

"What happened?"

Glancing at her interrogator, she saw nothing but friendly interest in his eyes. "My fiancé was killed a week before the wedding." Her voice was flat, as it always was on the rare occasions when she found herself recounting the past. "A stray bullet hit him during a robbery attempt. Michael was just passing by," she added, more to herself than to Boldt.

"Damned sorry to hear it. How long ago?"

"Two years." And three months and six days. But she'd already revealed more than she'd intended. He'd be thinking she wanted sympathy and understanding . . . maybe a further sharing of confidences. She didn't let anyone get close to her. Not anymore.

She stood. "If you'll excuse me, I think I'll go for a walk before the bus takes us back to the dock."

He pulled himself upright beside her. "Sure you don't want to stick around for the limbo contest? You don't have to participate to get a laugh out of the shenanigans. Ah, I can see you disagree. Well, never fear. These cruise people are determined souls when it comes to making us have a good time. Before long they'll come up with some activity that will get you involved. Be on your guard."

Silently she doubted that anyone could dream up anything that would pull her out of the past. Not if a week sailing in paradise—the cruise line's advertised claim—couldn't do the trick.

"Don't wander far," Boldt said with a worried nod. "Last tender leaves at nine, and that's not more'n a couple of hours away. Ship sails right after. I've seen crew members and passengers alike have to get themselves to the next port when they stayed ashore too long."

Beth glanced around at the sand and sun and swaying palms, at all the couples locked in each other's arms, their occasional laughter echoing above the reggae resonance of the steel drums. Never had she felt more alone.

"Don't worry," she said with a poor attempt at a smile. "I'm very good at keeping track of the time. I'll be the first one in line to leave."

Her voice broke, and setting her drink on the sand, she turned from him to strap on her fanny pack. Were those really tears burning her eyes? Impossible. She hadn't cried in a long while.

It was this cursed island and its even more cursed drink. She picked up the plastic glass once again and glanced at the clipper ship stenciled on the side. This was her second Painkiller—or was it her third? She never drank more than an occasional glass of wine. What had gotten into her to accept the beverages a very hospitable waiter kept placing in her hand? Goodness, she was positively light-headed as she made her way past the waiting buses and onto the dirt lane that led back to Road Town.

Concentrating on putting one foot in front of the other, she followed the flat surface for a dozen yards, then on impulse took a rutted path on the left that meandered through a grassy hillside. The grass soon gave way to low shrubs, then to thick, flowering bushes that rose like rough green walls on either side of her, blocking out the world.

She liked the feeling of seclusion the shrubbery

provided. Some of the plants—oleander, jacaranda, lantana—she could identify, gardening being one of the few activities she enjoyed outside of work. Most of the plants, however, were strange, exotic wonders, and she breathed in their sweet, fecund scent. From the taste of coconut, orange, and pineapple on her tongue to the heat of rum in her blood and the heady floral fragrances tickling her nose, she felt as far from winter-plagued Manhattan as it was possible to be.

She walked with a fair degree of steadiness, stepping carefully lest the unfamiliar sandals catch on unseen roots. Then she paused to glance back down the hill and saw an expanse of tropical beauty ending in white sand and azure water.

Never one to wander heedlessly into the unknown—not even a free winter vacation—Beth had researched the history of the Caribbean before flying down to Fort Lauderdale for the cruise ship's departure. She knew that Columbus had discovered these islands on his second voyage. She knew the names of pirates who had eventually followed in his path, knew they were not romantic figures but outlaws who raped and plundered and at the slightest provocation fell on their own kind.

She did not excuse those who broke the law, especially when it was at the expense of innocent people.

Michael's smiling Irish face suddenly flashed before her mind, and a small cry lodged in her throat. Everything reminded her of him, even thoughts of buccaneers who'd been dead three hundred years.

What a wonderful man Michael Flaherty had

been. She'd known him three years, working beside him in the law firm right after she'd passed the bar exam. Going against all the precepts of what a lawyer should be, he'd laughed easily, joked at unexpected times, treated her like a queen when he wasn't teasing her about her proclivity for somberness. Slowly, sweetly she'd fallen in love, and on the third anniversary of their meeting she'd agreed to become his wife.

She hadn't witnessed the tragedy that took him from her six months later, but her inventive mind had replayed it a thousand times, the gunshots echoing repeatedly in her nightmares. Not so often now, yet on unexpected nights they returned, a haunting reminder of what she had lost. Even the beat of the steel drums, drifting up the hill on the ocean breeze, carried his name.

Michael . . . Michael . . .

A giggle from the shrubbery behind her broke into her thoughts. Her heart quickening, she turned and stared through the thick leaves. A rustle, another giggle, and a pair of white-rimmed black eyes stared back.

A child, Beth thought with a sigh, and her anxiety eased. "It's awfully lonely out here," she said. "I wish I had someone to talk to."

The eyes disappeared, and she felt a sharp disappointment. She turned to retrace her steps and saw a boy no older than ten blocking her path. His skin and hair as dark as his eyes, his only clothing ragged, baggy cut-off jeans, he grinned up at her as if he hadn't a care in the world.

"Is the lady lost?" he asked in a rhythmic singsong voice. "Joseph show her the way back to the ship for only five dollar. Special deal."

Smiling down at the skinny child, Beth realized she could count his ribs. "Goodness, that sounds like a bargain. The only trouble is," she said, purposefully taunting him, "the lady already knows the way. A bus is waiting for me down at Smuggler's Cove."

The boy's face twisted in thought. His smile returned. "Joseph know a new way to get to the cove. Many pretty flowers. Does the lady like flowers?"

"Oh, very much." Almost as much as she liked children. She and Michael had planned to have four.

She tugged at the zipper of her fanny pack. The boy watched. She knew he would expect her to bargain. "Now that I think of it, five dollars is a great deal of money."

He eyed the empty plastic glass in her hand, particularly the replica of the sailing ship on the side.

"I'll tell you what," Beth said. "I'll give you this glass and a dollar. That's all any island guide should ask for."

The boy took the glass and the proffered bill before she could change her mind. "Follow me," he said with authority. Stuffing the bill into his pocket and gripping the glass in one hand, he skipped around her and headed higher up the hill.

She glanced back down the trail. "I must return very soon," she said worriedly, not entirely relaxed by the effects of rum and Joseph's charm.

"The lady is not to worry."

He spoke with an innocent confidence, and strangely, she believed him. Practical, workaholic, New York-smart Beth trusted this island boy.

He led her higher, through tangled brush that almost obscured the path, coming to a halt in a clearing on the far side of the hill. A wide grin split his face, his teeth starkly white against the darkness of his skin. "I show you my treasure."

He looked so proud, so young, she wanted to take him in her arms. Instead, she glanced at her watch. "I must be back to the cove in less than an hour."

"The lady is not to worry." He stepped away from the clearing and pushed aside a thick stand of flowering shrimp plants. Then he knelt before a pile of flat, plate-sized stones and moved them one by one until a burlap bundle was exposed. He folded back the corners of the material.

The first thing he pulled out was the stiffened, flat carcass of a long-dead frog. Then came a few age-encrusted coins that Beth could see were worthless, and at last a bracelet of poptops from aluminum cans. At each disclosure, she murmured appreciative compliments and tried not to look at her watch.

"The best is last," he announced just when she was about to rise for a quick departure.

"I really must—"

A chill breeze ruffled the surrounding bushes, sending a shower of pink blossoms to her feet. She paused and shivered for the first time since she'd left New York. The boy's hand lifted. A curious piece of tarnished metal covered his palm.

"This comes from a special place, high on the island."

Beth thought over the route of her noontime tour of Tortola. "Near Skyworld Restaurant?"

The boy nodded solemnly. "Where the cars stay. I find it when the men dig."

"Dig? Oh, you mean when they built the parking lot."

Joseph rubbed at the metal until a patch of silver gleamed in the sunlight. "It protects my secret treasure. No bad guys steal from Joseph."

Beth's heart twisted at the mixture of island lilt and American slang. How much was lost to her, she thought as she stared at the boy's youthful face. For the second time in an hour tears burned her eyes, and she knew that after two years, three months, and six days of masking her feelings, an island paradise, a couple of drinks, and a friendly child were destroying all her hard work.

"Why does the lady cry?"

Kneeling beside him, Beth brushed the tears away. "Because the lady must say good-bye to a very nice young gentleman and sail back to her home in New York."

"Do bad guys live in New York?"

His innocence was like a fist squeezing her heart. "Oh, yes," she said, "bad guys with guns—"

Her voice caught, all her self-possession dissolving in a wave of bitterness and desolation. "Oh, Michael," she whispered and without warning crumbled in a flood of tears. For more than two years she'd held these tears at bay, but she had no defense against them now. Her body wracking with sobs, she hugged herself as if she could hold in the misery until after her grief was spent.

"The lady—"

She barely heard the boy.

"Joseph!" a woman's voice called, its shrillness echoing over the hill.

"Mama," the boy said. "I must go." He stood and hitched the cut-off jeans higher on his bony hips.

But Beth's breakdown was complete, and she was helpless to stop the tears.

Joseph shuffled nervously. "Here," he said, placing the metal beside her on the ground. "The lady must not cry."

Through blurred eyes, she saw his offering and struggled for control. "I can't . . . accept this," she said brokenly.

Joseph shrugged his thin shoulders. "There are other pieces of treasure at the top of the hill."

Again came the call of his name. "Always I forget the time." Hastily he tossed the rocks onto the burlap.

Picking up the silver piece, Beth stumbled to her feet. "But the trail," she said.

"The lady is not to worry. The path leads to the beach."

"Joseph!" There were anger and anxiety in the mother's loud cry. Without another word the boy disappeared into the foliage, leaving Beth to stare after him.

Her gaze fell to the uneven surface of the metal burning against her palm. What a fool she had made of herself, falling victim to a drunken crying jag. And in front of an innocent child. Pulling a tissue from her pouch, she wiped at her eyes and blew her nose.

With a sigh, she moved the rocks Joseph had tossed so carelessly in his haste to leave. She folded the burlap around the frog carcass and the other valuables, adding the abandoned plastic glass and a five-dollar bill. But for some reason she was unable to return the silver. It had been a gift. She could not give it back.

As an afterthought, she threw in her watch. Inexpensive, it would help him remember the passage of time. And perhaps its absence would enable her to forget it.

When the cache was hidden once again, she hurried down the hill along the overgrown path, ignoring the pull of branches and the expanse of flowers, concentrating on the sea beckoning from below. Just as he'd promised, within minutes she stood at the edge of a pristine beach and stared in relief at the path of golden sunlight reflected on the water twenty yards away.

From around the bend to her left came the sounds of the steel drums, thrumming the rhythms of the limbo, in the background a round of applause. There was plenty of time to catch the last bus . . . time to catch the last tender . . . time to board the ship and sail for Florida and then home.

Mostly she heard the sound of the surf as it broke on the shore. Again and again. Eternal, beckoning, hypnotic.

She untied her scarf and let her hair blow free in the breeze. A gust of wind tugged the scarf from her hand and sent it tumbling across the sand. She watched as it came to rest at the water's edge. A wave dampened the silk, another pulled it into the undertow, and within seconds it was gone. Perhaps she should go the way of the scarf, stride into the ocean and let the waves decide her fate, since she seemed unable to do so.

A strong swimmer, she could get far from land and then simply quit fighting to survive. The idea held much appeal. Work, she saw clearly now, was no substitute for a real life. And she was tired . . . so tired.

Who would miss her? To her parents, she was a worry; a younger daughter and two grandchildren were their joy. To her law firm, she was a dependable worker who could always be counted on to handle the tedious tasks. To her friends . . .

She thought sadly that she had allowed her friendships to lapse. And there was no man in her life. Not after Michael.

What an ugly thing self-pity was. Teardrops fell onto the metal she held tightly in her hand, surprising her because she'd thought she had no more tears to shed. Absentmindedly she rubbed at the surface, enlarging the shining patch of metal Joseph had exposed. A design emerged, the outline of a turreted castle etched into the antique silver. Having first appeared to be scrap metal, it was really some sort of medallion.

She stared in fascination at the simple outline, then held the medallion to her chest just as the wind increased, the gusts harder than any she'd experienced on the cruise, dragging in an unexpected cloud to cover the setting sun and darken the sky. Sand stung her cheeks, burned her eyes, and all around her the palms thrashed wildly as day became night. It all happened with such fierce suddenness that for the first time in a long, long while, she was afraid.

This was foolish, she told herself. It was only wind.

Her attempt to move forward toward the revelers around the bend proved futile against nature's onslaught. The gale gathered strength, threatening to push her back into the brush. She dropped to her knees and huddled close to the ground, making as small a target as possible as the windstorm wrapped her in its power. The deafening roar made thought impossible, and she was captured by the other-worldliness of the moment. Even the ground beneath her seemed to sway.

She thought the storm would last forever, but then the wind died just as suddenly as it had arisen, taking with it the clouds. All was quiet. No sound of music, no laughter, not even a rustle of leaves in the shrubbery at her back. Just the whisper of water at eventide, her uneven breathing, the dizzying residues of grief, and an overdose of rum.

"*Alto!*" a man's voice shouted, and the momentary peace was shattered by an explosion.

Beth's eyes flew open. A man stood at the water's edge, waves lapping at his calf-high boots. He held a pistol in each hand. To his left, halfway up the beach, an unmoving body sprawled stomach down on blood-stained sand.

"Bastard, ye've killed me mate!" a second voice shouted above the echoes of the explosion. Beth stared in horror as a man wielding a knife appeared as if from nowhere and launched himself at the man with the guns.

A pistol lifted, fired, and the force of the shot propelled the assailant backwards. He fell, spasmed once, then lay still.

Beth's whole being vibrated with the force of the gunshots, and she stumbled to her feet, her thoughts shattered by the sight of falling bodies in the midst of an echoing roar, the scene both a distortion and a re-creation of her nightmares.

"Michael!" she screamed, and the name soared

above the spectacle. Here was the violent death she'd always imagined, except that now it was all too real. She couldn't think, couldn't reason away the horror of the scene as she stared at the body closest to her, twisted in death. For a moment he became Michael, his death a fresh knife wound in her heart.

Her eyes shifted from the sand to the man at the water's edge . . . to the black boots and the tight black pants that encased his muscular thighs and narrow hips, to the full-sleeved white shirt unbuttoned halfway to his waist. His suntanned skin was darkened further by his curly chest hair. She noticed his sinewed neck, the dark-brown hair falling to his shoulders, and his strong features. Her gaze settled finally on the deep-set brown eyes staring back at her.

The eyes of a murderer. She shrank from them. He stepped toward her. She screamed and dropped the medallion. Without thinking, she turned and ran back into the brush, hearing the thud of his boots as he bounded after her.

2

Caramba, Antonio thought as he pushed his way into the shrubbery. This woman could run. But, *en verdad*, not quickly enough to evade capture. Much depended upon his success in the chase. She would not escape.

Thorny limbs pulled at his shirt, and he saw they grazed her bare skin, but she did not slow her step, not until she stumbled into an unexpected clearing and fell to her knees.

He was upon her in an instant, clamping his hand about her wrist and jerking her to her feet.

"*Bastante*," he ordered. Enough. She glared up at him, defiance in her eyes as she struggled to breathe.

Antonio stared in surprise at his prisoner— Anne Bonny, Calico Jack Rackam's woman. On the beach she had been an unforeseen element in an already complicated circumstance. In this island wilderness he saw that she was also the beauty she was reputed to be. Her untamed hair was the color of a Spanish sunrise, her skin like polished ivory—except for the faint scratches from the brush. Her wide brown eyes revealed a soul both terrified and rebellious. A creature of the wild, but one, alas, who had allied herself with the devil.

He could snap her in two, as he would a twig, but he had other, more rewarding uses for her.

Beth read the triumph in his eyes. She felt his breath on her cheek, felt her halter brush against his white linen shirt as he bound her close to his side. *Killer* thrummed in her mind, and she trembled at the power of his masculinity and at the madness of this moment.

She had never been so afraid in all her life. Closing her eyes, she struggled for air and tried to make some sense of what was happening. Her head reeled with unwanted images . . . the gunshots . . . the bodies . . . the chase.

Hallucinations? They must be, yet the firm hand on her wrist and the heavy silver ring that cut into her skin were all too real. So was his raspy breathing. What was happening to her? What had she done by wandering to a deserted stretch of beach?

They'll come up with some kind of activity that will get you involved.

Roland Boldt's voice echoed in her mind as clearly as if he were standing beside her.

Be on your guard, he had warned.

In that instant sanity returned. Disgust replaced the horror that had driven her into the jungle— disgust for both herself and the cruise staff responsible for this charade. A lethal mix of alcohol and depression had taken control of her back on the beach and made her think of Michael. It wasn't his body that had fallen. In truth, no one had died. The gunshots she'd thought part of her nightmare were fake.

And her captor? She opened her eyes to stare at his bristled, stony face. A younger, more virile version of Boldt, hired to entertain the lonely single women. An actor. Nothing else figured. She shoved him away, and he lost his grip on her wrist.

In the dappled late-afternoon light his eyes raked over her. He took in her gaudy, meager apparel, the adornments unlike any he had ever seen, including the strange pouch she wore at her waist. Mostly he saw the woman who wore them without shame. She was a beauty to inflame the most passive of men, and he was far from passive. But he was civilized, he reminded himself, a descendant of noblemen who did not violate the women under their control. Even a woman who had played a part in his brother's disappearance.

But he could not look away. *"Madre de Dios,"* he said. *"Venga aquí."*

"I will not come there," she responded, her voice shaky. "I must say, you enjoy playing your role."

He looked at her in puzzlement. A man who traveled the world, he spoke a half-dozen languages, including English, but he understood only some of what she said. "My role?" he asked.

"Look," she said, "you've earned your money. Now I must return to the beach."

What a woman. Were others of her crew waiting to fall upon a second member of the Alvarez family? Antonio had slain two of the *bastardos.* He'd slay more men to discover the truth of his brother Rodrigo's fate.

He let her lead the way along the path down which he'd pursued her moments before, keeping her within easy reach, holding back the edge of anger she aroused.

Beth did not pause until she was once again on the stretch of sand where the make-believe shooting had taken place. She was surprised to see the two members of the supporting cast still sprawled where they'd fallen. Calmer now, she inspected them and saw they were both clad in bright, rough pirate costumes. All part of the show, she thought. She should have heeded Boldt's warning and been on her guard.

She paused beside one of the bodies. "You can get up now."

The man, lying face down, did not stir. She marveled at the realistic color of the stage blood seeping from beneath him.

She shrugged. If he liked eating sand, that was

his concern. She glanced at the other body, as still as the first, and wondered how much they were getting paid. Finally she looked back at the sole survivor of the scene. Goodness, his skin was a glorious golden color. Must use a tanning lamp on a regular basis, she decided. No one could naturally look that good.

Despite his appearance, she couldn't forget he'd frightened her into a state of hysteria, and all in the name of entertainment.

"Look, buddy, cut the crap," she said, hoping her bluntness would put an end to this ridiculous episode.

"You speak boldly, *mujer*. I would sooner cut your throat."

Definitely an actor, Beth decided. No one else could have that deeply modulated voice. Rather like Ricardo Montalban. No, she amended, Edward James Olmos was closer to it.

And those eyes. The contempt they mirrored seemed almost real.

She looked at one body and then the other. "Okay, Captain Kidd and Blackbeard, you can get up now."

Antonio laughed sharply and without humor. "The captain's tarred body hung for months from a London gibbet, the victim of English justice."

Beth looked at him in surprise.

"And," he added, "Blackbeard's head swung from the bowsprit of his conqueror's sloop."

He took a step closer to her, and another, moving with a powerful grace until he was within arm's reach. " 'Tis a wonder men still seek the sweet trade with such examples before them."

She waved a hand in exasperation. "All right,

you've done your homework. Tell the guys they can get up now. I've got a bus to catch."

She turned from him. An iron hand clamped her wrist and brought her to a halt.

"You've got to quit doing that," she said over her shoulder, but instead of easing his hold, he pulled her closer. Beth hadn't been in such intimate contact with a man in a long time, and never one quite so . . . so commanding. He wasn't all that tall, at least four inches short of six feet, nor even spectacularly built, but the hunks who paraded their muscles on the movie screen could take lessons from him in raw masculinity.

He wore no cologne or aftershave. Just the natural scent of sand, sea, and sweat, not so strong as to be offensive. On the contrary. And then there was his coppery skin tone. Obviously he hadn't read about the dangers of skin cancer.

She had never liked long hair on a man, but in his case, it seemed to suit him. He was quite an actor to have made her think him a murderer. And yet, she decided, there was something about him that hinted of barely restrained violence.

None of his obvious attributes, however, excused his mishandling. "You're hurting me," she said, leveling him with her best courtroom stare.

What a woman, he thought, to stall him with talk. He needed to focus on his mission— retrieving the treasure that would bring the people of his land the prosperity they once knew . . . *la medalla* that would return hope to his father's heart. And his missing brother. This woman held the secret to his whereabouts . . . to whether he still lived. Antonio tightened his grip.

Fear flickered back to life in Beth, replacing her

irritation. "I said you're hurting me," she repeated, more forcefully this time. "The cruise line will not be pleased."

"Where is your lover? I will know the truth."

Beth's breath caught. He spoke to her in such harsh tones and his fingers cut so deeply into her wrist that she began to doubt her assessment of what was going on. But if that were the case . . .

Unable to allow the thought to continue, she felt an impatience that was close to panic. The sun was practically touching the far horizon. She had probably missed the bus, damn it. She couldn't miss the last tender going out to the ship or else she'd have to find her own way back to Florida.

"I know your problem," she snapped. "You've watched too many reruns of 'Fantasy Island' on late-night TV. But Ricardo Montalban would never treat a woman like this."

"Ricardo Montalban? Is this another of your men?"

Beth abandoned all attempt at conversation. She had to escape. With her free hand she loosened the catch on the fanny pack, smiling sweetly to distract him. When she felt his hand loosen, she flung the pouch in his face and jerked free. She bounded toward the bend, calling out a frantic "Help!" as she ran.

He caught her in a flying tackle that would have done credit to a football lineman, landing beside her on the warm sand, which for once didn't feel particularly soft to her.

"Oof!" she said, tasting grit. She fought to get away but succeeded only in turning on her back, where she could get a better—and unwelcome—

look at her attacker with his thick brown hair, chiseled features, and challenging eyes.

He grasped her wrists and held them tight on either side of her head. She squirmed. It took only one of his powerful legs to pin both of hers in place. She felt the scratch of wool against her bare thighs and the cool slickness of a leather boot resting across her calves.

She twisted beneath him, her skin grinding against the warm sand, her fingers curled clawlike. But her attempts to escape resulted in frustration and a terrifyingly familiar look of triumph in his eyes.

As she ceased her struggles, he eased back a fraction and stared down at her sarong. To her shame, it had fallen open to reveal her pink bikini panties.

Her temper flared, for a moment stronger than her terror. "You hurt me, buster, and I swear your head will hang like Blackbeard's. What's more," she added, "I'll sue you for everything you own."

"Sue?"

"Don't play dumb. You're fooling with a New York attorney here. Unless you let me go this instant, I'll drag you before a judge and take you for all you're worth."

"I am sad to say my family's fortune is not what it once was. As you must know. Allow me to introduce myself. Don Antonio Estebanillo de Alvarez, *a su servicio*."

He saw no sign the name meant anything to her.

"A Spanish don, are you?" she said. "I should have guessed. Just don't tell me what kind of service you have in mind. I'm interested only in getting back to the ship."

Ignoring everything she said, he bent his head, his lips inches from hers. "And the *señorita* is called ... ?" he asked softly.

Beth swallowed. "Elizabeth Dixon."

He'd been taunting her, holding back his wrath, but her lie, even though he had expected it, enraged him. He bounded to his feet, dragging her up after him.

Beth's head swam and her legs scarcely held her weight as she struggled to stand. The contempt in his eyes became a force she could not deal with, and she stared past him. An icy chill raced through her. Was it possible that the two men on the beach would never rise again?

Much too possible. No living men, she realized, could lie so twisted and still. She stared in horror at her captor. "You really killed them."

"Before they could drive their cutlasses through my gullet. An act it is clear you would have preferred."

"What's going on?" she said, scarcely above a whisper. "Who are you?"

"The rightful owner of the treasure your lover has stolen. Did he kill my brother as well? It is what my father and I have been told."

"My lover?" Beth asked. She seemed to have wandered into some kind of time warp in which nothing made any sense.

"*Señor* Rackam," Antonio said contemptuously. "Known as Calico Jack."

Beth clamped a hand over her mouth to keep from crying out. Rackam was one of the pirates she'd read about, the last to sail the Caribbean, a lusty, bloodthirsty buccaneer who terrorized the seas. He'd been named for the calico clothes he favored. Equally famous was the woman who plundered alongside him—Anne Bonny, a redhead like herself, outspoken and daring for her time.

Could this brute possibly think she was Rackam's woman? The pirate and Bonny had been dead for almost three hundred years.

Fighting against panic, Beth stared back up the hill where she had left the island boy, then toward the bend in the coast. Only a short while ago, nearly a hundred people had been dancing and drinking and laughing in the nearby cove.

Or was the time so short? She had no idea. Desperation seized her. She felt disoriented, fearful, doubtful she even knew her real name. Surely this self-proclaimed don was an apparition, as were the bodies on the beach.

She wanted to flee. But where could she run? Would other terrors await her wherever she went?

"They were dancing," she said, looking back at her captor, praying he could see the desperate innocence in her eyes. "Over there in Smuggler's Cove."

"*Quién?*"

"The others from the ship."

Once again he took Beth's wrist and led her across the sand. He followed the line of grass and palm trees that marked land's end, rounded the curve of beach, and stopped at the edge of the cove.

A very empty cove. Beth stared in despair. Not so much as a single plastic glass remained as evidence of the festivities she had witnessed two hours ago. A jungle of underbrush bordered the curved expanse of beach, the sand wind-rippled in rows all the way to the water.

No foot had trod this beach in days, perhaps weeks or months, and there was no sign of the road where the buses had parked. Yet even in the waning daylight the rest of the scenery seemed right. Perhaps it was just her muddled mind, but she thought she could spot the palm tree under which she had sat when Roland Boldt joined her for a chat.

Questions piled one on top of another. She was a successful tax attorney, a woman in control of her emotions—until today. Had she lost all her reasoning ability as well? Facts. She needed facts. Forget the bodies, she warned herself. Forget the blood.

Forget, too, the masculinity of the man who held her wrist. Forget the fact that his shirt was opened practically to his waist. Study the shirt itself.

Collarless and made of fine linen, it was not the pure white she had thought at first glance. Black silk embroidery, entwined with silver threads, edged the front opening and the ruffles at the cuffs. She'd never seen such detailed work. It could only have been done by hand.

The neckline was bound by a narrow band ending in a long string tie, hanging loosely against his chest. The buttons were of silver filigree matching the silvered embroidery.

The fitted trousers were actually breeches of coarse black wool, ending just below the knee in buttoned bands that met the tops of cuffed, square-toed leather boots. Where the trousers' zipper should have been was a placket laced tightly with a strip of black leather.

"Does the *señorita* approve of what she sees?" Sarcasm sharpened Antonio's words.

Her eyes met his. Must he always stare at her with such contempt? She was the victim here, not he. She was the one being terrified. "The *señorita* is trying to figure out what in the hell is going on."

"You have, my little Ana, the mouth of a true pirate's woman."

Ana, the Spanish form of Anne. Beth shivered. He truly believed she was Rackam's mistress. She hugged herself, fighting the bile that rose in her throat.

"*Vamos,*" he ordered. "We waste time."

Tears ran down her cheeks as she stared up at him. "I need a ride to Road Town," she said, as if she could return to the way things were.

"I do not know this place."

"It's—"

Antonio would not listen to any more lies. His hand circled her arm and, his boots sinking into the damp ground, he headed toward the bodies. He felt her slap at his hand but ignored her.

Just past the bend, a glint in the sand brought him to a halt. *Impossible,* he told himself, but he dropped to his knees, pulling her down beside him, and with his free hand picked up the small piece of metal.

He rubbed his thumb over the silver surface, following the simple outline of his ancestral home. He thought of the southwestern coast of Spain, of the village of Sanlúcar de Barrameda, of the castle that stood on a hill.

And of the only member of his family left to await him, Velez de Alvarez, widowed patriarch of a noble clan—and Antonio's beloved father.

Here was *la medalla* that Don Velez treasured, the very one that had decorated the chest of gold Antonio sailed the oceans to find. The silver bore the crest of the Alvarez family. Never would his brother Rodrigo have allowed it out of his possession. At least, not without a great struggle.

Beth watched him in silence, struck by the deep emotion that etched his face. Then he looked at her with such hatred, as powerful as a blow from his fist, and instinctively she pulled back.

"A young boy gave that to me—" she began.

"*Mentira*," he ground out.

"I'm not lying," she said, her tears falling faster now.

He lifted her wrist, turning his hand until she saw his silver ring. Then he held up the jagged metal beside it. Both were engraved with an identical turreted castle.

"As we feared, my brother is dead," Antonio said in a voice that bore the weight of a great sorrow. "Never would he have parted with the Alvarez crest unless his life's blood was spilled. They told me in the taverns of Nassau and Jamaica that *el pirata* had taken my brother's treasure, confirming the rumors we heard in Spain. I know now he has taken Rodrigo's life as well."

In that moment, kneeling beside the Spaniard on the sand, Beth knew beyond a doubt that this man was not playacting, and that her life was in danger.

"I have sailed these islands for many months," he said, looking out to sea, its brilliant blue muted to gray in the twilight. "Here I came across two of his men, left perhaps to guard the treasure." His gaze shifted to her. "But then I saw his woman.

Was he punishing you, Ana, by abandoning you on this island? Have you somehow displeased him in bed?"

"No!" she shouted. "I'm not Anne Bonny!" She tried to twist out of his grasp, but all her fighting was in vain, and slowly, under his savage grip, she felt her hysteria subside. Surely, she thought, her wrist would shatter from the pressure he maintained. Surely terror would burst her pounding heart.

Slipping the medallion into his boot, he stood and pulled her close, his eyes roaming over her skimpy clothes and her exposed skin.

"I believe you play the part of a demented woman, or else you are a very clever one who wishes to taunt men with her shameless dress." His lips hovered near hers, and the terror in her heart increased as she wondered what he might do.

He backed away and regarded her with contempt. "I have no urge to taste the leavings of a scoundrel. There are better uses for you. It is said in the taverns of the Caribbean that your lover values you above all others. If so, then we must learn if you are worth my family's gold."

3

Antonio refused to consider the fear in the woman's eyes, or the vulnerability she wore like a cloak over her bare skin.

Women lied. He knew it well enough.

This one was *una bruja*. A witch with wild red hair, and a pair of *senos* that spilled from the poor scrap of cloth, full and tempting enough to make a man forsake his sanity. But she was a pirate's woman and must be treated as such.

Unlike the priests of the Inquisition, Antonio did not believe in witches, but she made him reassess his belief. For all his scornful words, she was, in truth, a temptress who aroused him. He'd been celibate too long. A man outside the priesthood was not meant to live in such a state, even a man who grieved for a lost wife and child.

Bastante! He'd been distracted enough. He touched his cheek where she'd clawed him, felt the thin line of blood. *Madre de Dios.* He ought to throw her to his crew. They'd show her soon enough how to behave.

He let go of her while he scooped up the pair of pistols from where he'd dropped them. He tucked them into his waistband, threw her over his shoulder, then clamped his arm tightly around her legs so that she could not kick. He strode along the hard-packed sand at the water's edge, leaving behind the bodies of the two pirates as he left the cove.

"Let me go," she cried, pounding her fists on his back, wiggling her body in the most provocative ways.

He was tempted to strike her well-rounded bottom. He stared at the flowered silk riding tightly across it. Too well he remembered her pale pink undergarment. Never had he seen such a provocative scrap of silk, not even in the brothels of Seville.

He followed the curve of the shore, his captive threatening him all the while. At last he reached the small boat he had rowed from the *Manzanilla*, which was anchored half a mile away beyond the island's treacherous shoals.

Without ceremony, he dumped her onto the seat in the bow and shoved the boat into the surf. He scrambled into the stern and manned the oars as the first swells lifted and lowered the small craft and sent it skimming out to sea.

In the fading light, Beth fell silent and watched him row, her arms hugging her knees. She could not help comparing him to the male attorneys with whom she worked. She'd thought them arrogant, but they were humble compared to this Spaniard.

He seemed to control the sea itself as his muscled arms worked the oars, the sinews of his neck bulging, his strong legs spread wide.

Her muscles ached from balancing herself against the pitch and roll of the boat. Already her clothes were soaked and clung to her cold skin. "Where are we going?" she asked at last.

"To the ship."

She brightened. "The ship?"

"*Sí. La Manzanilla.*"

She frowned. "Either you're crazy, or I am."

"Sanity has been the curse of my people for many years. Perhaps if we had a touch of *la demencia*, we would treat our enemies as they deserve."

She rolled her eyes. "I haven't noticed you fighting for self-control."

"The battle for control is one I wage with necessary constancy. It is a wonder that Rackam does not fear mutiny with his woman aboard his ship."

Beth felt a sense of helplessness as the boat sped over the waves, taking her farther and farther from all she knew. New York seemed a million miles away. Her parents . . . her sister . . . her precious nephews who visited in her Manhattan apartment . . . Would she ever see them again?

In that moment, she vowed that she would. No matter what it took, or how long.

"Look," she said above the wind and the slap of the prow against the water, "all I'm asking is that you take me to Road Town. I know, I know"—she fought to keep the panic out of her voice—"you claim not to know of any such place. It's on the southern coast of the island, at the edge of a natural harbor. A large ship will be anchored a few hundred yards off shore. That's where I want to go. Take me there and I'll see that nothing happens to you."

"A ship? Do you tempt me into an *ambuscade?*"

"I mean you no harm," she said, trying to sound placating, although she would have hit him in the head with an oar if she had the chance. "I just want to understand what's happening to me. You get me to Road Town and I'll treat you to all the Painkillers you can drink. If a few of those don't give you a touch of *la demencia*, you're beyond help. Look what the stuff has done to me."

He looked beyond her, and following his gaze, Beth looked over her shoulder at the ship rising high out of the water, a life-size version of the one that had been stenciled on the plastic glass. A dozen lanterns illuminated the deck, and she could see men running about. "Oh, my God," she whispered. She had never seen a more daunting sight. Every time she thought she might find a way out of this madness, an insurmountable object barred her path.

She turned back to him. "Who are you? What is happening to me?"

Antonio did not answer, but concentrated on bringing the boat alongside the *Manzanilla*. A ladder dropped over the side. He lifted her until she was able to grasp and climb the slippery ropes, then followed closely behind her.

The ropes cut into her hands, and she swayed dizzyingly between the wooden hull and open space. She thought of letting go and falling into the water, but he would surely come after her.

A young boy helped her over the side. His curious black eyes darted to Antonio, but he said nothing. Neither did the men who gathered on deck, assessing her. She shrank back, wrapping her arms around her.

Antonio ordered a cloak from his first mate. Within moments the garment appeared, and he tossed it to her. She accepted it without a word.

"Captain," the first mate said in Spanish, "when you did not return right away, we feared for your safety." He glanced at the woman, then at Antonio's cheek. "It is an unusual remembrance you have brought from the island."

"I promise, Fortunato, to explain her presence before the night is done."

"Were there signs of Rackam?"

"Two of his men attacked me, but I was prepared for them. It is unfortunate they died before they could tell me about the gold. It is possible our search will end here." He thought about the medallion resting in his boot. "I feel certain we will return."

He gave orders to set sail, and slowly the men moved away. He glanced at his captive as she stood at the port rail and gazed out at the island, fast disappearing into the night. The wind caught in the canvas, the boards creaked, and the waves slapped noisily against the hull as the ship plowed through the dark water, following the coastline to the natural harbor, where the pirate's woman claimed a ship awaited.

Antonio prayed she was right, for the vessel might belong to his enemy, the man reported to have captured Rodrigo's ship and slain him sometime in May or June, taking the gold that would restore their fortune.

The man known as Calico Jack Rackam.

Hate for the pirate boiled within Antonio. He would take great pleasure in severing his evil head.

And as for his woman . . . He must give the matter great thought.

It took less than an hour to sail the length of the island, from the western end known as Smuggler's Cove to the eastern tip. There were no lights, no ships, no signs of civilization, and Antonio directed that the ship be set on a northwesterly course toward Nassau, where Rackam was known to visit.

He could tell that the woman was listening as he gave the orders in Spanish. He doubted she understood much of what he said.

At last she turned to face him, and he saw on her face a look of such confusion and despair that he was moved deep in his heart.

"Who are you?" she asked.

"I have already told you. Don Antonio Estebanillo de Alvarez."

"But who *are* you?" She spoke as if her life depended on what he said.

Perplexed, he gave her the only answer he could, speaking above the wind, the creaks, and the shouts of the men as they scrambled among the sails.

"I come from the town of Sanlúcar de Barrameda on the southwestern coast of Spain. In the Alvarez vineyards grow the finest grapes. From them comes manzanilla, the finest sherry in the world. But a drought devastated our vineyards, and the grapes turned bitter. Once the land recovered, we were able to produce and sell our sherry again. It was from the sale of manzanilla here in the New World that my brother Rodrigo amassed the fortunes that would return our people to their former prosperity. Rodrigo gave his life for that fortune. It is he who begs to be avenged."

"And the date?"

"It is February, in the year of our Lord 1720."

Beth covered her mouth with her hand, suppressing a scream. She could no longer doubt that somehow, for reasons she could not fathom, she had slipped two hundred and seventy-four years back in time. She who had found satisfaction in her work, in the flowers of her apartment window boxes, in her nephews' occasional visits.

Hysteria bubbled within her. She was an unlikely candidate to handle this calamity, especially when at its center was an eighteenth-century don, a genuine control freak who alternately scorned her and undressed her with his eyes.

As if puzzled, Antonio watched the play of emotion on her face. "Does not *Señor* Rackam allow his woman a calendar?" he asked.

Beth summoned the last reserves of her strength. "You really do think I'm Anne Bonny."

"Who else could you be? The medallion is proof enough, but I found you on the beach with your lover's men. Your hair, too, Ana, and your eyes. I have heard them described. It would have served you better to admit the truth from the start."

Clasping the railing, she stared into the darkness and felt sea spray sting her cheeks. The rise and pitch of the deck, the slick, wet wood beneath her fingers, the snap of wind-caught sails were all very real. The year was 1720. She could believe nothing else.

An icy fist squeezed her heart, but otherwise she felt empty inside. She closed her eyes for a moment, then opened them to the don's implacable stare.

"My name is Elizabeth Dixon," she said flatly. Perhaps if she spoke the truth often enough, he would believe her. Futile though it might be, she had to try.

"I come from a place called New York City," she

said slowly so that he could grasp every word, calmly so that he would not view her as a hysterical female. "A small town in your day, but in mine one of the greatest cities in the world."

For all he reacted, she might have been talking to the wind. Brushing the hair from her face, she determined to be as unruffled as he. And as stubborn. "Would it be possible to get a cup of coffee?"

He shrugged. "I have on board such beans from Java."

"Good. Because I've got a lot of talking to do, Don Antonio. My guess is we'll be up most of the night."

4

Antonio's cabin was a third the size of Beth's cruise ship stateroom. A porthole opened onto the starless night; a lantern on the wall provided light. He directed her to sit on the narrow bed, then left. A short time later he returned with two tin mugs of steaming coffee. He sat in a chair behind a small desk, settling back and stretching his legs nearly to the bunk.

Sitting on the edge of the bunk, still wrapped in the cloak, the hot mug balanced between her trembling hands, Beth looked around and saw brass fittings and dark wood. A woven straw basket on the floor by the desk held a collection of tightly rolled maps, and beside the basket was a brass bucket. A spittoon? she wondered. Or perhaps it was a receptacle for something much more basic.

She recalled from her reading that the eighteenth century was known for sailing ships, struggles over domination of land and sea, revolutions, and, later, the development of democracy. It was not, however, renowned for its technological advancement.

Nor for its fair treatment of women. They were chattel, little more than servants even in the wealthiest households, providers of pleasure and male heirs. Men possessed the power. She knew she had cause to be afraid.

She sipped the coffee, welcoming its heat and bitterness, and looked over the mug at her captor. He sat straight-backed in the chair, his elbows resting on the arms, his legs extended, one boot crossed over the other. His shirt remained unbuttoned halfway to his waist, but he had washed the blood from his cheek and had bound his hair at his nape.

How gentlemanly, Beth thought. If only he'd taken a razor to the bristles shadowing his cheeks, he wouldn't look quite so menacing as he stared at her, so virile, so dangerous. Somehow he managed even to *sit* powerfully. As well he should, she reminded herself. He was an eighteenth-century sea captain, the owner of Spanish vineyards, a titled nobleman. He was in control.

But he had never dealt with a twentieth-century woman before. Beth used the thought to fight her rising sense of powerlessness. She had to sound reasonable—at least she had to try. Maybe he wanted only to frighten her into revealing where he could find Calico Jack. Well, if it was fear he wanted to arouse, he was doing a hell of a job.

Taking a deep breath, she began. "In a hundred years or so an English poet is going to write about a 'willing suspension of disbelief.' That's what I'm asking of you. Do not doubt what I am about to tell you. Wait until I am finished to judge my story."

His eyes widened slightly. "A hundred years from this day?"

"See there, you're already picking at the details, and I haven't even begun."

It was a detail, he thought, worthy of "picking at." There would no doubt be others to follow. He would attempt to suspend his disbelief of them, but he knew already his captive asked much.

He stared at her, and she stared back with dark and pleading eyes. They touched something deep inside him, something that had lain dormant for a long time.

And such magnificent hair, he thought, remembering its silkiness beneath his fingers. Too, he remembered the softness of her skin. Even wrapped in that voluminous black wool cloak, Ana continued to intrigue him.

He finished his coffee, set the cup on his desk, and crossed his arms across his lap. "Begin," he said. "I will not interrupt."

She told him of her life in the twentieth century and recounted the strange day, including her overindulgence in a drink she called Painkillers. When she fell silent, Antonio studied her carefully before he spoke.

"It is just as I feared. *La calentura.*"

"What's that?"

"A fever of the islands. It is marked by delirium and hallucinations."

"I am not ill," she snapped. "When you touched me, did you feel heat?"

His lips twitched. "*Por Dios*, that I did."

She blushed. "I mean, did I feel as if I suffered from a fever?"

"Possibly. Perhaps I should touch you again."

"Watch out. If this illness really has struck me, I might give it to you."

Antonio shrugged. "A leader of men must be prepared to face all risks."

"How noble."

"I am descended from a long line of noblemen."

"So it's *noblesse oblige*, is it?"

"I do not know this term."

"I guess it's after your time. It means the obligation of the high-born to behave with honor and generosity to those less fortunate."

He felt a moment's anger. "Do not mock me, Ana. I care for my people without need of a Frenchman's phrase to instruct me."

In addition to his honor, she saw clearly, he was a man with a quick temper and an oversupply of pride. She shouldn't be surprised, since she'd already had hints of both.

He was also a man of passion, a fact that brought her little comfort, since they were alone on a ship he captained and she was sitting on his bed.

The lady is not to worry. Hadn't young Joseph told her that repeatedly when he'd guided her along her fatal path? She wondered what he would tell her now.

Gathering the strength to stand, she crossed to

the porthole. A cool breeze ruffled her hair as she gazed out. It was dark, and she could not discern the meeting of sea and sky. Beneath the porthole ran a narrow walkway. If she strained a little, she could make out a couple of lanterns hanging from posts on the deck to her right, their light turning the ship's flapping sails ghostly white against the blackness of the night. A sailor who worked at the edge of the shadows seemed like a creature from another world.

An eighteenth-century world. Impossible. But all too true.

She turned to face Antonio. At this moment he was every judge and jury she'd ever encountered, every opposing counsel, every client who'd ever doubted her ability because of her sex.

Her mind raced as she saw him turn the medallion in his hand. Perhaps if she retold her story in greater detail he might believe her.

"As I said, a little boy gave that to me. I carried it down to the shore. I was so unhappy, Antonio. My tears fell on the silver and you suddenly appeared, shooting down those men. Naturally I panicked and ran. You chased me. I told you my name, which unfortunately you do not believe is true. You think I am your enemy, so you drag me on board a ship that's right out of a maritime museum and make me your prisoner."

"Most of this I do not dispute."

"How could you? Most of it you witnessed. Given the necessity of gaining my freedom, don't you think I would come up with a better story than the one you just heard?"

"*Por supuesto.* Would you care to try again?"

Exasperated, Beth rolled her eyes. "The only thing I care to do is to go back home."

A lump formed in her throat, and she felt despair clutch her heart. Turning from him, she stared into the night and fought for control.

"I know little of Spanish history," she said, a tremor in her voice. "Except for our countries fighting a war over Cuba just before the turn of the century."

She faced him once again. "The twentieth century, that is."

Growing desperate, she began to pace alongside the bed, twisting her hands in front of her.

"The truth is, your country has known its glory days. They won't return."

Antonio listened, marveling at the fantastic tales of war that fell from her lips as she continued to speak of things he could not even imagine.

"You paint a picture without light, *señorita*. And this you expect me to accept?"

"Oh, but there is much that is wonderful about your land and your history that does not involve conquest. You will produce great artists and musicians who will bring pleasure around the world. Haven't you seen the paintings of El Greco?"

His dark eyes regarded her with great care. "His work resides in Toledo, deep in the heart of my country. How do you know of him?"

"By my time, the whole world knows of him. And of Velázquez and Goya and Picasso. Their paintings are treasured in New York and London and Paris, as well as in the Prado in Madrid. I haven't mentioned anything in detail about the music and the dancing, the wines and the oils, but they are equally valued. Spain has truly enriched the world."

He stood, and his presence filled the room.

"You are a strange woman, Ana," he said, stepping to her side. "You almost make me believe."

Without thinking, she touched his sleeve. Through the fine linen she could feel the heat of his skin.

"You must believe me, Antonio. You are my only hope."

The ship took an unexpected pitch, and she fell into his arms. She wanted to pull away and stand under her own power, but she'd been doing that for more than two years. How wonderful it would be for just a moment to lean on someone else.

She held on to his arms and rested her cheek against the bare chest exposed by his open shirt. Wiry hairs tickled her skin, and she could hear the beat of his heart. She felt inexpressibly wearied by all that had happened and, too, she felt reassured by the presence of a man whose existence could not be.

Nothing made sense to her logical lawyer's mind. And she didn't care. *She didn't care.* What a relief it was to accept the way things were. She'd panicked and fought and denied, not just today and tonight but ever since Michael died. She hadn't planned ever again needing anyone as much as she needed him.

But she needed Antonio Estebanillo de Alvarez in ways she didn't try to understand. She'd done all she could in this mad situation. The rest was up to him.

Antonio held her gently. There were those who would say she used her woman's wiles to trap him into acquiescence. But she'd made no demands upon him, save that he believe she was from another time.

It was much to ask, and he could not bring himself to believe such was so.

Thrusting his hands in the glorious red mane, he lifted her face and looked into her eyes. She, too, had known great sorrow, which pierced his heart. But in which century? *Por Dios*, he wished he knew.

He kissed her, then rubbed a thumb across her cheek and felt her tears.

"Do not cry, Ana," he whispered against the dampness. "I mean you no harm."

"I'm not crying because I'm afraid."

"You speak to a confused man. Please explain."

Once again she rested her face against his chest, and he felt his heart beat faster than before.

"I've been alone in the night for a long time. I don't know what all of this is about, any more than you do. What I do realize is that I don't want to be alone right now. I'm so tired, Antonio. So very, very tired."

He lifted her and cradled her close. Laying her on the bed, he turned to the small, brass-bound chest on the floor behind his desk. He lifted the lid and, slipping his hand inside his boot, withdrew the medallion and hid it under his clothes. He picked up a shirt, straightened, and walked to the bed.

"Here, *querida*," he said, thrusting the garment into her hands, hardly aware of the endearment by which he addressed her. "Sleep in my shirt. We will talk more in the morning."

Then he was gone. She watched with a sense of

loss as the door closed behind him. It took her an eternity to get undressed, to shed the heavy cloak, to remove the foolish parrot earrings and the scanty clothes, giving up after fumbling long minutes over the ankle bracelet clasp. She seemed to be moving in slow motion as she put on Antonio's shirt.

She hardly knew what to think of him, any more than he knew what to think of her. Except that for some unknown reason, she was not as afraid of him as she had been. At least for a while he'd stopped throwing accusations at her. But her sense of hopelessness had not dissipated, and wearily she stumbled to the porthole to catch the scent of the night breeze.

A whisper carried on the wind. *The lady is not to worry.* Again young Joseph's words came to her. He'd also told her the medallion would protect her from bad guys. She only prayed he was right.

"I will get away, Joseph," she whispered into the darkness. "Whatever it takes, I will return to my time."

She lay down on the bunk and rested her head against the pillow. Almost immediately she fell asleep.

On deck, Antonio stared into the darkness and thought of his captive. She must be mad to think he would believe such claims of future centuries where women were allowed to plead before the courts. Impossible, as was everything else she said.

Yet there was something about her that disturbed him. He would have expected the pirate's woman to curse and rave and reach for hidden knives to carve out his heart.

Yet she had resorted to mild curses and feeble assaults, to preposterous stories, and at last to falling helplessly into his arms, and allowing him to kiss her. The memory of her sweet lips wrenched his heart. Oh, if only he could believe all that she had said! But how could he? Her appearance, Rackam's men, the island where he'd found her, the medallion—all condemned her as the woman Bonny.

Antonio admitted to a great weariness, and to a sadness at the loss of Rodrigo, his carefree, reckless brother who had served with such great success in the sale of the fine Alvarez manzanilla. In May, ten months ago, he had set sail for home, bearing a great chest of gold. But two months after his departure, only rumors of his death had reached Spain, and at the end of August Antonio set sail to investigate these rumors. Rumors he now knew were true.

At heart Antonio was a man of the soil, who sometimes found it necessary to take to the sea. Now was such a time.

Too, he knew the ways of women. Had not many sought to console him after the death of his wife and child? Five years ago, a fever had taken them. His marriage, arranged between their parents, had not been a union of love, but they had cared for one another, and Antonio had valued his young son above all else. He doubted he would ever know such contentment again.

And so he fought to help the people who toiled on Alvarez land, and to bring a smile once again to his father's eyes. Not once had Velez de Alvarez known joy since he heard the rumors of Rodrigo's death at the hands of *el pirata*. His father believed that the crest Rodrigo took with him held mystical powers, powers that would return prosperity to Alvarez land. For Don Velez, Antonio had vowed to return the piece of silver to Spanish soil, and he had managed to keep that promise, for the medallion lay safely at the bottom of his trunk.

Then his thoughts returned again to his beautiful captive. Could the woman he had held in his arms and kissed be an accomplice to Rodrigo's murderer? Though his mind knew it was so, his heart denied it.

Beth awoke to the sound of the door opening, and she bolted upright. She brushed the hair from her eyes and leaned against the wall as she watched the young sailor who had pulled her on board enter the cabin. He carried a tray of food and a bundle of clothes. Without a word or glance in her direction, he set them on the desk. Then, as if he did such things every day, he picked up the brass bucket and left, closing the door behind him.

The food was water, stale bread, and dried meat, the origin of which she didn't care to know. Ravenous, she ate every bite, then unfolded the clothes—a shirt and a pair of loose-fitting trousers, both obviously the boy's. She thought of Antonio's kindness in providing her with these clothes and food as she took off Antonio's shirt and put on the young boy's over her halter. She pulled on the pants and fashioned her sarong into a belt, praying that her sandals would be sufficient for walking on a wet, rolling deck. If, that is, she ever got out of this cabin.

Late in the afternoon, Antonio reappeared. He stared at this bold woman who now wore boy's clothes. She did not wear them as the young sailor had, but instead filled them out in unorthodox places. A maddening woman, and a foolishly brave one to keep up her charade. While he was on deck, his thoughts had kept turning to her.

"I have come to tell you that we sail for Nassau. The journey is not long, but we will navigate among the islands in search of your lover. Do not think you can escape."

Over the next week, Antonio continued to question Beth, and she answered again and again that she was not Anne Bonny. She also managed to insert in their conversations something about the world that for him was yet to be—sports, inventions, even wars. He never commented, although he listened as she spoke, and during the second week of the voyage, he dined every night with her, strolled the deck with her, keeping a close watch on the crew, and no longer slept on deck but on the floor next to her bed. Now that they shared the same quarters, their discussions had become more intimate, and some of Beth's tension eased.

One night while they were eating, Beth decided to ask the question that had been nagging her.

"Tell me, Antonio, do you have a wife and children waiting for you back in Spain?"

"Once I was married. The fever took my wife and son."

"I'm sorry," she said, instantly regretting her need to know.

"It was a long time ago. And you, Ana? Have

you left in this distant world of yours a man who mourns your absence?"

"I was engaged once. Betrothed, you'd probably say. He was killed. Of course there were no children."

He didn't ask, but she went on to tell him of her family, of her work, of her life, adding bits of information she had not told him during their previous conversations. She tried to make her life sound fulfilling, even exciting, but she feared he could hear the truth behind her words.

"It is strange, this idea of women who work beside men far from home. In my world, a woman's life is bound by marriage. After my wife Consuela's death, many *mujeres* expressed sorrow at my loneliness. They offered to provide solace. One in particular, a member of the powerful Duke of Medina Sidonia's family, seemed willing to take Consuela's place. I considered the possibility, especially during the drought, but word of our difficulties spread, and she was not so interested."

Beth caught the anger in his voice.

"Did you love her?"

"No. But I am a proud man, Ana. I learned that, like men, women can be deceitful."

"And you don't trust any of us?"

"We should not talk of such matters now."

But Beth wasn't satisfied to change the subject away from him. "This gold that was taken from your brother Rodrigo. Where did it come from?"

"Rodrigo served as our intermediary in the New World, setting up the distribution for shipments of our fine *manzanilla*. The governor of Nassau has praised our sherry. Through the years it has brought high prices among the wealthy purchasers in the Caribbean. Rodrigo completed his sales of the best that we could produce, given our new circumstances. Even though the risks of piracy were always great, Rodrigo had to bring home the great chest of gold. My father believed he would be protected by the crest of silver as he had been during previous journeys."

Antonio fell silent, remembering that the crest had been found on the beach where Ana had first appeared. He doubted her story of a child giving her the silver, but he went on.

"This small piece of silver has been highly regarded by my people. The Holy Father himself blessed it many years ago, when my father's father made a sacred journey to Rome, and it is said that before Cristóbal Colón began his second voyage into the vast oceans, he held it in his hand. Did you know that this great explorer set sail from Sanlúcar de Barrameda?"

"I didn't," Beth said, amazed by his story.

"*Es verdad.*"

A pounding at the door interrupted her response.

Reluctantly, Antonio rose from the table. "I must go."

He left quickly, giving her no chance to ask him if he now believed her story of who she was and where she had come from.

Gradually she grew accustomed to her life on the ship, but she never accepted that it was her prison. Observing the ship's routine through the inadequate porthole, she never stopped considering her escape. In the night she reviewed her short time on Tortola, searching for a clue to explain her state, but there was so little to remember. Mostly she thought about Joseph and all he had said.

Each day or two the ship anchored off a different island and she watched as she took her daily walk with Antonio on deck and sometimes through the porthole as a few men rowed a small craft to shore to spread the word that Anne Bonny was on board. She watched these journeys with growing despair, for they were evidence of Antonio's continued belief that she was Calico Jack's woman. Considering Rackam's reputation as a bloodthirsty pirate, she would have admired the don for his courage—if he weren't using her as bait in his trap.

And so her despair continued to build, along with her confusion as to why he was almost always on her mind. Perhaps it was because of the days and nights they spent confiding their personal histories, so that Beth had come to look forward to the time they spent together. Perhaps, too, it was because she slept in his shirt and thus kept his scent against her skin.

She even became jealous of the ship and of the islands that took his time, because they robbed her of opportunities to be with him and to try to convince him of the truth about her. Even though the discussions so far had proven futile, they were her only hope of persuading him.

One morning close to a month after her capture, an explosion awoke her. Her heart pounding, she fumbled at the door. She hurried down the narrow passageway and emerged onto the deck to see a second ship racing parallel to the *Manzanilla*. The other ship rode low in the water twenty yards to starboard, a row of guns trained, it seemed, directly at her.

Beth's gaze flew upward. From the marauding ship's mainmast, a flag waved furiously—white skull and crossbones against a black background.

5

A pandemonium of gunshots, smoke, shouts, and pounding feet erupted, and Beth covered her ears, trying to block out the tumult. Smoke stung her eyes, and she tasted the gunpowder's residue.

A rough hand clasped her arm.

"Por Dios! Are you *lunática?"*

She looked into a pair of furious brown eyes and breathed a sigh of relief. Not until that moment did she realize that Antonio's safety had been uppermost in her mind.

"Thank God you're all right," she said.

He didn't take time to respond until he'd dragged her to his cabin and, with little gentleness, thrown her inside. His eyes raked over her. She looked fragile in the oversize shirt, her hair a tangle, her expression one of shock and confusion.

"I will throw you in the hold if you do not do what I say. You will not leave this cabin again. Do you understand?"

Beth knew he meant his threat. "Yes, I'll stay here."

The cabin shook from the force of a nearby explosion. She grabbed his arm. He forced her fingers to release their grip. Their eyes met and something passed between them. Something she couldn't put a name to, although it was a familiar feeling, as though he had aroused within her an emotion from the past.

He stroked her hand and then he was gone.

She rushed to the porthole, frustrated that it opened onto the wrong side of the ship. Thrusting her head outside, she could see little more than smoke and a confusion of sailors scurrying about the port side of the deck. On the horizon, a lacy gray sea lay beneath an overcast sky.

Fear gripped her as she pulled back inside and paced the cabin. Antonio could die. He was her only link with safety, the only one who protected her, even if his reasons were all wrong. If he died, she would be left alone on a ship of strangers. It mattered little to her whether the pirates or the Spaniards won the battle—if Antonio died.

The idea was unthinkable. She had come to believe him invincible, and she could not forget the look in his eyes when she had agreed to remain in the cabin. She'd seen the remnants of anger there, but also concern, and something else . . . something that came from deep inside him. Something that spoke silently to her heart.

She stopped. Were the explosions dying away?

She sat in the chair and listened. Yes, the guns of both ships had definitely stopped firing. And as far as she could tell, the *Manzanilla* rode as high as ever in the water. Surely the Spaniards had been victorious. Surely Antonio lived.

She drummed her fingers on the arm of the

chair, then tapped her bare foot against the plank floor, staring at the foolish gold ankle bracelet. She hadn't been able to unfasten the clasp since her journey back in time.

Where was Antonio? What was he doing now that the firing had stopped? At this moment was he striding aboard the pirates' deck? Or were they striding aboard his?

A glance through the porthole told her nothing. She had to know what was happening, and it didn't matter if he threw her in the hold.

Leaving the cabin and retracing her steps along the passageway, she peered cautiously outside. The pirate ship was gone. Two men from the *Manzanilla* lay on the deck, a companion hovering over them. The grin on his grizzled face indicated that neither man was seriously hurt.

Beth looked beyond them toward the bow. Through a maze of ropes, barrels, and masts she saw the unmistakable figure of Antonio. Still in shirtsleeves and breeches, he stood in the midst of his crew, laughing. Laughing! She didn't know whether to cry from relief or find a harpoon to throw at him.

She watched as Antonio and his men passed out cups which she doubted contained coffee. Rum, or maybe their famous sherry. She decided to leave them to their celebrating.

Drawing a breath of fresh air, she retreated to the passageway and followed its length. It led to a ladder that dropped steeply into the hold where he had threatened to put her. Well, now she was going down there under her own steam, for this was her chance to explore, to see if she could find anything that might help in her escape, while the men and Antonio were distracted.

She returned to the cabin for the lantern. Hastily donning her daytime clothes and her sandals, she hurried to the ladder and cautiously climbed down. The air was close and sour, and in the poor light she saw barrels, stacks of boxes, and ropes. Rope that she could use to lower herself over the side of the ship into the sea.

Here the ship's rocking was strong, and she struggled to maintain her balance. Around her the wooden hull moaned eerily, and from the shadows came a scuttling sound that shredded her nerves. Something brushed over her bare toes, and with a cry she darted for the ladder, bounded to the passageway and, her heart pounding, scurried to the cabin.

She cursed her cowardice for not trying to get one of the ropes, but she realized how foolish she'd been. Where would she have hidden it, for there was no question of her returning to the hold to get it? Frustration, fear, and anger made her pace again. There was one bright spot. Antonio hadn't seen her and made good his threat.

At midday, the young sailor brought her meal, but when she tried to ask him about the battle, he burst into Spanish she couldn't understand.

Night had fallen when Beth, dozing in Antonio's shirt, heard the door close. She sat up. His hair was as disheveled as hers, and more than ever he needed a shave. The coarse bristles, combined with his tired expression, made him appear vulnerable.

She was happy that he finally had come to her, though she was uncertain as to his mood. She sighed. "Obviously the good guys won," she said, smoothing the shirt as far as it would go over her knees.

A weary Antonio studied the beauty who was his prisoner and wondered at the emotions crossing her face. "You have a curious way of speaking," he said. "Am I one of these good guys?"

"'I don't know. I hope so. All I know is that those guns were firing at us, and I hope you sent them to the briny deep."

He raked a hand through his hair and remembered the fray. He had spent the day examining the ship's damage, tending the wounded, and mostly celebrating the victory, the details of which he would never forget.

"We brought ten of our guns to bear on him, though it was apparent that he had expected far fewer. We poured a broadside upon him. He could not equal the fire and sheered off. We will see no more of this man-of-war."

"Who was he?"

"A pirate captain. He was unknown to me."

"And to me. Whether you believe it or not, as far as I'm concerned, Rackam and his kind are nothing but villains in a history book."

"*El pirata* is a bad guy?"

"One of the worst."

Studying the tilt of her chin and the resolute light in her eyes, Antonio wanted to believe her. He liked this woman. He admired her impertinence and her mystery and the way she looked at him eye to eye, instead of slyly like other women. And there were other, more physical traits he liked as well. He very much liked her in his shirt. She was right, he decided, to bare her magnificent legs, even if she was not wise.

The fire of victory still pulsed in his veins, heated by the sight and sound of the temptress he had found on a golden beach. His caution melted in that fire, along with his reserve and his noble intentions. At this moment, he craved this woman, a creature of many facets, each one more intriguing than the last.

Beth watched as he moved to the bed and took her hand, turning it and kissing her palm. She stared up at the hot eyes that bore through her, and shivered with anticipation.

She swallowed hard. "You said you didn't want a scoundrel's woman."

"And you claim to be someone else."

"Elizabeth—"

He stopped her with a finger on her lips. "It matters not who you are. Not for now. I will call you Elizabeth, if that is what you wish."

It was the first time he had said her name. She liked the way he drew it out. He made it sound like a song lyric. Looking up at him, Beth felt stir inside her a desire she had not experienced since Michael's death.

All the banked passions of her lonely years flared into existence. All her doubts and insecurities slipped from her as easily as the centuries had disappeared. For whatever reason she'd been transported back in time, it wasn't to deny herself a slice of happiness. In truth, denial was far from her mind.

He bent to kiss her and run his hands over her back, kindling a heat within her that aroused her hunger for him. He lifted his head, and his smoldering brown eyes disintegrated the barriers between them.

She touched his chest, looked at his copper skin dusted with curly black hair, at the strong column of his neck, his parted mouth, and his handsome face.

Antonio unbuttoned her shirt and covered her breasts with his hands. She swelled to fill his palms, her nipples sensitive and eager for his touch. Her fingers splayed in his hair and she brushed her lips against his.

The light touching, the teasing, became torturous, and she ached for more as he pulled the shirt from her body and kissed her thoroughly. His tongue entwined with hers and his hands stroked her arms and the subtle curve of her back.

Cupping her buttocks, he eased himself between her legs and pulled her against him. She wound her arms around him, her thighs trapping him in place. She returned his probing kiss, her tongue playing with his, answering his deep moan with soft cries of her own. She wanted to taste him, to touch him, to be a part of him. She wanted him to be a part of her—didn't care, even with her logical mind, that it was impossible.

He broke the kiss, but only to trail his lips across her eyes, her cheeks, her throat. He bent to taste her hard-tipped breasts. Such sweetness was almost unbearable.

Beth tore at his clothes. Unfair, she wanted to cry, that he should remain dressed while he tormented her with his sweet-savage lovemaking. She thrust her hands inside his shirt and stroked the contours of his chest, rubbing her thumbs across his nipples, which were as hard as hers.

She stroked lower, and her fingers groped at the lacing of his breeches. He covered her hand with his and pressed her palm against his erection.

"Antonio," she whispered.

He lifted his head from her breasts, and their eyes met. "*Querida*," he said, "this is right."

He stepped back to undress. She submitted to the complete madness of the moment and watched him, marveling at his beautiful body, at his taut muscles, at the small scar below his waist, a provocative diversion to his perfection.

When she opened her arms, they embraced and he eased her to the narrow bed gently lowering himself over her. He caressed her body and at last his hand ventured along her inner thigh, finding all the erotic places that aroused her, his fingers teasing until she could no longer stand the torture.

"*Ahora*," she demanded.

He moved inside her with great care, and she grasped his powerful shoulders as their hips rocked in unison.

Beth lost all sense of time and place. Swept by rushes of passion, she squeezed her eyes closed and hugged him tightly, letting his rapid thrusts carry her to a world where only the two of them dwelled.

She reached a climax first, her world splintering into a million particles of pleasure. He exploded a moment later, his thrusts fast and hard, the completion all-consuming.

They held on to each other, neither willing to part from an embrace that had brought them a totally unexpected sensation, the feeling that they had experienced something unique, something that might not come to them again.

It was a silently shared feeling, their only communication a gentle touch of his lips on her brow and a languorous stroke of her hand down his arm.

Antonio wished only that he could prolong the time he held her in his arms. There was something magical about this woman that had nothing to do with her journey through time. She had come to him as if through a miracle, and if she really came from the future, she might want to return there, leaving him alone. And if she were Ana ...

At last, he lifted his head, and once again their eyes met. "Ana," he said in a low, husky whisper, "I want to believe you are who you claim to be."

Her heart quickened with hope and joy, but a knock at the door interrupted her response.

Reluctantly, Antonio eased from her side. "I must go." He covered her with a blanket, and she watched as he dressed. She remained very still, savoring the ecstasy they had shared and the happiness his words had roused.

He paused in the doorway. "We sail for an inlet of an unnamed island nearby. There are repairs to make and damage to assess. Until I know that all is well aboard ship, I must sleep on deck. A day, maybe two. Then I will return not to the floor but to my bed, Ana, where I belong with you."

She said nothing, and the door closed behind him. Clutching the blanket to her throat, she felt some of the heaviness in her heart lift. She only wished he had eased her fear completely, for he had not said one word about not using her to bring Calico Jack to him. If only all the distrust had melted away in the passion of their lovemaking. If only love could replace fear ...

* * *

She spent the next day studying the maps in the basket and viewing the limited scenery from the porthole, all the while unable to forget the ecstasy of the previous night. She watched the waves, saw the island Antonio had mentioned, felt the ship drop anchor a short distance from the beach. *Close enough to swim to,* she thought as she stared at the curve of sand in the sunlight.

Antonio did not return to her until the morning of the second day, to announce that they would be setting sail shortly. He caught her at the porthole, staring at the beach.

"I will be busy for some time yet, with the repairs of the ship," he said from the doorway. "For your safety it is necessary that you remain in the cabin. But be assured, Ana, I will be back."

Watching the door close behind him, Beth trembled, not from fear of him but from fear of what the future held. She had surrendered to him without any reassurance that he would find some way to entrap Calico Jack other than using her. She'd grown accustomed to everything aboard ship except the uncertainty of her existence . . . and of her feelings for the don.

When she was with him, she knew the finest moments of her life . . . and yet she knew he was holding back. And that made good sense on his part. After all, he believed she was Anne Bonny. How could she expect him to plan a future with her, to take her back to Spain and introduce her to his father?

No way. And unless she could convince him he was wrong about her, she would definitely have to leave him. She could only hope that their lovemaking had meant as much to him as it had to her, and that it had altered things between them.

As the time for sailing neared, there was much scurrying on board, and Beth heard two men's voices coming from the passageway near the porthole. She had never heard any conversations before, but the shift of the wind carried the sailors' words clearly.

At first she picked out only an occasional phrase, but the longer she listened, the more her college Spanish came back. The crew were growing restless because they had not found *el pirata*. Surely he would appear when the captain brought *la puta* to Nassau. Perhaps then he would kill Rackam and reclaim his gold.

The men moved on, and in deep pain, Beth lowered herself into the chair before she collapsed. So Antonio had not changed his mind. She knew it now without a doubt. His own men had spoken of his plans. Despite their intimacy, his duty to his father and to his people was more important to him than she was.

How could she have thought otherwise? How could she have let herself believe that he might care for her?

She knew how. Forgetting the lessons of the past, she had allowed herself to feel again, to open her heart. She forced herself to move. She could not allow her situation to defeat her, or else she would fall into the same lethargic trap in which she had remained far too long after Michael's death.

She had been unable to prevent the shooting. But she could keep from being used by Antonio. She hadn't chosen to come aboard the *Manzanilla*, but she was choosing to leave now. And she would take one item of his with her—the medallion. If there was a chance she could return home, she must hold the medallion in her hand once again.

She felt its presence inside the cabin. Knowing she must hurry, she began her search.

6

Once Beth decided on a plan of action, there was no turning back. She didn't let herself think, except where practical matters were concerned. In New York she was known as a problem solver, and now she had ample problems to solve.

But escape came more easily than she had expected. With all the commotion involved in setting sail, no one noticed a youth in baggy pants and shirt scurrying along the edges of the deck and down the seldom-used port-side passageway. Her hair was hidden under a floppy hat. The medallion, which she'd found in Antonio's chest, was bound in a handkerchief tied to her halter.

She waited in the shadows of the passageway, grateful for the clouds that had rolled in, darkening the day. She quickly removed the hat she had found in the cabin and tucked it in her waistband. She then removed her sandals and tied them around her neck. At the moment of most activity, when the sails unfurled to catch the wind, she forced herself to ease over the side, and jumped feet first.

All the long way down to the water, she reminded herself she was a good swimmer. Holding her nose, she broke the surface cleanly and sank like a stone to the bottom, where her feet, already stinging, hit hard rock.

Bounding back to the surface, she fought a sudden coldness that struck to the bone. Her heart pounding, she struggled for air. Shock was a danger, she knew, and she flailed her arms and legs in the water to stimulate her circulation. The sandals broke loose from round her neck, and before she could grab them they floated out of reach, caught by a wave that took them close to the ship.

She looked up, expecting to see a scowling face glaring down at her, or at least an excited sailor or two. But no one had noticed her jump, and she knew that even if she screamed out for rescue, no one would hear, not with all the shipboard noise and the roar of the wind.

But someone might glance into the water. Despite the cloud cover, she felt exposed so near the ship. A heavenly gift—a load of refuse from the galley—dropped from above, tossed carelessly overboard by a sailor who did not look to see where it fell.

Garbage landed on Beth's head and shoulders, littering the surface around her. She crammed the hat securely on her head and held her nose as she lowered her face under the water. From above, the hat would look like part of the refuse, and the garbage would obscure her body, suspended in the all-too-clear inlet waves.

When her lungs threatened to burst, she came

up for air. The sea stung her eyes, but she could see the blurred outline of the *Manzanilla*'s shrinking stern as the ship headed for open waters. She swam toward shore, not stopping to question her actions until she was sitting on the beach, wishing the sun would come out to warm her and subdue the wind with its heat.

Thrusting the hat back into her waistband, she hugged her knees to her chest and stared at Antonio's ship, now a vague silhouette in the distant gloom. Expecting exhilaration to overcome her, she experienced a strange emptiness instead, as if she'd missed an opportunity that would not come again. How ridiculous, she told herself. She had every reason to hate Antonio now ... every reason to regret what she'd done with him ... every reason to celebrate her escape.

If only she understood why she'd been transported through time. She prayed her guess about repeating the miraculous shift across the centuries was right. Only this time she must go forward, and she hoped she had the strength to try it.

She certainly hadn't had the strength to fight Antonio. In only a few weeks he had taken her to his bed. With Michael, nine months had passed before she'd admitted her feelings and given him her virginity.

But Michael had been different in every way. Sensible. Orderly. *Normal.* Nothing about her relationship with Antonio resembled those traits. And she'd loved Michael. But did she love Antonio?

All she knew was that for a short while, she had wanted him passionately. He had aroused her to an ecstasy she'd never known.

Except when it came to being used as bait. It

tore at her to realize that if he found her here, he might do it yet.

For that moment she felt as devastated as when she had received the news about Michael. Stupid, stupid, stupid, she thought, running her fingers through her wet hair. She shouldn't allow Antonio to wound her so. She didn't understand why he could.

Panic overwhelmed her. She must find a place where she was safe, a place far from this cove where she could try to go home.

She quickly rose and ran to the water's edge, where her footprints disappeared in the dying waves. Her legs, used to the sway of the ship, trembled, but she managed to follow the line of surf. Soon leaving the cove, and finding another and then another, she scrambled across stretches of ground where vegetation and rocks obliterated the sand. At last, exhausted, she came to a small inlet that bore an uncanny resemblance to the inlet where she had first traveled through time.

Wearily she made her way across the sand, stopping at a cluster of palm trees backed by a wall of shrubs. Turning, she pulled out the medallion, warm from her body, and stared at the endless, empty sea. On Tortola, she had cried and rubbed the silver. Could she summon tears again?

With the metal resting in her palm, she knelt in the sand and thought of the recent days . . . of all the energy expended in anger and fear and the futility of trying to reason with her captor. Remembering the hurtful things that had passed between them, she felt her tears. She held the medallion close, waiting for her second journey to begin.

* * *

Antonio found her at sunset, the time of day he had first seen her on a similar beach.

She lay curled up like a child in the shade of a palm tree, her hands cushioning her face, her matted hair spread across the sand. Emotions tore at him. He wanted to thrash her to within an inch of her life, but he wanted even more to embrace her, and to cover her body with kisses.

He cursed himself for a fool. Never before had anyone, man or woman, so completely destroyed his peace of mind. Not since the death of his son had he suffered the agonies of the frantic backtracking to the cove after discovering her gone.

He had thought she'd drowned; instead, she slept.

Ah, she deserved to be thrashed.

He grabbed her by the shoulders and lifted her to her feet. She came awake fighting, her fists flailing, striking out. Mostly she lashed the air. He held her firm, and gradually she grew still.

Her eyes focused on him. "You."

"You were expecting *el pirata?*" He spat out the words.

Slowly her fingers opened. "Here," she said, her voice bitter. "Take it. Then go away. Get out of my life."

He stared at the antique silver, and a great sadness overwhelmed him. For a short while on his ship, when he had held her in his arms, he had forgotten all the barriers between them. Her lovemaking had been passionate and she had shown great tenderness. Her concerns had been for his pleasure, and she had responded to his touch and his kiss with an innocence that could not be feigned. It was as if she had seldom lain with a man.

Or so he had believed. But only for that too-short while. She had stolen the medallion, knowing what it meant to him, and she had risked her life to run away from him. His hands ached to circle her lovely throat. Instead, he took the medallion and thrust it into his boot, just as he'd done the first time he found her.

"We must go," he said.

"Leave me."

He looked at her with contempt, at her tangled red hair stiff with dried sea water, at her sand-sprinkled face, at the boy's clothes that hung limply on her body. For all that he saw, he felt his passion for her, and that enraged as much as it inflamed him.

"*Es verdad*," he said with purposeful cruelty, "you are poor bait to trap *el pirata*. But you are all that I have." He grabbed her arm.

Fury gave her strength, and she wrenched free. A wall of jungle blocked her retreat, and without thinking she ran for the water. He caught her halfway to the surf. They fell to the ground. She writhed in his arms, determined to break his hold, but stretched out on top of her, pressing her shoulders to the ground, his weight pinned her down. In frustration she kicked, but her bare feet landed weakly against his leather boots. Her hips rubbed against him, her loose trousers in friction with his tight breeches. Her breasts heaving as she gasped for air, she grew quiet and her hysteria passed.

She could not meet his eyes. While he could still strike anger in her heart, she didn't fear him as much as she feared herself, or at least the woman she became when she felt his touch. He drove her to emotional extremes, one of which was desire, and she could easily become enslaved to her passion.

Having failed to return to her time and with nothing left to lose, she would make one last attempt to gain her freedom. She'd thought of it during the long nights in the cabin, when she remembered every detail of her day on Tortola and reviewed everything the island boy had said. If Rackam's men confirmed that she was not Anne Bonny, then perhaps Antonio would allow her to use the medallion to try again to return to her time. Or better yet, would he ask her to stay, to be with him? Would he admit his love for her?

Taking a deep breath, she gazed into his eyes.

"You win," she said. "Let me up and I will take you to him."

Easing from her, he pulled her to her feet. She stepped away from him and looked out to sea. She saw a setting sun that turned the ocean to gold and glanced around the inlet at the jungle of flowering shrubs, the white sand, the progress of waves upon the shore. It should have been the paradise the cruise brochure had promised she would find in the islands. But could she still discover happiness here?

Her gaze met his. "Take me back to where you found me, Antonio. There, if anywhere, we will find the pirate you want and I will take you to your gold."

7

The boat landed on the north side of Tortola, at a point closest to the highest point on land. Beth had been specific. She wanted to reach the peak, where a few hundred years later a place called Skyworld Restaurant would stand. Joseph had said there were other pieces of treasure where he found the silver. Beth prayed he had known what he was talking about.

Two sailors from the *Manzanilla* accompanied Antonio and Beth on their trek. They carried cutlasses, as did Antonio, to hack their way through the undergrowth. He led the way. They had gone no more than a hundred yards into the interior when they found a rough path. He looked back at Beth, who walked between the two men.

She saw his inquiring look and nodded for him to continue up toward the hill. As if she knew what she was doing. As if she wasn't terrified of keeping her promise to lead them to Calico Jack. But Calico Jack could swear she wasn't Anne Bonny. So could his men. If she was right, Calico Jack had replaced his dead guards with other pirates, who might be there to capture and question them. If Antonio didn't shoot them before they could talk.

Or—she shivered at the thought—if they didn't shoot him.

She had tried to warn him of the danger.

"Take all the men," she had begged as they stood on the deck preparing to board the boat.

"We've sailed the perimeter of the island," Antonio had responded. "There is no pirate ship as you said there would be."

"All right," she had said, nervously aware of the crew watching her with open skepticism, "so maybe Rackam isn't close by. But he left men there before, and it's possible he's left them again."

"They were no more than a minor problem."

Now, she watched Antonio hack through the brush, then pause in his upward progress. She and the other men followed suit. Except for the rustling leaves and a screeching gull overhead, all was quiet. He appeared uneasy, as if he knew something was wrong.

Antonio resumed walking, and Beth, moving between the two sailors, followed, trying to get used to the borrowed boots that were much too large. She felt Antonio's eyes turn to her occasionally, but she couldn't bear to look up and see the grimness shadowing his face.

Within half an hour they reached a small clearing on what appeared to be the crest of the island. Like a sparkling jewel, the Caribbean spread to the horizon, but there was no time to appreciate the view. Beth studied the area, trying to remember which way the restaurant had faced—or would be facing in two hundred and seventy-four years. With the sun directly overhead, she had to ask Antonio which way was south.

Concentrating intensely on the problem, then figuring the placement of the parking lot, she gradually became aware of the stillness of Antonio and of his men. She glanced up at him. He stared past her with cold, steely eyes. She turned in the direction of his gaze and found herself looking into the barrel of a gun. The man holding it appeared much like the pirates Antonio had slain a month ago on the beach.

So did the two men hulking behind him, armed with similar weapons.

"By Gawd," the one in front said, "Calico Jack said you'd be back." He grinned and spat through blackened teeth. "M'boys, looks like we'll get our revenge."

Beth whirled back to Antonio. "I was afraid of this—" She broke off, anguish and fright tightening her throat.

He looked back in sad resignation that he'd been right about her all along. Beth read his thoughts, and her own mind screamed the protest that had so often been on her lips. Suddenly what he believed became more important to her than life itself. Damn her future and damn her past.

She turned to the pirates, forgetting caution, forgetting common sense, and taking off her hat, shook her hair loose. "You've sailed on Rackam's ship. Have you ever seen me before?"

All three pirates blinked at her.

"By Gawd," Black Teeth said, "it's a woman." He looked her up and down, grinning.

"Aye," one of his companions said, leering. "So 'tis."

Beth panicked at the thought that they would all die and the truth would never be known. "I asked if you'd seen me before."

"Quiet, wench," Black Teeth roared. "We'll hear from ye soon enough when we've got ye alone."

"You don't know me, do you?" she cried, beyond fear of harm. "Tell him. Tell them all. I'm not Anne Bonny. I'm not."

The pirate barked in laughter. "Ain't likely since the two of 'em's a hunnert miles away. 'Pears we'll be gettin' us a fire-haired bitch, too." He aimed his gun at her middle. "Unless ye don't quit yer whinin'."

Oh, God, she thought, why was she agitating these cutthroats like this? The men of the *Manzanilla* were armed with cutlasses, a weak defense against the pirates' guns.

One of the pirates was watching Beth with a look that was not comforting. It was, however, encouraging. She directed her attention to him. Fingering her hair, she smiled. "I'll bet Rackam keeps all the women for himself." She took a step forward, past the *Manzanilla*'s two crewmen, and stood between Antonio and the three guns.

She smiled at the pirate. "You know the old saying. To the victor go the spoils."

The pirate blinked in confusion.

Beth turned to Black Teeth. "Doesn't this one ever talk? I rather like a man who can express himself well. But I guess pirates aren't noted for that, are they?"

"Gawd almighty, woman, don't ye ever shut up?" Black Teeth snarled. "Git back wi' the others."

"Well, I can't. You see, they're not very happy with me right now. I was thinking that if you didn't mind—" She broke off, hearing a growl from behind her.

Moving quickly, she tossed her hat into Black Teeth's face, at the same time dropping to the ground and rolling against the legs of one of the other pirates. He didn't fall as she had hoped he would, but the jolt sent his gunshot high into the air.

Sound exploded around her as other gunshots followed. "Antonio!" she cried, springing to her feet and searching frantically for him through the smoke.

The air cleared. Antonio stood just out of arm's reach. At his feet sprawled one of the pirates, the hilt of a dagger impaled in his throat. Beth covered her mouth and looked at the two other bodies in the clearing. Both pirates were covered in blood, their guns useless in the dirt. Beth's gaze traveled to the red-stained cutlasses of Antonio and his men. They stood like statues, their eyes on her.

Forgetting the death surrounding her, she thought only that Antonio was alive. He stood much as she'd first seen him—his legs apart, in shirtsleeves and dark breeches and knee-high boots, his hair ruffled, a dark, wild look in his eyes.

She swayed toward him. "Antonio . . ."

"You saved my life." There was wonder in his voice, and more she could not name.

She said nothing. They looked at each other for what seemed an eternity. "Elizabeth."

Elizabeth. The sound of her name on his lips echoed in her mind. He had called her Elizabeth. She was filled with happiness because she understood what was in her heart.

She knew without a doubt that she loved him. She would risk danger a thousand times to keep him safe. And now that Antonio knew the truth, did he love her, too?

She kept her gaze on him. "Come, Antonio. We must find the treasure the little boy told me about. I promised to take you to it. You must know now that you can trust me."

They uncovered the buried gold after little searching, and as they descended the hill, Antonio stopped and took Beth's hand.

"Where did the little boy show you the medallion?"

Beth led him up to the spot where Joseph had revealed his hidden treasure. Antonio knelt and dug a small hole in the earth. He took the medallion from his boot, dropped it into the ground, and quickly covered it.

"What are you doing, Antonio? You promised to return the medallion to your father."

"It is my gift to Joseph for bringing you to me. When I tell my father of my love for you, he will understand."

They were back at the ship before dark, after burying the bodies of Rackam's men. When the sailors learned of Beth's role in regaining the gold, they cheered her and treated her with awe, fighting to spare her from the smallest task.

In the evening, she stood on the deck beside Antonio as the ship moved through the water under full sail. He was dressed in his usual black breeches and knee-high boots, but tonight he had added a brocade frock coat the color of a blazing noonday sky. His dark-brown hair hung below his collar, and his face bore a rare contented look.

Beth had never seen a more romantic figure in all her life.

An oversized embroidered shirt was the best he had been able to do for her, although he had promised that one day soon he would clothe her in the finest silk gowns. At his request, she had also put on the parrot earrings.

"They remind me of the day we met. You were the most exotic creature I had ever seen," he had said. "And so you remain."

Side by side, they stared at the moonlit sea, each waiting for the discussion that had been postponed. Around them the wooden ship groaned, the sails billowed, and the water slapped against the hull. It was music to them both.

"My father will adore you," Antonio said.

"Your father?"

"*Sí.* I have changed our course for Spain."

"Why?" she asked.

"To take you to your home."

Beth closed her eyes. Home. It had long been her goal. Could home be Antonio's castle off the coast of Spain?

Oh, yes, if he were there with her.

She turned to face him. "I'm a woman of the twentieth century. Have you accepted that?"

His eyes burned with such emotion that she felt the heat. "I love you, *querida.* I want you for my wife. Does that answer your question?"

Her eyes blurred with tears. "Oh, Antonio, I love you, too."

He pulled her into his arms and kissed her. It was a long time before he broke the embrace. Stroking her hair, he stared solemnly at her. "I cannot change my ways to be like the men of your time."

"And I can't be a quiet eighteenth-century servant wife, either. We've got some adjustments ahead."

"With love in the heart, all is possible."

She winked. "You've got that right. Sorry, a little modern slang. I'll try to watch it."

"And I will teach you the language of Cervantes. You will learn that it is the language of love." He grew solemn. "You have known me as the captain of a ship, but it is the land I favor. When we wed, you will become a farmer's wife."

"No problem. I was the geranium expert on West Eighty-second Street." Then she, too, grew solemn. "What about your people? Will they accept me?"

"There will be times when they do not understand your ways, but they will love you as much as I do. Well, perhaps not so much, but you understand."

"I understand." She looked out at the dark, rolling waves and the boundless sky. Stars that shone down on her would shine down on her family hundreds of years from this moment. "I wish I could tell my mother that all is well with me. That at last I have found happiness."

"You came to me in a miracle. Can you not believe that this miracle extends to giving her peace of mind?"

She looked at him with new appreciation. "What a clever man you are. A philosopher, I do believe. And a darling." She snuggled close. "I've spent some time wondering why I was transported to your time. I think now it was to help you and your people. And to help me, too. There was no happiness for me in my time, just work and a false sense of contentment."

Resting her head against his chest, she listened to his heartbeat. "I also believe that everything happening now is as right as anything in the universe. It's as if the planets changed their orbits to send me to you. We belong together, and my life with you will always be paradise. I know it in my heart."

She looked up at him. "I was thinking I might read up on Spanish law. You never know what good I can do."

"Or what mischief you can incite."

"Listen, Antonio, if at any time on this voyage you have second thoughts, just say so. I won't sue you for breach of promise."

His gaze locked with hers. "Listen to me, Elizabeth. I have found the gold for my people, but the greatest treasure I save for myself. You."

"All your doubts about me are gone?"

"*Todo.* I have but two regrets, my love. Foremost is the suffering I caused you because I could not accept the impossible truth you presented." He stroked her hair. "I will spend my life in compensation."

"That's not necessary. If our situations had been reversed, I wouldn't have believed you, either."

His finger on her lips stilled her words. "Such protests will serve little purpose. To deny my debt would rob me of happiness."

"And the second regret?"

"The scoundrel Rackam has escaped."

"Only until December. He's hanged in Jamaica,

right after a very pregnant Anne Bonny curses him for being captured."

A look of relief came into his eyes. "There are uses to your knowledge."

"I'll try not to be a know-it-all." She shared a smile with him and in her heart felt true contentment.

Antonio took her in his arms. His lips met hers, the kiss deepened, and Beth forgot everything but her love and her happiness. Overhead the sails flapped in the breeze, as if applauding the scene, and the *Manzanilla* glided quickly through the night toward Spain.

Evelyn Rogers

EVELYN ROGERS discovered her strong romantic streak when she began writing romance novels more than ten years ago. In her fourteen historical romances and several short stories she has worked at capturing the most vital element of romance—love. Nowhere has it appeared more naturally or dramatically than in this time-travel story, "Always Paradise."

She finds that the time-travel concept really puts the *romance* in romance literature, bringing together two people who are meant for each other, even if they are centuries apart.

This, to her, is the most romantic idea of all.

Time-Stolen Love

Bobbi Smith

Prologue

He moved silently and unnoticed through the dark, dank streets of Whitechapel, London's squalid East End. Though he appeared to be one of its residents, he was in truth a predator, prowling courts and alleyways, watching, planning for the moment he would strike. Only bloodletting could satisfy his hunger, and here he had found the perfect hunting ground. The destitute women who walked these streets were more than willing to satisfy his needs for a few pence—until they discovered what his needs really were.

A thrill shot through him at the thought of taking another unsuspecting prey. He stepped back into the shadows. Carriages passed on the cobblestoned street, people walked within arm's reach of him, but no one saw him. He felt omnipotent, immortal.

He thought of the name he'd chosen to sign his letter to the press: Jack the Ripper. It suited him well. They didn't respect his power yet, but they would after tonight. Tonight he would leave his indelible mark of fear on all of London.

He stepped from the shadows and returned to the hunt, searching the streets for the woman who would quench the fire of his bloodlust.

1

Roni Mitchell walked down Whitechapel's Commercial Street and stopped at a shop window that advertised Jack the Ripper souvenirs. She laughed. In a manner of speaking, Jack had brought her here. For some time she had been considering taping an investigative report on serial killers, and these streets, the Ripper's stalking ground, would be her first location.

This morning she had finished her documentary on powerful women in government by taping an interview with Margaret Thatcher. Now, her work done, she had taken her time, enjoying the East End's nineteenth-century charm. Yes, she would definitely recommend the serial-killer idea to her producer.

It was nearly sundown when she reached Whitechapel High Street. A few blocks ahead lay the Underground station, and she quickened her pace, eager to return to her hotel.

She crossed a side street, glanced down it, and stopped. Narrow and shadowed, the street seemed to belong to another age. Halfway down the block, a weather-beaten sign that read "Antiquities" hung over a small shop.

Intrigued, she turned down the side street. Nearing the shop, she saw the words "Fortune's Treasures" painted on the window, and a battered "Open" sign propped on the sill. A small, dark passageway led to the door. It creaked when Roni opened it.

She felt as if she were entering a different world. The air smelled musty, and to Roni's surprise, the shop was quite spacious, its long aisles cluttered with all variety of books and bric-a-brac.

"Good afternoon," a deep voice called.

Roni turned to see a wizened old man perched on a stool behind the counter. He could have been anywhere between sixty and a hundred and sixty. His eyes, bright blue, sparkled with humor and vitality.

"Hello," she said. "I didn't see you sitting there."

"It seems my lot in life is to be missed by the most beautiful women."

She laughed. "Thank you. I'm just completely enchanted. Your shop is wonderful."

"There are those who would not agree with you."

She frowned at his odd comment. "Then they must not appreciate the past." She made her way slowly down one of the aisles.

"My name's Telyur, by the way," the man said.

"It's a pleasure to meet you, Mr. Telyur. I'm Roni Mitchell."

"No 'Mister,' just Telyur," he said, smiling. "You're an American?"

"Yes, I'm from California."

"I've never been there, but I've heard it's a lovely place, warm and sunny almost all the time."

"It is beautiful, but then, there's beauty in everything, if you look for it."

"Well said, my dear. Is there anything special you're looking for?"

"No." She paused to examine a stack of leatherbound books. "You never know what you might stumble across. I love the past. There are so many mysteries . . . I've always believed that if I tried hard enough, I could solve them . . ."

She looked up. Telyur was staring at her intently, as if trying to see into her very soul. She smiled uneasily. "You must love history, too, or you wouldn't have this shop."

"History is my life, my existence."

"Have you been in business a long time?"

"An eternity, I think." He gave an odd chuckle.

"It can't be that bad. You must meet a lot of interesting people." She picked up a mantel clock.

"There are moments when it does seem worthwhile . . . Are you interested in timepieces?"

"Yes. I always wonder what happened in the hours they were running. I suppose that's why I do what I do."

"And what is that?"

"I'm a TV reporter. I like to discover the who, what, when, where, and why of things."

"Sometimes it's impossible to find the truth, you know."

She looked at him. What an odd little man. "Do you really think so?" she asked. "I always think it's best to bring things out into the light for all to see."

"Perhaps some things should not be seen."

For some reason, his words chilled her. "What do you mean?"

"Pure evil, for instance. Would you want to be the one to set it free?"

She did not know what to say.

Telyur slipped off the stool and walked into a small alcove behind the counter. "I have something here . . . something you might find interesting."

"Oh?" Roni felt a sudden urge to leave, yet her curiosity held her there.

"Come here, my dear. I want to show you something I have never shown to anyone."

She approached the counter. He began to sort through a jumble of wrapped packages on the counter, studying the inscription on each one.

"Ah!" He held up a small package wrapped in brown paper and tied with string. "Yes, I think you will be interested in this," he said, brushing a thick layer of dust from the top.

Roni leaned across the counter. "What is it?"

"Let me unwrap it for you." He stopped and looked at her. "Remember, no one else knows of its existence. If word of this were to get out . . ."

"Then why show it to me?"

His gaze burned with an inner fire. "Because I think it was not by chance that you entered my shop. I believe that destiny has brought you to me."

She said nothing as he untied the string and tore away the brittle paper. Inside was a plain, lidded wooden box. He pressed it into her hands.

She lifted the lid. Inside lay a gold pocket watch and fob. The watch bore no decoration or inscription. She set the box on the counter and carefully lifted out the watch. The metal felt cold in her hand, and she shivered. Then she looked at Telyur. "Who owned this watch?"

"You won't believe me."

"I'll believe you."

"The watch has been in this shop for as long as I have. I do not remember how it came here, but I do know that it once belonged to Jack the Ripper."

In any other shop in any other neighborhood, Roni would have laughed aloud, but somehow his declaration wasn't funny. Walking the streets of Whitechapel, she'd seen Jack the Ripper knives, Jack the Ripper deerstalker hats, but this . . . this was different. "How could you know that?" she asked, her voice a whisper.

"I know. As I have told you, I do not remember how it came here. But I do know that it was found at the scene of one of his murders."

"Whoever found it should have turned it over to Scotland Yard. It's a valuable clue."

He shrugged. "Many things in the past could have been done differently."

"Do you know who the Ripper was?" She had to ask.

"No one knows for sure."

"You don't believe any of the theories the experts have put forth?"

"Each contains some particle of truth, even as each contains a fatal flaw. It was the great mystery of its time, and it remains so today. Perhaps the truth will never be known."

Roni looked down at the watch in her hand.

"There's always the chance that some new piece of evidence will be discovered . . ."

"Yes, there is that chance."

She looked again at the watch. "Does it still keep time?"

"It hasn't worked in all the years I've had it in my possession."

She opened the case and read the time: three o'clock. Then she carefully returned the watch to the box and closed the lid. "I would like to buy it."

Her own words surprised her. Logic told her the watch was a fake, that it had no more connection to Jack the Ripper than the rubber knives in the windows of the other shops she'd passed. Yet something compelled her to own it.

"Some things cannot be sold," Telyur said. "They must find the person to whom they rightfully belong." He studied her face. "What did you feel when you first touched the watch?"

In her confusion she could find no words to describe her feelings.

"You needn't say anything." He handed the box back to her.

"I can't just take it," she said. "I must give you something in return." She thought for a moment, then slipped a signet ring from her finger and pressed it into his hand.

"It is sealed, then," he said. "We have made a bargain, you and I. I am glad you came into my shop, Miss Mitchell."

"I am, too," she said, putting the box in her pocket. Then she bid him good-bye and left the shop.

It was dark outside. She turned to look back at

the shop and saw Telyur flip the sign in the window to "Closed." Then, without looking up, he turned and vanished into the shadows.

2

Dampness hung in the air, and thick fog blanketed the street. Roni was glad she'd worn her trenchcoat. She buttoned the top button and hurried toward Whitechapel High Street and the Underground station.

Telyur's strange words still echoed in her mind, but she determined not to dwell on them until she was safely back in her hotel room. She quickened her pace, the fog swirling around her. It seemed to muffle all sound and left her slightly disoriented.

She was about to turn the corner when she heard the faint, muted sound of a chime. She stopped, wondering where the sound had come from, then realized it was the watch in her pocket. Stopping beneath a street light, she pulled out the box. Just as she lifted the lid, it chimed again. Her hand trembling, she lifted the watch out by the fob and held it to her ear. The watch was ticking. She opened the case and strained to read the time in the semidarkness. Three o'clock.

A gust of chill wind swept down the street, moaning eerily as it passed. At the same time the street light overhead dimmed, and Roni looked up to see a flickering gaslight. She could have sworn it had been an ordinary street light when she'd sought its protection.

It had grown strangely quiet. The sounds of traffic were gone, replaced by an unsettling stillness. Still clutching the watch by its fob, Roni hurried on toward Whitechapel High Street.

Footsteps echoed on the street behind her. She walked faster, knowing that safety was as near as the corner. The footsteps quickened to match hers. Her heart began to race.

Then she laughed to herself. She was being ridiculous, she thought, and turned to see who was behind her.

She came face to face with a man who emerged from the fog. He was far taller than her own five feet eight inches. His long cape and the clothing beneath it were dark, and he wore a deerstalker hat that shadowed his face, though she could see that he had fair hair and a mustache. Then, for a fleeting second, she caught a glimpse of his eyes. They were cold, emotionless.

She paused, stunned. Then the long blade of a knife gleamed in the distant lamplight. Gasping, she turned to flee.

With lightning speed he grabbed her by the arm, the knife poised in his other hand, his black cape billowing around him.

Her self-defense training told her she wouldn't be able to overpower her attacker, but if she were quick enough she knew she had a chance of getting away. She tried to yank her arm free and run, but he was surprisingly strong. His hand tightened painfully on her arm and he spun her around, slamming her against his chest.

She felt his hot breath on her cheek. Knowing

her very life depended on her next move, she reached back to gouge at his eyes, at the same time stomping with all her might on his instep. He let out a grunt of pain, and in the split second when he loosened his grip, she jabbed her elbow into his stomach and broke free, her purse falling to the street.

Cursing, the man reached for her again, but he succeeded in grabbing only the watch she still held in her hand. Releasing it, she turned and ran toward the Underground station and salvation.

"Help!" she cried, running into Whitechapel High Street. The fog was even thicker here, and she wondered what had become of the cars and buses that had crowded the street only a short time ago. Her breath rasped loudly in her ears as she ran, not daring to look back to see if the man was following her.

From out of the fog loomed a horse and carriage. With a cry of panic, Roni tried to dodge the rearing horse. Her foot slipped on the damp pavement and she fell, hitting her head with a jarring thud. Dazed, she lay where she had fallen. The world swam around her, and she closed her eyes.

"Easy, boy," a man's voice said.

She heard the sound of a latch opening. "Bellamy, what the devil is going on?" another man said, this one younger judging by the sound of his voice.

"It's a woman, sir. She ran right out in front of me. Nearly ran her down, we did."

"A woman? What was she thinking of, running out in the street that way?"

"Is she dead, sir?"

"No, thank heaven. She's alive, but it seems

she's hit her head. She's going to have a nasty bruise."

Roni felt someone touch her forehead, and she winced with pain. She opened her eyes and saw a man's face hovering near her. Her vision blurred, and suddenly she saw the face of the man with the knife and the stone-cold eyes.

"No! Let me go!" She struggled wildly, striking out at him with her fists.

"What the—!" Two strong arms pinned her hands at her sides. "Miss, calm down! I'm not going to hurt you."

"What . . . ?" Panting, she blinked several times, struggling to clear her vision and her head. When at last her eyes focused, she realized that this was not the man who had attacked her. This man was young, fair-haired and clean-shaven, his features lean and handsome. His eyes were deep, smoky gray, and they reflected intelligence and concern, not the deadly intent she'd seen in the other man's gaze.

"I said calm down," he said gently.

"But you've got to help me! I've got to get away from here!" She imagined her attacker closing in on them even now. This man who held her looked big and strong enough, but the other man had had that knife . . .

"Easy now, miss. You've had a bad fall and hit your head." He released her arms.

"But you don't understand! He's after me . . ." She struggled to sit up and look around. Pain pounded in her head.

"Who's after you?"

"I don't know who he was. But he was right behind me and he had a knife!"

The man went still. "A man was chasing you with a knife?"

"Yes! I had just come out of a shop and he came up behind me. I got away, but—"

"You said you saw him?"

"Yes."

"Did you see him clearly?"

"Yes! His hair was a little lighter than yours. He had a mustache and the coldest eyes . . ."

The man lifted his head and looked around, his piercing gaze seeming to take in every detail of the street and buildings. Then he slipped his arm around Roni's shoulders and helped her stand. "We'd better get in the carriage."

"Carriage?" Now she wondered what in the world this man was doing with a horse and carriage, but she felt too weak and dizzy to ask. She took a step and then the world spun crazily and she clutched at her rescuer for support. When he swept her up into her arms to carry her, she was grateful. She felt safe and protected, and for that moment she gave herself over into his keeping. It was an odd feeling for her; she was so used to taking care of herself.

He settled her in the carriage, then climbed in and leaned his head out the door. "Bellamy, get home as fast as you can!"

"Is she that bad, sir?"

"No . . . But I think she may have seen him. I must keep her safe." He spoke in a low voice, as if someone were near, listening.

"Yes, Mr. Grayson!"

The man called Grayson pulled the door shut and settled himself beside Roni as the carriage lurched into motion.

The man went still. "A man was chasing you with a knife?"

3

Though it was dark inside the carriage, Kent Grayson could see that the woman was pale. Yet he could also see she was quite beautiful. Her hair was the color of gold, long and loose around her shoulders. Her features were delicate—her mouth soft and vulnerable, her nose straight and feminine.

Suddenly she sat up and looked at him, her eyes wide. "That man's a madman! I may have gotten away, but somebody else may not be so lucky. Stop this thing so I can get to the phone and call the police!"

Kent had no idea what a phone was, but he was determined to put her at ease. He must get her safely away so he could question her about what she'd seen. "Miss, there's nothing to fear. I am the police."

"You?" She peered at him through the dimness.

"Yes, I'm Inspector Kent Grayson of Scotland Yard."

"If you're an inspector, why on earth didn't you go after him? He had a knife, and the way he was dressed, he looked like some kind of Jack the Ripper impersonator!"

Kent went rigid. He stared at her. There was no way she could have known that name unless she were directly involved in the case. The letter, written in red ink and signed "Jack the Ripper," had arrived at the Central News Agency two days ago on the twenty-eighth, and so far the Yard had taken great care to keep the letter's contents out of the press. The public still referred to the killer as "Leather Apron" because of an apron that had been found at the site of the first murder.

"We'll talk about that later," Kent said. "Right now the most important thing is to get you to safety."

"Just take me back to my hotel, then," she said. "Once I get there I'll be fine."

"Which hotel are you staying at?"

"The Hilton at the airport."

He stared at her in confusion. He knew of no hotel in London called the Hilton. And what the devil was an airport?

He wondered if she was an escapee from Bedlam or some other private institution, come to the East End to play on the police's desperate attempts to catch the killer. Perhaps she had written that letter! Disturbed people often took credit for crimes they hadn't committed. He wanted desperately to challenge her knowledge but decided to wait until they reached his house, where she could not run from him.

"My townhouse is close by," he said. "My driver is taking us there. My physician lives nearby, and I can send for him to come and see to your head."

"My head is fine," she said. "I don't need a doctor."

"I insist."

She eyed his suspiciously. "If you're the police, let me see some ID."

"I beg your pardon?"

"I want to see your police badge or whatever you carry around to identify yourself. How do I know you're not connected with that lunatic?"

Kent said nothing as he drew out his identification and handed it to her. She studied it closely, trying to read it in the dark.

"Trust me, Miss ... What is your name, by the way?"

"Roni. Veronica, really. Veronica Mitchell."

"I'm pleased to make your acquaintance, Miss Mitchell."

"Look, Inspector, I'm really not in the mood for chit-chat. I've just been attacked. I've lost my purse, the watch ... And why are we riding in this thing. Don't you have a car?"

He frowned. "A car, Miss Mitchell? Do you mean a railroad car?"

She exhaled in exasperation and turned to look out the window. For several moments she was quite still. Then she looked back at him, her face pale. "Where are we?" Her voice was a hoarse whisper.

"I don't understand what you mean ..." Kent said. Clearly her injury was serious.

"I mean the people in the old-fashioned clothes and all those other horses and carriages. Is this some kind of tourist thing?"

"Miss Mitchell," he said sympathetically, "you've had a bad fall and I can see that you're a little confused. Why don't you just rest until we get to my townhouse? After the doctor sees you, I'm sure you'll be as good as new."

"Mr. Grayson, do not patronize me. I want to know what's going on."

He glanced out at the street, confused. "I'm

sorry, but I'm afraid I still have no idea what you mean."

"I mean everything's changed!"

"What is it you're looking for?" he asked. "Perhaps we're in a part of the city you don't recognize."

"I don't care what part of the city we're in! Where are the cars and buses and . . ." She glanced out the window again and broke off as another brougham went by.

"Cars? Buses?" he repeated.

She turned to him hopefully. "Are we on a movie set or something?"

He shook his head. "I'm afraid, Miss Mitchell, you are making no sense at all."

She stared at him as if he were the one making no sense. "Everything looks as if we're in the 1800s."

"But we are."

"We are what?"

"In the 1800s. It's 1888. Really, Miss Mi—"

"You're saying it's 1888."

"Well, yes, of course!" he said impatiently. Was this some sort of strange joke, or was she truly daft? Perhaps she had been drinking. He smelled no liquor on her breath. "September thirtieth, to be exact."

"Let met out of the carriage—now!" She moved toward the door.

Kent grabbed her arm and pulled her back against the seat. "Please. In just a minute we'll be at my townhouse."

"I don't want your townhouse. All I want is to find a phone so I can call a cab. I'll take it from there."

"I'm afraid that's not possible."

She stared at him. "Not possible! I don't think so. This is Roni Mitchell you're dealing with. Thanks for all your help. It's been interesting. This next corner looks great. Just let me out here." She reached for the door handle.

"I can't let you do that, Miss Mitchell." He spoke in a low voice, but his arm held her back firmly.

She gave him a look of panic. "What are you talking about? You can't let me do what?"

"I can't let you leave."

"Why not?"

"Because you've seen the killer."

"The killer?"

"As you said, you saw Jack the Ripper. No one else has ever seen him and lived to tell about it."

"You're saying the man who attacked me was Jack the Ripper? First you try to convince me it's 1888, and now . . . You're out of your mind!"

"No, Miss Mitchell, I am quite sane. You have seen the killer, and therefore he has seen you. The only safe place for you is with me. You will remain under my protection until I discover what connection you have to all this." He looked out the window. "Ah, here we are now," he said, and the carriage drew to a halt.

4

"**S**hall I carry you inside?" Kent asked as he helped her descend from the carriage.

"No, I'm perfectly capable of walking now," Roni said irritably and moved past him. She looked up at the three-story townhouse and paused. Once again she felt that something strange was happening.

As if sensing her hesitation, Kent took her arm. "Let's go inside. Bellamy, you can put the carriage away. And then I'd like to see you."

Roni froze. "I told you, I am not going in that house with you. Why don't you take me to the Yard and we can talk there?" She tried to pull away from him.

"Miss Mitchell, I think it would be more prudent if we went inside and discussed things privately." He tightened his hold on her arm and propelled her straight up the steps. As they reached the door, it opened, startling her. Then she saw an elderly, kindly-looking man in a butler's uniform and breathed a sigh of relief. At least she wouldn't be alone with Grayson.

"Good evening, sir," the butler said.

"Good evening." Kent released Roni's arm as soon as they were inside. "Hargrove, this is Miss Mitchell. She'll be staying with us, and I'd like you to tell Mrs. Randall and Mrs. Reilly and anyone

288

else who asks that she is my American cousin who's come to visit.,"

"Very well, sir," Hargrove replied.

"I never agreed . . ." Roni began, but Kent shot her a quelling look.

"Hargrove, I suggest you prepare the front guest room."

"Yes, sir. Let me take your coats," Hargrove said, and waited as Roni removed her trenchcoat. Both men stared at her. She frowned. She knew her outfit was current and fashionable. The fuchsia wool jacket over a white silk blouse and black slacks had been perfect for her day's outing in Whitechapel. Why were they looking at her so strangely?

"You're dressed like a man . . ." Kent said.

Roni had had enough. "If you think for one minute that I'm buying this 1880s act of yours, think again!" Exasperated, she marched out of the foyer and into the front room. Once she found Kent's TV and VCR, his telephone, and newspapers with the date June 2, 1994 on them, she would tell him he was full of it and get the hell out of here.

But there was no TV, no VCR, and no telephone. The furniture was heavy Victorian, and tiny flames flickered in the Tiffany lamps lighting the room.

At that moment, the truth hit her, shattering her anger and leaving bewilderment in its place as she tried to grasp the magnitude of what had happened to her. She knew that a lesser woman would have panicked. But Roni was not given to panic. On the contrary, if she had achieved the impossible and traveled through time, then this was truly the challenge of a lifetime, terrifying but also fascinating.

"Damn, it really is . . ." she murmured. But how had it happened?

"It really is what?" Kent asked, closing the doors behind him.

She faced him with as much bravado as she could muster. "I'm hoping you have some liquor in the house, because when I'm finished telling you, we're both going to need a drink."

"Telling me what?"

"We need to have a talk . . . a long one. I don't think you're going to believe much of what I have to say, but you have to hear it anyway. Since you're a detective and I'm a reporter, maybe together we can figure this out. You got any whiskey?"

"Whiskey? Well, yes."

"Good. I'll take a straight shot. This has been a long day, and I've got a feeling it's going to get even longer before it's over." She dropped onto the sofa.

Kent crossed to a small liquor cabinet, returned with two shot glasses, and handed her one. Then he sat down at the other end of the sofa. "You say you're a reporter? Are you with the Central News Agency?"

"No, I'm a TV reporter. I live in California. I flew here to do an interview with . . ." She could see from his face that he was completely bewildered.

"Why don't we start at the beginning," he said. "Suppose you tell me what you were doing in Whitechapel tonight."

"That's what I was trying to do," she said in exasperation. "I'm here in London on business. I finished my project early and decided to go sightseeing in Whitechapel."

He stared at her. "No one goes sightseeing in the East End."

"In 1994 they do."

"Nineteen ninety-four?" he repeated, scowling.

For the first time, she smiled. "Good. I'm glad to see you looking so perplexed. Now you're as confused as I am. While I was walking around the East End, I found this antique shop run by a very interesting man named Telyur. I bought a watch from him, left the shop, and the next thing I knew I was being chased by that wild man with the knife. The rest you know."

"You actually want me to believe that you came here from the future?"

"Look, you're the detective, you figure it out. I sure can't. All I know is that one minute I was in Whitechapel chuckling over Jack the Ripper souvenirs and the next minute I was running for my life in 1888. If you can give me a logical explanation as to how I got here, I'll be glad to listen to it."

Kent downed the rest of his whiskey in one gulp, then got up and poured himself another.

Roni watched him, sensing his doubt. "Look, I know it sounds wild. I know it doesn't make sense. Lord knows, I had no great desire to be whisked back in time like this. I feel like Michael J. Fox without the car. At least he could get back to the future."

Kent returned to the sofa. "Michael who?"

"Never mind." She sighed in frustration, seeing the uncertainty in his eyes. She sipped her whiskey and enjoyed its fiery effect. "Look . . ." she began again. Then she remembered something. Setting her glass aside, she stood up and shoved her hand into the pocket of her jacket. She almost shouted for joy when she felt the five-pound note she'd stuffed there earlier after paying for her taxi.

"I know my words aren't convincing you, but this should!" She pulled the bill out of her pocket and handed it to him. "Look! Queen Elizabeth's picture is on it. That'll prove I'm not out of my mind."

"Queen Elizabeth has been dead for years," Kent scoffed, taking the note from her hand and staring down at it. He frowned.

"Not Elizabeth the First. This is Elizabeth the Second!"

"Elizabeth the Second?"

He studied the bill for a long moment and then glanced up at her. His face had grown pale, and she could see undisguised amazement in his eyes.

"Now check the date," she said.

He did, and she heard him draw a sharp breath. "Nineteen ninety-two," he murmured. "This is incredible."

"I know."

His gaze met hers, searching, questioning, and finally believing.

She gave a little smile when she saw the acceptance in his eyes. "I don't know how this happened to me, but it did. The question is, what do we do now?"

"I think our first step is to pour you another whiskey." He retrieved the bottle and refilled their glasses.

They drained their drinks in silence.

There was a knock, and Kent rose and opened the doors. He stepped out into the foyer, and Roni could see him speaking to Bellamy. Kent reentered the room and pulled the doors closed. He sat down again on the sofa and studied her.

"If you're from the future, how do you know about Jack the Ripper?" he finally asked.

"*Everyone* knows about him in my time. The Jack the Ripper murders are one of the greatest unsolved mysteries of all time."

"Unsolved?" he said, clearly shocked.

"No arrests were ever made. Let me try to remember what I've read. I think he murdered a total of five or six women. On one night he actually killed two. I wish I could remember the dates..."

Kent shook his head in wonder. "So far he has killed only two... The letter he wrote to the press hasn't even been released to the public yet. No one knows the name 'Jack the Ripper' except those directly involved in the investigation—and the killer himself."

"And someone from the future," she added simply.

"Yes, and thank heaven you're here with me. You heard what I told Hargrove to tell my cook, Mrs. Randall, and my charwoman, Mrs. Reilly. And I have given the same instructions to Bellamy, so there will be no uncomfortable questions about you, and I can keep you safe here until we catch him."

"But you won't catch him," she pointed out.

"Yes, I will. If it's the last thing I do, I'll see him pay for what he's done."

"And will do," she said. "You can't change history, so what do you want to do now?"

"I want you out of harm's way until the Ripper is in custody. Just because there is no record in your time of his being caught doesn't mean he wasn't. Perhaps over time, facts about this case and the Ripper's arrest were lost. If so, I wouldn't be changing history after all. Nevertheless, when we have him locked up, I want you to see him so that we can be sure we have the right man."

"Now hold on a minute. There is no way I'm going to sit in this house like a prisoner and wait for you to find the Ripper. Look, let's assume for the moment that your theory is right and that you will catch him. I can help you with the investigation. I'm trained to uncover information. It's what I do for a living."

"Miss Mitchell . . ."

"Roni."

"Roni, I don't want you to leave this house. I . . . I've seen what the Ripper does to his victims. You'll stay right here where it's safe."

She shook her head. "I'm going to help you. Have you gotten any fingerprints or blood samples? Were there any hair samples? Any skin or blood under the victims' fingernails?"

"What are you talking about?"

She stopped, realizing she was over a hundred years ahead of herself. "Never mind. Look, I want to help. Tell me what you have."

"I don't want you involved."

"I'm already involved. I became involved the minute the Ripper attacked me. I am going to work with you."

"No, you're not."

"Why not?"

"Because you're a woman."

"Oh, really?" she said, amused.

"Yes, and it's a man's duty to protect a woman from the ugliness of life."

"But I'm the only real witness you've got."

"Not if you're dead, and that's exactly why I want you to stay here. What if he came after you again? You'd be helpless against him."

"No, I wouldn't. I can take care of myself."

"Of course you can, my dear. But . . ."

"But nothing. Try me." She stood, ready to demonstrate her prowess after seven years of tae kwon do.

He looked at her in dismay. "I have no intention of trying to harm you."

"I didn't say you were going to. I said you should try. Come on. Try to grab me."

"This is ridiculous."

"Are you afraid?"

Reluctantly, Kent followed Roni into the foyer.

"Now," she said, "pretend you're the Ripper and you're after me. Come at me." She motioned for him to charge her.

"This is pointless. I know I'm bigger and stronger than you are, and I don't want to hurt you."

"You won't. I thwarted Jack's attack on me, didn't I?"

In a lightning move, Kent charged Roni and tried to grab her. She was ready for him. Timing her move perfectly, she shifted her weight to the side, grabbed him, and tossed him. He was heavy and it wasn't easy or pretty, but she had proven her point. He might not be unconscious, but he was on the floor, and had he been the bad guy, she would have had time to escape.

"Satisfied?" she asked, feeling slightly more in control of her situation.

"I don't think I'd like living in the 1990s," he muttered as he got up.

"I'm working with you on this case," she said. "You may be right that you will catch the Ripper but that we will never learn of it in my time. There is also the possibility that you will not only catch him, but that once his identity is discovered, a massive coverup will occur—another reason why there would be no record of the case being solved in my time. Either way, he must be stopped.

"Here's how our partnership will work. I'll tell you everything I can remember, and you'll share your information with me. It's fifty-fifty. Have we got a deal?"

"I don't like it."

"I didn't ask you if you liked it. I asked you if we have a deal. Well?"

"All right, but on one condition. You are not to go roaming the streets looking for him, and you will confine yourself to discussing theories and whatever clues I might find. Besides," he added, smiling, "I can't have you hunting him down with me. How would I ever explain you to the Yard?"

5

"Mr. Grayson?"

Hargrove's soft call, accompanied by

his knock at the bedroom door, brought Kent instantly awake.

"Yes? What is it?" Kent sat up in bed as Hargrove entered the room and lit a lamp.

"One of your associates from the Yard is downstairs, sir. It seems there's been more trouble."

Kent swore violently under his breath. Quickly he got out of bed and pulled on his pants, then at a run he grabbed a shirt and suitcoat and hurried from the room. When he reached the top of the staircase, he saw his friend, Rod Davidson, waiting for him downstairs in the foyer.

"What's happened?" Kent tucked in his shirt as he descended.

"It's horrible, Kent. He's struck again, and not just once this time . . . He murdered two tonight!"

Kent reeled. Roni had known about the double murder before it had even occurred. Any doubts he had had about her story vanished. "Let's go," he said, shrugging into his suitcoat and then his overcoat.

"It is gruesome, sir," Rod said.

"I didn't expect it to be otherwise." Kent followed his colleague into the predawn darkness.

Roni sat in the parlor of Kent's townhouse, trying to occupy herself. When she'd awakened early that morning, Hargrove had informed her that Mr. Grayson had gone out during the night. After the huge breakfast Mrs. Randall had prepared, Roni had read the newspaper, marveling at the events of October 1, 1888. Since then, however, she had been at loose ends. She wondered where Kent had gone and whether his sudden departure had anything to do with the Ripper. He had made no mention last night of having to go out.

It was midday when she heard him come in, and she hurried to the foyer, eager to see him. He was handing Hargrove his coat when she reached the parlor doorway. When he turned to her, his face was grim and haggard.

"The Ripper again?" she asked.

"It was just as you'd said. He struck twice just before dawn."

"Oh, God . . ." Agony filled her at the thought that if she had remembered more, she might have been able to prevent the killings. "Did you find anything?"

"Nothing. It's as if he disappears into thin air."

"What are we going to do?" she asked.

He glanced at her, dressed in her own clothes, and gave a little smile. "The first thing we had better do is buy you something to wear. Those clothes would draw too much attention in public."

"In the future a lot of women will be running around in slacks, but I guess you don't want me to be a trendsetter."

He couldn't help laughing. "No, not right now."

"But I don't have any money."

"I'll pay for them."

"I appreciate your generosity. I'd like you to keep track of everything you spend so I can pay you back." But even as Roni spoke, she wondered how she would ever be able to do so, stranded here with no career prospects and no way of returning home.

"It's not necessary," he said.

"I insist. It's the way we do things in my time."

"Very well. I'll order the carriage and join you in a few minutes."

Kent went upstairs to wash before his outing with Roni. He felt contaminated by the ugliness he had just seen. He yearned to get away from the case for a while, and today was the perfect opportunity. He would take Roni to buy an appropriate wardrobe, and then they would dine out. She was a breath of fresh air in his life—something he needed now. The long hours he had spent working on the murders had tarnished him, dulling his heart and soul. Roni, he hoped, would bring the shine back into his life.

After washing up, Kent donned a dark suit and waistcoat and descended the stairs to the foyer.

Roni was waiting for him in the parlor, and when he joined her, she smiled at him. "Are you ready to go?" he asked.

"If you are."

The dress shop was a short carriage ride away.

"These clothes are wonderful," Roni said, looking through the window at a display of hats and bustles and parasols. She laughed. "What great antiques!" Abruptly her smile vanished. "You really think it's necessary for me to wear these things?"

"Yes, if you want to move around freely and go unnoticed."

She nodded, but her expression was doubtful as she gazed at the selection of bustles.

A short time later Kent watched as Roni emerged from the fitting room at the back of the dress shop to model yet another outfit for him, a visiting dress of dark green wool. Demure in style with its high neck and long sleeves, it fitted her to perfection, the skirt nipping at her waist and then flaring out over the bustle in the back.

He smiled broadly, "You look lovely."

"Do you really think so?" She tugged at her corset. "I feel like a sausage."

"You'll get used to it," he said, then turned to the proprietress. "We'll take it. And the lady will also need something for evening wear."

The woman frowned. "While some of our day dresses are ready-made, I'm afraid our formal gowns are still sewn to order." She paused, then smiled. "I do have something in back that just might fit . . . The gown was made for another customer who cancelled the order at the last minute. I think with a few alterations the gown might do. Come with me, my dear . . ." She ushered Roni into the fitting room.

A half-hour later, Roni emerged from the back again, this time wearing a low-cut gown of lace and royal-blue velvet. Kent stared at her, mesmerized, as she walked slowly toward him. The seamstress had helped her arrange her hair in a sophisticated style, and although he had thought her lovely before, he now thought her positively ravishing. The color of the gown suited her fairness, bringing out the blue of her eyes and the highlights in her upswept pale-golden tresses.

Kent's gaze dropped to the decolletage and his breath caught in his throat. The gown had obviously been made for a much smaller-busted woman. Roni more than filled out the bodice, her breasts swelling temptingly above the lace. As much as he was enjoying the view, he reminded himself that the proprietress thought Roni was his cousin and he forced his eyes away from the enticing display.

"As you can see," the shop owner was saying, "I'll need to let the seams out at the bodice. Otherwise, it fits beautifully."

"How soon can you have it ready?"

"By the day after tomorrow."

"That will be fine. We'll take it."

Kent met Roni's eyes and knew while he was with her he could put the ugliness of the murders out of his mind. He was pleased that the current fashions suited her so well, but then he'd had little doubt. Her figure was slender yet womanly, and her manner, for all her strange ways, was ladylike. He had never met anyone like her, and he doubted he ever would again. She was the perfect combination of beauty and intelligence, and he grew more intrigued with her every minute.

"As soon as the alterations are completed, deliver the packages to my home," he instructed the proprietress as he paid the bill.

"What would you like us to do with her other clothes?" the woman asked, eyeing the parcel. She had barely concealed her shock at seeing Roni in men's trousers when she and Kent had arrived.

"I'll take them with me," Roni said as she emerged from the fitting room, where she had changed into the dark green visiting dress. To Kent she looked every bit an 1880s woman.

But clearly the clothes did not feel as right as they looked, for as Kent escorted Roni from the shop, the parcel containing her old clothes under his arm, she chafed uncomfortably.

"Incredible," she muttered, and struggled to climb into the carriage.

"What is?" he asked.

"This corset! In my time, we would burn the damn thing. What evil, sadistic person created it? No doubt it was a man. How's a woman supposed to breathe in it, let alone move?"

"I've never given it much thought."

"You should. This is cruel and unusual punishment. How could a woman run in this if she were in trouble? It would be next to impossible for her to protect herself."

"Why would a lady need to protect herself? Her husband would protect her."

"Some women don't have husbands to protect them. The women in Whitechapel, for example."

"You're right," he said grimly as he helped her into the carriage. All thoughts of the murders dissipated as he caught a glimpse of her shoes, and realized that they had one more stop to make.

"Bellamy, take us to a ladies' shoe shop," he directed as he settled himself beside Roni.

"Yes, sir."

"I guess I do need shoes," Roni remarked as she glanced down at her practical low-heeled pumps.

"After we get them, we can dine out, if you like. Are you hungry?"

"I'm famished, and, yes, I'd love to eat out." Roni smiled at him, then turned to gaze out the carriage window.

To Roni, nineteenth-century London was even more fascinating in the daytime than at night. As strange as it was for her to be here, she was determined to enjoy every minute.

But why was she here? She thought back to her actions the previous night, just before she had realized she was standing under a gaslight. She remembered hearing the watch chime, opening it, and hearing it tick. Then the fog had come up and she had found herself still holding the watch in the gaslight's dim glow.

Her heart pounded and she felt a sheen of sweat break out on her forehead. It was the watch that had caused her to travel in time! But her realization brought no relief, for she knew that without the watch, she could not go home.

Then another thought assaulted her. Even if she had the watch, would she want to leave?

Kent glanced at Roni as she peered out the window, and again he was struck by her beauty. He had found her attractive when she had worn trousers, and now, dressed in the current fashion, she completely entranced him. He stared at her profile, wondering what act of fate had brought her to him. Though she had been with him less than a day, the thought that she might leave him someday made him uneasy. She captivated him, and didn't seem to possess the flirtatious artifices he'd suffered through with most of the unmarried women he knew. Despite their bizarre meeting, he was strongly drawn to her, and was actually looking forward to having dinner with her—after they bought her shoes.

Two hours later, after finishing their meal in the quiet establishment Kent had chosen, they finally took up the subject of the murders, reexamining everything they knew about Jack the Ripper, trying to find the clue that might reveal his identity.

"Who were considered the most likely suspects in your time?" Kent asked.

"You may not want to hear this . . ."

"Go ahead," he encouraged.

"History has focused on five suspects. One was a poor, single man from the Whitechapel area. One was a lawyer from a good family who was rumored to be insane. One was the queen's physician, and the last two . . ." She hesitated, knowing that what she was about to say was surely close to blasphemy. "The last two were the queen's grandson, Prince Eddy, and a friend of his, J. K. Steven."

Kent nodded. "We're investigating all those leads," he said noncommittally.

She understood his discomfort that one of the royals might be involved. If one of them was, then that would explain a coverup in this time. "All I know is that the last murder will occur some time in early November—around the tenth, I think, though I'm not certain."

"Early November . . . So we have about a month's reprieve," he said.

She nodded. "If you're going to catch him, you'll have to do it between now and then. If we could save that one woman's life, all this will have been worth it." She looked down at the table. "His last murder . . . was his most savage."

"I'll do everything in my power to stop him before then," Kent promised.

"I believe you."

In the soft, muted light of the restaurant, she met his gaze across their secluded table. She could see the fierceness of his determination in the depths of his gray eyes, and her admiration for this special man grew. She knew that his dedication to solving the case wasn't motivated by a desire for fame or accolades, for he knew now from what she had told him that he would get no recognition for his success. He wanted to catch the Ripper for only one reason—to save lives.

There was a long pause as they gazed at each other enraptured, as if seeing each other for the first time . . . as if their coming together had been destined.

"Let's speak of something else," Kent said at last. "Tell me about your life . . . about you . . ."

She was relieved to be distracted from thoughts of the murderer. He haunted her every waking moment as it was. She began to tell Kent about her life in California. She told of how she had built her career, and of her desire to become the best investigative reporter in television news.

"Do you have any family?" he asked.

"My mother lives in Chicago. Whenever I can, I fly out to see her, but—"

"Fly?"

She smiled. "We have airplanes . . . jets, actually. We can fly from coast to coast in a matter of hours."

"Amazing. What about your father? Is he dead?"

"No . . ." Roni paused, remembering the pain of her parents' divorce when she was twelve. "He and my mother were divorced. I rarely see him anymore."

"Oh."

She heard the shock and surprise in Kent's voice; she knew that divorce was practically nonexistent in his time.

"And you have no husband or fiancé?" he asked.

"No. I guess I'm too busy to think about romance. There's not much time for a relationship with all the traveling I do. Plus, I'm not really sure I want to get married."

"Why not?"

Her expression was tinged with sadness as she looked at him. "My mother loved my father with all her heart and soul. Her entire life was centered around him, and when he left her . . . Well, she was never the same after that. I don't think I want to put myself in that position . . . to give a man that kind of power over me."

"But marriage isn't a matter of one partner having power over the other. A husband and wife should complement each other, not dominate each other. A marriage is sharing both the good and the bad, with complete and total trust. What man wouldn't want to come home to a loving wife?"

"Plenty of them," she said with a hint of bitterness, thinking of all the nights she'd listened to her mother cry herself to sleep. "That's why I'm determined to be independent. I don't need a man to take care of me. I'll take care of myself."

"So you never want to marry? Surely you want to have children someday."

"Who says I need a husband to have children?"

He stared at her, aghast. "Have things changed so much in the next hundred years?"

"Well, there was the sexual revolution in the sixties. Women are no longer repressed as they are in your time. They no longer believe they exist purely to satisfy a man's desire."

Kent chuckled. "Repressed is hardly a word I

would use to describe the women I've known. I've never met a woman yet who thought she existed simply to satisfy my desires, unless you'd like to be the first." There was a gleam of wicked amusement in his gaze.

"I'll pass, but thanks for the offer," she countered.

"Most of the women I know would be insulted to think that you considered them somehow less than their husbands' equals. What could be more important in this world than raising children and keeping a warm, loving home for a family? Family is the most important thing in the world, you know."

Roni sensed that Kent meant every word he was saying, and she was touched by his ardent devotion to marriage and family. She found herself wondering what it would be like to be married to a man like him . . . a man who truly believed in the vows he would take, a man who would put his wife and children first in his life, and she decided it might not be so bad. "What about your family?"

"My parents are both dead, but I have a brother who is happily married and has three sons. I see him at the holidays."

"No fiancée?"

"No. I suppose I'm like you. I'm wedded to my job. There is satisfaction in knowing that I'm helping people . . . But tell me more about the 1990s. What else is exciting?"

Roni paused, not sure where to start. "Well, we have cars—horseless carriages is what they used to call them, and they run on gasoline. We have television—it's an electronic device that projects a picture with sound, so instead of relying on newspapers for information, you can just turn on the TV and get all the news you want. We have highways, skyscrapers, air conditioning, electricity . . ."

"Do you miss it all?"

She paused to consider his question. Of course she missed it. That was her life. But she was here for whatever purpose. "Yes." She heard the loneliness in her own voice.

Kent reached out to cover her hand with his. She was surprised by her reaction to his touch. She felt drawn to him, and knew instinctively that she could trust him with her life.

"Could you be happy here?" he asked.

"It's a slower-paced, more romantic time, but . . ." She found herself wondering about her life . . . if she would ever find the watch, which seemed impossible . . . if she was destined to stay in the 1880s. The whole situation was so strange, so unlike anything she'd ever experienced, that she was uncertain how to answer him. The question that flitted through her mind was whether she wanted to spend the rest of her life here with him. She could form no definitive answer. "I'm not sure."

"Perhaps I can convince you that you could be happy here," he said warmly, and lifted his glass to her. "To the future . . ."

She raised her glass to his, joining him in the toast.

6

Later that night, Kent bid Roni good night and she started up the stairs. Halfway up, she paused. "Kent?"

Heading for his study, he stopped and glanced up at her.

"Remember the night you found me, I told you I lost my purse and a watch? Well, the Ripper took the watch from me during the attack, and I have finally figured out that it was the watch that brought me here. Without it, I can't get home . . ."

He heard the vulnerability in her voice, and it touched a chord deep within him. His determination to protect her became a burning need. Despite her objections, he would keep her safe—for however long she decided to stay with him.

"We'll take everything a day at a time, Roni. I will be with you for as long as you need me."

"Thank you," she said, smiling tremulously.

He returned her smile. "I'll always be here. You needn't worry."

She hesitated, as if intending to say more, then seemed to change her mind. "Well, good night."

"Good night." He watched her climb the stairs and wondered if she was real or if he were caught up in some kind of dream. If it was a dream, he had to admit that he was enjoying it. And it comforted him to know she would not disappear from

his life. Only the knowledge that the Ripper was
still out there and might be looking for her tem-
pered his good mood.

He entered his study and settled himself at his
desk, intending to go over his notes on the case.
Instead, he found himself staring out the open
doorway at the stairs, thinking of Roni and what
they could do together tomorrow. He wanted to
show her London, wanted to show her more of life
in his time. Most of all, he just wanted to be with
her. The idea surprised him, for his work had always been his obsession. It had been his life, his
reason for being, and now . . . Despite that he'd
known Roni for only one day, he would miss her
terribly if she were to go.

The weeks that followed passed in a sweet,
steady rhythm of discovery for them both.

At first, while Kent was working, Roni passed
much of her time reading. She eagerly devoured
the London newspaper every day and then started
on the books in the library.

Kent met her for lunch as often as he could, and
he did take her to see the sights, but there were
still long hours when he was gone and she was
alone with the servants. Eventually, just reading
wasn't enough to keep Roni occupied, so she
started to pitch in and help Mrs. Reilly and Mrs.
Randall with their work. Both ladies protested that
she was a guest and, as such, shouldn't assist
them, but Roni was so persistent that they ultimately capitulated.

As Roni worked with them, she listened to them
sing Kent's praises. It seemed he was invariably
kind and generous with those he cared about, hav-

ing taken good care of both women through the years they'd been in his employ. Roni came to like and respect him even more.

There were days, though, when Roni longed for her home, her work, and her own time. She wondered if anyone missed her and if her mother, friends, and colleagues were looking for her. Some nights, she would lie in bed, trying to figure out what she was going to do. Certainly, a career of her own was out of the question in this time period, but she wondered if Kent might let her help him with his cases. Roni was certain that her abilities could aid him in solving crime. All she had to do was convince him to let her work with him behind the scenes.

Sometimes at night, the thought of how truly alone she was in this strange world haunted her. Then Kent would slip into her thoughts and somehow calm her fears. There were even some nights when she drifted off to sleep trying to imagine what it would be like to be married to him. The idea was not unpleasant.

For his part, Kent put in long hours on the job, but he grew increasingly frustrated by the department's failure to catch the Ripper. Despite his dedication to his work, he always found time for Roni. He enjoyed their sightseeing almost as much as she did, for experiencing the city through her eyes renewed his love for it. In the evenings when he came home, they would discuss the case and any new information he had learned that day.

One evening, Kent arrived home to find Roni at the desk in his study, reading the newspaper. Her concentration was so intense that he was curious to find out what she was reading.

"Is something troubling you?" he asked.

"Hmm?" She was surprised to see him, for she hadn't heard him come in. "No, no, nothing's bothering me. It's just that . . ." Abruptly she laid the newspaper aside in frustration.

"That what?"

"There's a picture of Prince Eddy there . . . As you know, he is considered a suspect in my time, and I was trying to see—"

"Is he the one?" Kent tensed as he awaited her response.

"What if he is? Even if you arrest him, he will never be punished, and the public will never know what he's done." She gave him an agonized gaze.

"Is he the one who attacked you?"

"You'll be ruined if you try to do anything about it . . ."

"I don't care. Nothing is more important than finding the killer before he strikes again."

Roni picked up the newspaper once again and concentrated as she stared at the likeness of the prince. She sighed in exasperation. "I can't be sure. I wish I could be, but I can't . . . There's so much difference between a picture and seeing the real man who attacked me that night. What I mean is that the Ripper wore a hat and his features were shadowed. I just can't be certain. I'm sorry."

"There's nothing to be sorry for. The whole department is just as frustrated as you are. We've tried everything from bloodhounds to decoys to catch him, without success."

Roni sat perfectly still, then lifted her gaze from

the newspaper to him. "Kent, what about using me?"

"I have been. Your knowledge of the Ripper has been extremely helpful."

"That's not what I mean. You said the Ripper might be after me because as far as we know, I am the only person to survive one of his attacks and I can identify him. So why don't I make myself conspicuous? You could use *me* as a decoy. I'm more than willing to go to Whitechapel and help you trap him."

"No."

"Why not?"

"Because, as I told you before, you could be killed, and I won't allow you to be deliberately set up for that to happen. I simply won't be a party to it. Besides, even if I were willing to go along with your idea, I would need my superiors' approval to use you in a stakeout, and they would never give it. You're going to stay right here where Hargrove or I can protect you should the need arise."

"Do your superiors really have to know?" she asked. "I mean, if we catch him, you don't have to tell them of my involvement. You also forget that I wouldn't be alone in the street. You'd be there, watching me."

"All right, forget my superiors for the moment. What if I were watching from a distance and he proved to be faster than I was? You'd end up dead."

"You have very little faith in my ability to defend myself. Didn't I prove to you that I could do it?"

"You proved that you could defend yourself against a man who attacked you head-on. But what if he came upon you from behind? What if he stabbed you before you knew what was happening? No, it's best to leave things as they are."

"But Jack did grab me from behind, and I escaped," she persisted. "And just to be safe, I could carry a gun. Don't you have one?"

"Certainly, but what good would it do you? You must have time to aim and fire. If he surprised you . . ."

"You're determined to keep me out of this, aren't you?"

"I'm determined to keep you alive, and if that means keeping you in this house out of harm's way, then that's what I'm going to do. So leave it alone. Now, for a change of topic, would you like to go for a walk tonight? It's clear out and the weather's mild."

Though Roni was tempted to continue arguing with Kent, she conceded good-naturedly. In the few weeks she had been with him she had learned to gauge his moods, knew just how far she could press him. As much as she wanted to help capture the Ripper, she realized that Kent was probably right. His superiors would never go for the idea of using her as a decoy.

She smiled at him. "I'd love to take a walk with you."

Outside, walking beside Roni, Kent found himself as enchanted as ever by her witty conversation. Well-versed in many subjects, as he had discovered from their many conversations, she was stimulating, and he told himself again that she must be a dream, for no real woman could have fit so perfectly into his life. But then, whenever he touched her, he knew she was no figment of his imagination. He did not know why she had come into his life, but he would always be grateful that she had.

He felt her gently squeeze his arm and looked at her.

"You're so far away," she said. "Is something wrong?"

He smiled, slightly embarrassed at the direction of his thoughts. "No. I was thinking about you."

"Me? Why?"

He stopped walking and reached for her hand. She felt vibrant, alive. He wished he could keep touching her for all eternity. "I was just telling myself that I'm here talking to a woman who hasn't, by all rights, been born yet."

"If that's the case, then I'm talking to a man who's been dead for a number of years. Do you realize how old you'd be if this were my time?"

He thought about it and laughed. "Old. Very old."

"I'm glad you're not. I don't usually date older men." She was laughing, too.

"I don't know how this has all come about, but I'm glad you're here, Roni . . ."

"I am, too." Her reply was a whisper on the gentle night breeze.

They stood still on the quiet street, caught up in the intimacy of their confessions.

Kent studied her upturned face in the moonlight. She was everything he'd ever wanted in a woman. He longed to take her in his arms and hold her close. He wanted to kiss her, to keep her near and never let her go. With an effort he maintained a grip on his desire, determined to continue his role as a gentleman. It wasn't easy. She was so lovely . . . He wanted her with a passion that surprised even him.

Roni gazed up at him and she knew in that moment that she wanted to kiss him, to be in his arms. At times she had found his protectiveness almost smothering, for she wasn't used to anyone keeping tabs on her. But during their time together, she had come to appreciate his concern for her and her safety. She had to depend on him for her very existence, yet he had never tried to take advantage of her in any way. No man she had ever met could match him.

Ever one to go after what she wanted, she closed the distance between them. Without a word, she looped her arms about his neck and drew him down to her for a kiss.

Kent was momentarily shocked. No woman had ever taken the initiative with him. He'd been battling his own need for her, and she had come to him. After his initial disconcertment, he quickly decided he was delighted that she had. As her lips sought his, he embraced her, his arms encircling her and bringing her against him.

Their lips met, and in that dark London night, they shared their first kiss. It was a passionate blending of desire and restraint as they tasted the sweetness of their newfound feelings for each other. The world around them faded.

Kent wanted to crush Roni to him and claim her in all ways. Just this one kiss sent heat flooding through his body, settling in his loins, urging him to claim her, to make her his own. Only a last shred of sanity saved him. As much as he thrilled at having her in his arms and feeling her soft curves pressed against him, he knew it couldn't be. She was a lady. He had her honor to uphold. He could not and would not take advantage of her.

With a fierce effort, he broke off the kiss and stepped back. Staring down at her once again, he could see passion's flush on her cheeks, and he knew she had been as deeply affected by the embrace as he was.

"I'm glad you kissed me," she said in a low voice, wanting him to know that she had enjoyed every second of it.

"We'd better go . . ." he said, feeling a little awkward as he faced the truth of his feelings for her. She was becoming important in his life . . . so very important.

"Are you sure?" Her tone was inviting.

"No, I'm not sure at all. That's why we're going," he admitted. Then, unable to bear the thought of not touching her, he took her arm and linked it through his.

Roni smiled contentedly as she walked slowly at Kent's side. She felt right, as if this was where she was meant to be.

They strolled quietly for some time, before he turned to her. "Do you like the opera?"

She nodded.

"Good. I'll get tickets and we can go this weekend."

When they returned to the house, Roni bid him good night. With all her heart she wanted him to kiss her once more, but he did not.

Sleep was long in coming. She tossed, remembering every blissful moment of being in his arms. She fantasized again about being married to Kent, and smiled. He was compassionate, gentle, devoted, and caring, not to mention handsome, sexy, and intelligent. As she closed her eyes, she thought that perhaps being committed to a man like Kent wouldn't rob her of her independence after all.

In his room, Kent lay awake, staring at the ceiling. His thoughts were of Roni. By some incredible happenstance, she had come to him through time. He didn't know how or why, but he did know that he didn't want to lose her. Images of coming home to find her waiting for him appealed to him, yet even as he pictured sharing his life with her, he worried about what the fates had in store for them. As always, the specter of the Ripper hovered in the back of his mind. The realization that November would soon be upon them gave him a nagging sense of dread. He feared that something terrible was going to happen, and that he would be unable to stop it.

There! She'd actually done it! Roni smiled as she stared at the perfectly set dining-room table with its white linen tablecloth, highly polished silver, sparkling crystal, and delicate china.

That morning, right after Kent had left for work, she'd decided to fix a special dinner for him, since it was the cook's day off. Now, a great sense of feminine pride filled her as she stared at her handiwork.

Roni's heartbeat quickened as she realized that Kent would be coming home soon. She hoped he would enjoy the dinner she'd prepared. She knew she would. It seemed an eternity since she'd last had pizza, and she'd labored all afternoon making the dough and trying to find the right ingredients. It hadn't been easy, and she still wasn't certain just how it was going to taste, but the pie smelled delicious in the oven.

Taking such pleasure in cooking for Kent gave Roni pause. Domesticity had never been her strong suit. Some nights when she'd been working late, there had only been time for a microwave dinner or a peanut-butter sandwich. Roni frowned as she mentally debated the merits of eating a microwave dinner alone in her apartment after a hard day at the TV station or having a homemade pizza here with Kent. Dinner with Kent won. She was considering that revelation when she heard the front door.

"You're home . . ." she said brightly as she hurried to greet him in the foyer.

"Finally." Kent had passed another frustrating day following up on the endless and ultimately useless leads in the Ripper case, and he had been more than eager to head home to Roni. Seeing her now, smiling in warm welcome, he had to fight down the urge to take her in his arms and kiss her. "What smells so good?" he asked.

"I cooked dinner for you tonight."

"You didn't have to do that. Didn't Mrs. Randall leave something? She usually does on her day off."

"She did, but I wanted to make something special for you. I cooked my favorite meal for you. I hope you enjoy it. I don't think you've ever had anything like it before. Everything's just about ready. Come sit down, and I'll get you a glass of wine." She took his hand and led him into the dining room.

"Roni, the table looks lovely. You must have spent hours preparing for dinner." He was impressed. As he took his seat, she poured a glass of wine and handed it to him.

"I did."

"You mean to tell me, you actually enjoyed doing a domestic chore?" he teased.

"I have to admit, I did. I wanted to do something special for you."

"You have, just by coming into my life."

His words left her breathless and she smiled tremulously as her gaze met his. For a brief moment, the universe narrowed to just the two of them. There was no past or future. There was only now—the time that they shared.

"Thank you," she said.

"Have some wine with me?" he invited.

"Just as soon as I get the salads and the pizza."

"Pizza?"

"You'll see."

A short time later, Roni was watching with pleasure as Kent devoured the last slice with gusto.

"Your pizza was delicious."

"I'm glad you liked it. I was worried that it might not turn out right. I've never made it from scratch before."

"You did a marvelous job. What other recipes do you know? I may fire Mrs. Randall."

"Oh, don't you dare! She's a wonderful cook, and after pizza, there's only tacos and hamburgers from McDonald's left in my repertoire."

"McDonald's?"

"A fast-food restaurant." At his quizzical look,

she said, "When I don't have time to cook, I go to the drive-through and grab some burgers to take home."

"You actually drive through a restaurant?"

She laughed. "No, there's a window you drive up to, and after you pay, they hand you your food in a bag."

"I think I like this type of dining better," he remarked thoughtfully.

"So do I," she admitted, thinking how wonderful it was to be sitting with him, sharing an intimate dinner. "Well, I'd better start washing the dishes."

"We'll do the dishes together." He stood up and picked up his plate and glass.

Roni was startled by his willingness to help. Every man she knew high-tailed it when it came time to clean up after a meal.

"Thanks."

"My pleasure."

Later, after Roni had bid Kent good night and gone upstairs to bed, she couldn't help wondering if being married to him would be as wonderful as this evening had been. His conversation had been interesting and intelligent. He'd helped with all the housewifely chores without complaint, and he'd even liked her cooking. She had to admit he was close to being the perfect man. She was smiling as she drifted off to sleep.

The following Saturday evening they attended the opera. As they took their seats, Roni was pleased that they had a good view of the stage and the rest of the theater. When everyone stood and began to applaud, she noticed Kent gazing at something across the theater.

"What is it?" she asked.

"His Royal Highness is here." He nodded toward the box where Prince Eddy stood with his entourage.

The prince acknowledged the audience's welcome, and when he was seated, the audience sat. Roni stared at him, trying to discern if he was the man who had attacked her on that dark night, if he was the one whose violent use of a knife would mark him as the killer of the century. If he was, then that would certainly account for the necessity of a coverup.

As if sensing Roni's gaze upon him, the prince suddenly glanced in her direction, frowning slightly. Roni quickly looked away, unnerved by the thought that he might have known she was watching him. Now she felt even more confused as to the Ripper's identity.

After the opera, Kent took her to a fine restaurant.

"This place is wonderful," Roni told him as she sat across from him at the candlelit table.

"After your pizza, I felt I owed you a special night out."

"The opera was special enough. You didn't have to do this."

"But I wanted to."

The waiter came to take their order then, and after he'd left them and their wine was served, Kent lifted his glass to Roni.

"To us," he said with quiet intensity.

Roni lifted her glass to his, and they drank to the toast.

"Do you think you could be happy here? Can you accept our way of life?" Kent asked. He knew she would be remaining in his time if they couldn't find the watch, and he wanted to protect her, to keep her safe.

"I don't know," she answered hesitantly. "I've tried to change my way of thinking, to come to grips with the fact that I may never go back ... but everything is so different. I'm used to being independent and taking care of myself."

"Could you be content without your career? Could you be satisfied being a wife?"

"I've learned so much from you in just the short time we've been together, and I realize that I was wrong about a lot of things about marriage. A marriage doesn't necessarily have to be the way my parents' was."

"No, it doesn't. It can be a wonderful thing ... two people working to make a life together. It's a challenge, and not an easy one, but worth the effort, I think—if there's love."

"There has to be love," she agreed as she looked up at him.

"Without it life means little." He gazed at her, wondering if love was the elusive emotion that was filling him, keeping visions of her dancing softly through his mind.

"I know. I watched my mother try to exist without my father after he left her."

"But that won't happen to you."

"No. I won't allow it to. I'm firmly convinced we're each responsible for our own happiness. We can choose to be happy or we can choose to be miserable. I choose to be happy. Life's too short to be anything else."

She smiled at Kent as the waiter served their first course.

It was hours later when they returned to the townhouse. Hargrove had already retired for the night, so they were alone in the foyer.

"Thank you for a lovely evening," she said as Kent took her wrap.

"It was my pleasure." He put her cloak away with his own. "I had a wonderful time."

"So did I." She turned to him as he came to her.

"Did I tell you that you look lovely tonight?" His deep voice was a velvet caress to her senses.

"Thank you." She lifted her gaze to his and in that instant saw a flare of desire in the depths of his eyes. She stood poised and motionless, wanting him to kiss her, wishing she could once again know the pleasure of his touch. She had come to care about him deeply, but except for that one kiss she had given him, he had made no move to touch her again. He had been the perfect gentleman, and it was driving her crazy.

Her wish was granted, for Kent could no longer deny the need that had been building within him. She haunted his thoughts by day and his dreams by night. He had never felt this way about another woman, and the power of his feelings for her surprised him. Logically—his whole existence was built around logic and good, methodical police work—she shouldn't even be here with him. And yet . . .

"Kiss me . . ." she finally whispered, unable to bear being so close without touching him.

It was all the invitation he needed. He took her in his arms and held her. His mouth found hers, and Roni gave a soft sigh as she instinctively nestled against him. She arched with need for him.

The kiss sparked a flame inside Kent that quickly grew to a raging fire. He was lost in the glory of her embrace. It was heaven to hold her, and he realized almost painfully that if he didn't let her go now, he never would. With a Herculean effort, he ended the kiss and held her slightly away from him.

"Good night, Roni," he said, the regret in his voice unmistakable.

Roni understood, for she too was ready to cast all common sense to the wind and love him. She stood on tiptoes to give him one last quick kiss before moving away from him.

"Good night, Kent."

She started up the stairs. Kent remained downstairs, feeling the need for a drink before retiring. He watched her until she was out of sight, then stepped into the parlor and poured himself a shot of whiskey.

7

Roni entered her room and turned up the lamp on the dresser. She walked to the bed and turned back the covers. Something metallic gleamed on her pillow, and puzzled, she leaned closer.

It was the watch Telyur had given her, the

watch the Ripper had taken from her the night he had attacked her.

Her heart lurched in her breast and she backed away from the bed.

He had found her.

"Kent!" she screamed, and ran out into the hallway.

He came bounding up the stairs. "What is it?"

"He's been here!"

"Who?"

"The Ripper!" She pointed through the doorway into her room, and he stepped inside. "There," she said, "on the pillow."

Kent crossed to the bed and looked down at the watch. He picked it up and studied it, then looked at Roni. "This is the watch he took from you?"

She nodded. Revulsion shuddered through her. She felt violated.

"He's found me, Kent. He was here, in my room. This is his message to me . . ."

Kent came back out to the hallway and took her in his arms. "Are you all right?" he asked. "You're as white as a ghost."

She looked up at him sharply. "Oh, God, Kent, he may still be in the house!"

He muttered grimly, "Come with me."

They went down the hall to Kent's bedroom, where he took keys from his pocket and unlocked a chest at the foot of the bed. Inside were two pistols. He handed her one as he grabbed the other.

"Be careful," he said. "It's loaded."

As Roni took the weapon she felt a great relief. She wanted to be prepared when they faced the Ripper.

Kent led the way first to Roni's room. He made

a thorough search while she waited in the doorway.

"He's not in here. Stay with me while I check
the rest of the house."

"You don't have to worry about that," she told
him, shadowing his every step.

Hargrove appeared from his quarters on the
third floor. "What's happened, sir?"

"Someone's been in the house, Hargrove. Did
you hear anything unusual tonight?"

"Nothing, sir."

Hargrove joined them in their search. At the
back of the house they found that a window looking out on the alley had been forced open.

It took them the better part of an hour to ascer-
tain that the intruder was not inside.

"Even so," Kent said, "we're going to have to be
extra careful from now on. In the morning,
Hargrove, I want a second set of locks installed on
all the windows and doors."

"Yes, Mr. Grayson, I'll see to it first thing. Is
there anything else tonight? Would you like some
tea?"

"No, thank you, that'll be all for tonight."

Hargrove climbed the stairs to his room, and
Kent and Roni went into the parlor, still too
shaken to retire. Kent could tell that Roni was
fighting to be brave, trying to put up a good front
for him, but her trembling hands betrayed her.

"Would you like something a little stronger than
tea?" he asked.

"Definitely," she answered gratefully.

He poured her a small whiskey but didn't fix
one for himself. After what had just happened, he

had no intention of dulling his senses. He would take no chances with Roni's life.

Roni finished her drink and set the glass aside. She looked at Kent sitting close beside her. She didn't want him to think badly of her, but she couldn't face the prospect of being alone in her room tonight.

"Kent, would you stay with me tonight?"

He touch her cheek in a gentle caress as his eyes met hers. "Don't worry, my love. I'll keep you safe."

Bending to her, he kissed her with infinite care. Then he rose, taking her hand and drawing her up with him. He picked up both of the pistols and led her from the parlor and upstairs to his own bedroom. There he placed the guns within reach in the nightstand drawer, then turned back to the woman he loved more than life itself. When he had heard her cry out his name earlier that night, the terrifying thought that something had happened to her had shaken him to the depths of his soul.

"I love you, Roni," he said, standing before her. "I don't know what will come of our time together, but I can't deny what I feel for you any longer."

She smiled tenderly at him. "I feel as if I've known you forever. It's almost as if you're a part of me . . ."

"I want to be part of you," he said, his gaze darkening as he lifted her in his arms and kissed her passionately. He looked into her eyes. "I want to be with you every minute. I want us to be together always."

"So do I." She linked her arms around his neck

as he carried her to the wide, inviting softness of
his bed.

He lay her upon it and then stretched out beside
her. "You're the most beautiful woman I've ever
known."

"I want to be beautiful—for you . . ." She
reached out and rested a hand on his chest, feeling
the solid, heavy beat of his heart beneath her
palm. "What we have is so precious . . . Kent, I'm
so afraid I'm going to lose you . . ." The words
were agony for her to say.

He cradled her to him. "Don't be afraid, love.
I'll be with you always."

"But what if . . ." She rose for a moment to look
down at him, committing to memory the manly
beauty of his features. She was giving her heart
and soul to this man, and the fear that the Ripper
could hurt him and that Kent might be taken from
her filled her with pain.

He silenced her with a kiss. "I'll never let you
go," he vowed. "No one will ever take me away
from you. No matter what, we'll be together . . ."

For now, they would forget everything else—the
uncertainty of their lives, the cruelty and violence
of the Ripper. For now, it was just the two of them,
giving of themselves as neither had ever given before, pledging their devotion with words and ca-
resses.

Kent helped Roni to undress, stripping away the
many layers of clothing that he now cursed for
their inconvenience. His frustrated mutterings
drew a sensual chuckle from her as she helped
him with the many ties and buttons. She had worn
her hair up tonight, and he took great pleasure in
freeing her golden mane. As the pale curls cas-

caded down her back, he raked his fingers through the silken length. Gazing upon her unclothed for the first time, he knew she was feminine perfection. Her breasts were high and firm, her waist slender, her hips round and inviting.

Unable to deny himself any longer, he stripped off his shirt and went into her open arms. His mouth slanted across hers in a possessive exchange that left them both breathless with the promise of what was to come. There would be no stopping this night. Driven by desperation and fear and love, they would come together, pledging with their hearts the truth of their devotion. They were one and would be one forever.

He shed the rest of his clothes, then moved over her to claim her in love's most perfect way. She whispered his name and then their bodies melded in rapturous union. They moved together, their sole reason for being to love each other.

A spiraling crescendo of desire took them higher and higher until ecstasy exploded within them, sending them both to heaven and beyond. They drifted in love's aftermath, joined in body and spirit. They had given to each other their most cherished gift, and they knew paradise.

They did not speak, but lay together, their limbs entwined, their hearts beating in union. They had no future and no past. They celebrated the moment and cherished each touch, each caress. Theirs was a love that had been stolen out of time.

"I love you, Kent."

He drew her even closer and kissed her deeply. "And I love you."

There was no need to say more as she felt the heat of him again deep within her.

Kent had wanted and needed her for so long that just having her near aroused him. This time setting a slower pace for their lovemaking, he savored every moment of having her silken body beneath him. He caressed and kissed her, teaching her of love's delights and encouraging her to learn more.

She proved an apt pupil, and she eagerly experimented, touching him as boldly as he had touched her. Her boldness won her his passion, and he began to move more quickly inside her, his pace frenzied in his need to claim her once more.

The crest came upon them in a rush of glory, and they clung together, mindless in the pleasure that had swept over them. They lay sated, neither having known a love so sweet.

After that night, Roni did not return to her solitary bed. Each day that followed held new delights as they learned more about each other, and each night was idyllic as they lay in each other's arms.

Time passed far too swiftly for them. They wanted only to be together. Roni never even thought of testing the watch to see if it would send her back to her own time. She had decided that she belonged with Kent. He had shown her the beauty of true sharing and devotion. Any doubts she'd had about committing herself to a relationship were gone. In all of time, there would be no other man for her.

But as November neared, the final murder loomed closer, and Kent had to force himself to leave Roni more and more often. He worked from dusk to dawn, prowling the streets of the East End in his constant search for the vicious murderer. Kent and Roni both knew this was his last chance to catch the Ripper.

Prepared to be away from Roni at night, Kent arranged for Hargrove to keep watch. He also left one of the pistols close at hand for her, in case she should need it. He hated leaving the paradise of her arms and going out into the dank, filthy streets, but the Ripper had to be stopped before it was too late.

Night after night, alone in his bed, Roni turned restlessly as she anxiously awaited Kent's return. She feared for him and ached to have him back with her, safe from the bloodthirsty killer.

Seven days and seven long nights passed during which Kent worked the streets in his search. Roni found she couldn't even rest in her bed. Nervous and worried, she paced late into the night. She didn't know why she was so upset, but instinctively she felt that something was wrong.

She had avoided going into her own bedroom since the night of the break-in, but for some reason she was drawn there now. She entered and lit a lamp. Nothing had changed. Hargrove had put the watch the Ripper had returned to her on the dresser. From where she stood in the doorway, she could see the gold glimmering in the semidarkness. Instinctively she went to the dresser and picked up the watch.

When she'd held it in Telyur's shop, it had felt cold. Now, as it lay in the palm of her hand, the watch felt warm, almost hot. The change startled her. Nervously she opened the case and found that the watch had stopped.

And as she stared down at the watch, remembering Telyur and his strange shop, a date suddenly came into her mind. November 9.

That was today.

Sometime before dawn, the Ripper would kill again.

Her hand closed around the watch as she turned and fled the room. She must find Kent and warn him!

She hurried back to Kent's room and dressed quickly, pausing only long enough to get the pistol he had left her. Then she crept from the room. Sneaking past Hargrove would be the hardest part.

She made it to the foyer without waking the butler and donned her cloak. It was well past midnight when she slipped from the townhouse and headed for Whitechapel and the stakeout area where Kent had told her he'd be. In the pockets of her dress she carried not only the gun, but the watch as well. Not only had it sent her back, but it had also brought Jack the Ripper to her. Perhaps it would do so again tonight.

The trek to the East Side took her a while, but finally she arrived. Her nerves stretched taut, she moved off into the darkness of the narrow, deserted streets.

Several drunks staggered by, but no one paid any attention to her, and she was relieved. Walking quietly, she searched for some sign of Kent but found no trace of him. A fine misty rain began to fall, adding to the night's chill.

It seemed she'd been walking for hours when she heard heavy footsteps. The memory of the first time she had heard footsteps in the night was alive and terrifying, and this time she wasn't sure whether to stop and confront whoever was behind her or continue moving at her steady pace. Slipping a hand into her pocket, she gripped the pistol. As the steps came closer, she tensed. The man drew alongside her and with her heart pounding she turned to him.

It was a bobby, walking his beat.

"Evening," she said.

"Good evening, ma'am." He looked puzzled to see her there but continued walking, disappearing down a side street.

Roni realized she was shaking. It hadn't been the Ripper. It had been a policeman. She almost laughed at her overreaction and was glad to move into the dim glow of a gaslight.

"I knew you would come."

The sound of that deep voice shattered her momentary calm, and she spun around, pulling out the gun as she faced the man she knew to be a cold-blooded murderer. Viciously he knocked her arm aside, sending the gun flying.

She turned to flee, but he grabbed her around the neck and yanked her back against him. She screamed, the echo reverberating through the streets and alleyways.

"Why, you . . ." he hissed. He tried to throw her to the ground, but knowing she was fighting for her very life, she kicked and clawed at him. His arm at her throat was choking her, and as she thrashed wildly in his grip, trying to break free of his deadly hold, she could feel her strength ebbing as darkness closed in on her.

"Roni!" Kent yelled, running from the side street where he had kept his vigil. He charged toward the Ripper. He wanted to use his gun, but he didn't dare while the murderer was holding Roni.

The Ripper saw Kent coming and threw Roni aside just as Kent launched himself at him. Roni went sprawling to the cobblestones but recovered immediately when she realized that Kent was in danger. She screamed for help as she got up and searched frantically for the gun she'd dropped.

Meanwhile, Kent and the Ripper struggled wildly. In the scuffle, the Ripper's deerstalker hat flew off, clearly revealing his face. Kent stared at him in amazement.

"You bastard!" he cried, attacking again in a mindless frenzy, wanting to make this man suffer for the pain he'd caused.

The Ripper still held his knife, and he struck swiftly as Kent lunged at him, the blade finding its mark in Kent's side.

Roni saw the Ripper stab Kent and screamed just as two bobbies came running toward them. The Ripper let out a blood-curdling laugh as he watched Kent fall, then gasped in surprise as the two policemen came at him from behind and knocked him off his feet.

"My God . . ." they said, staring down in disbelief at the man they held to the ground.

"Kent!" Roni ran to where he lay clutching his shoulder. She fell to her knees beside him, tears streaming down her face. "Are you all right?"

"Roni . . . did they get him?" he asked hoarsely, then shut his eyes in pain.

"Yes, they got him . . ." she answered, sobbing. "We've got to get you to a doctor . . . You're bleeding and . . ."

From her pocket came the muffled sound of the

watch's chime. She snatched it out and opened it. "It's working again . . ." she said in wonder.

"What is?" he asked, looking at her.

As she handed him the watch so that he could see it, the wind picked up, moaning as it rushed down the street.

"Kent . . ." She grasped his hand, knowing what would happen and fearing it. A sudden heavy fog swirled around them, obscuring the world and sweeping them away through time . . . together.

Roni clung to Kent, refusing to be parted from him, knowing that her life would be empty and pointless without him.

Then, in an instant, it was over.

They were beneath a street light in Whitechapel, and Roni could hear the sounds of traffic and see the lights in the windows of the houses. She still knelt beside Kent.

He struggled to sit up. "Roni . . . what happened? Where did they go?"

"It's all right. Be careful with your shoulder . . . Let me help you." She put an arm around him and helped him to his feet.

"Miss, are you and the gent all right?" an elderly man asked as he emerged from a building nearby. "Good Lord, he's bleeding."

"Yes. Please, would you call an ambulance? I've got to get him to hospital!"

"Straight away!" The man hurried back inside the building.

"Roni . . ." Kent's face was pale as he stared down at her. He felt a little light-headed, but he knew it wasn't from his wound. He looked around in awe. "It was true . . . everything you said . . ."

"Everything," she confirmed, as the blare of a siren grew louder.

"Was it the watch?" he asked.

"Yes . . . I never told you *how* I knew it was responsible for my traveling through time. The first time I heard it chime and then opened it was the night Jack attacked me and you found me. Tonight was only the second time I've heard it chime and opened it. Now the watch has brought us back to my time. Do you remember we talked about making a future together? Well, we're going to live that future now. Trust me."

She kissed him softly just as the ambulance turned down the street and came to a halt in front of them.

Epilogue

C lad in casual slacks, a polo shirt, and loafers, Kent sat on a chair in the hospital room, eagerly anticipating his release after three weeks of confinement. Within the hour they would have the doctor's signature and he would be free to go . . . free to explore a whole new world with Roni. So far he had been fascinated by modern inventions and the marvelous convenience of electrical gadgets and machines. He remembered wondering—it seemed so long ago—if he would want to live in the 1990s, and he decided now that it wasn't such a bad place after all.

Roni stood at the window, staring out at London's skyline. She couldn't imagine everything having turned out any better. There had been a few awkward moments in the ambulance when she had had to explain their clothes to the attendants by saying they'd come from a party and had been robbed. That white lie explained Kent's having no currently dated identification. From that moment, all had gone incredibly smoothly. Though Kent had lost quite a bit of blood, and had developed a serious infection that had required intravenous antibiotics, he had completely recovered, and today they were ready to begin a new life.

"I have only one regret," Kent said.

She turned to him, smiling. "What's that?"

"That there's no record of the Ripper's arrest."

His gaze met hers across the room, and they both knew what he meant. She had brought him all the books she could find about the Ripper, and he had been angered by the lack of information they had contained—especially regarding the Ripper's real identity. When Kent had discovered that many files had been destroyed in the hundred years since the murders, his anger had escalated into outrage and disbelief.

Later, when he had finally calmed down, he had realized that Roni's theory of a coverup of Jack's arrest had indeed been true.

"I've been thinking about that," Roni said. "You've been wondering what to do for a living now that you're here with me. Well, I'm sure I can get you a job at my station. You're certainly a qualified investigator—although it might take you a little while to catch up on the new techniques.

I've been wanting to do a TV documentary about serial killers, starting with Jack the Ripper. Interested?"

"Most definitely. I want the truth told. This is one secret that's been kept too long."

"I agree, but we're going to have to have factual proof. Believe me when I say our eyewitness testimony won't carry any weight with the network. All it would do is get us both locked up somewhere."

He frowned at the thought that no one would believe them, but then, he hadn't believed her either when he'd found her. He smiled. "I can't think of anything I'd like more than to spend the rest of my life working with you . . ."

He went to her. He winced a little as he moved, but he knew that the wound was not serious and that the soreness would be gone in another week or so. "I told you I would never let you go, and I meant it."

Roni put her arms around his neck and pulled him down to her for a kiss. "I'm glad you're here, Kent Grayson. Without you . . . I wouldn't even have a life."

He raised his head and smiled gently. "Will you marry me, Roni? Will you be my wife, my life, and my love for all time?"

She returned his smile and kissed him again. "Oh, yes, Kent. For all time . . ."

Bobbi Smith

BOBBI SMITH believes in love. Love is mankind's most powerful emotion, and she believes it has the ability to transcend time and space. She says everyone's life should have a happy ending.

An award-winning author, Bobbi Smith has been writing since the age of ten. She is married, has two sons, and lives in St. Charles, Missouri.

Avon Romances—
the best in exceptional authors and unforgettable novels!

FOREVER HIS Shelly Thacker
77035-0/$4.50 US/$5.50 Can

TOUCH ME WITH FIRE Nicole Jordan
77279-5/$4.50 US/$5.50 Can

OUTLAW HEART Samantha James
76936-0/$4.50 US/$5.50 Can

FLAME OF FURY Sharon Green
76827-5/$4.50 US/$5.50 Can

DARK CHAMPION Jo Beverley
76786-4/$4.50 US/$5.50 Can

BELOVED PRETENDER Joan Van Nuys
77207-8/$4.50 US/$5.50 Can

PASSIONATE SURRENDER Sheryl Sage
76684-1/$4.50 US/$5.50 Can

MASTER OF MY DREAMS Danelle Harmon
77227-2/$4.50 US/$5.50 Can

LORD OF THE NIGHT Cara Miles
76453-9/$4.50 US/$5.50 Can

WIND ACROSS TEXAS Donna Stephens
77273-6/$4.50 US/$5.50 Can

Avon Romantic Treasures

*Unforgettable, enthralling love stories,
sparkling with passion and adventure
from Romance's bestselling authors*

COMANCHE WIND *by Genell Dellin*

76717-1/$4.50 US/$5.50 Can

THEN CAME YOU *by Lisa Kleypas*

77013-X/$4.50 US/$5.50 Can

VIRGIN STAR *by Jennifer Horsman*

76702-3/$4.50 US/$5.50 Can

MASTER OF MOONSPELL *by Deborah Camp*

76736-8/$4.50 US/$5.50 Can

SHADOW DANCE *by Anne Stuart*

76741-4/$4.50 US/$5.50 Can

FORTUNE'S FLAME *by Judith E. French*

76865-8/$4.50 US/$5.50 Can

FASCINATION *by Stella Cameron*

77074-1/$4.50 US/$5.50 Can

ANGEL EYES *by Suzannah Davis*

76822-4/$4.50 US/$5.50 Can

The Incomparable

ELIZABETH LOWELL

"Lowell is great!"
Johanna Lindsey

ONLY YOU
76340-0/$5.99 US/$6.99 Can

ONLY MINE
76339-7/$5.99 US/$6.99 Can

ONLY HIS
76338-9/$5.99 US/$6.99 Can

UNTAMED
76953-0/$5.99 US/$6.99 Can

FORBIDDEN
76954-9/$5.99 US/$6.99 Can

And Coming Soon

LOVER IN THE ROUGH
76760-0/$4.99 US/$5.99 Can